SHADOW
OF THE
YANGTZE

GHOSTS OF SHANGHAI

SHADOW OF THE YANGTZE

JULIAN SEDGWICK

Hodder
Children's
Books

HODDER CHILDREN'S BOOKS

First published in Great Britain in 2016
by Hodder and Stoughton

1 3 5 7 9 10 8 6 4 2

The moral rights of the author and illustrator have been asserted.

A CIP catalogue record for this book is available from the British Library.

ISBN 978 1 444 92449 7

Typeset in Garamond by Avon DataSet Ltd, Bidford-on-Avon, Warwickshire

Printed and bound by CPI Group (UK) Ltd, Croydon, CR0 4YY

The paper and board used in this book are made from wood
from responsible sources.

Hodder Children's Books
An imprint of Hachette Children's Group
Part of Hodder and Stoughton

Carmelite House, 50 Victoria Embankment,
London, EC4Y 0DZ

An Hachette UK Company
www.hachette.co.uk

For Chalkley and Talullah, fearless women

Contents

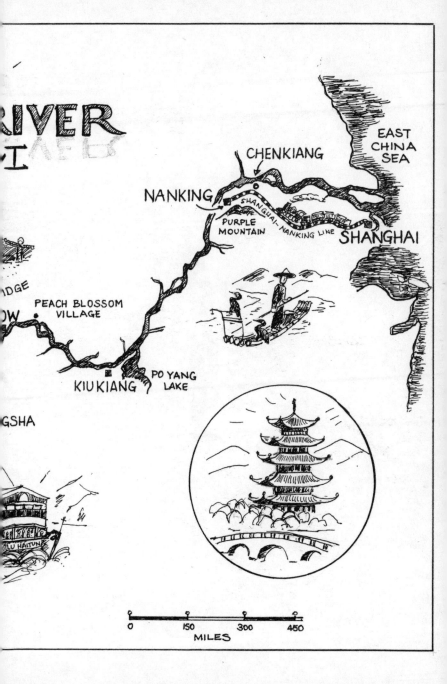

RIVER
（T）

EAST
CHINA
SEA

CHENKIANG

NANKING

SHANGHAI-NANKING LINE

PURPLE
MOUNTAIN

SHANGHAI

IDGE

OW

PEACH BLOSSOM
VILLAGE

PO YANG
LAKE

KIUKIANG

GSHA

LU HAITUN

0   150   300   450
MILES

Dawn breaks in pieces across Shanghai.

Hot gunfire and explosions are still shaking the air as the last survivors of the doomed uprising are crushed by gangsters from the Green Hand. Columns of smoke lift the sky like thick, grey pillars, the bodies of the fallen lying beneath; waiting to be carted off to unmarked graves.

Apart from Moonface's men, not a soul is braving the streets, and the shops and grand hotels are all locked up tight. Even the Great World Amusement Palace is closed, its nine floors of acrobats and dancers dark and silent – and it *never* shuts. The sun stamps the shadows of its towers on the deserted street as machine guns rattle, fall silent, rattle again.

But far away up Bubbling Well Road, on the outskirts of the city, something *is* moving. A green van

1

is nosing out through the gates of Liska Bakery, its driver still uncertain whether to risk the morning or not. Underneath the company name on the van's side, a jaunty cartoon fox waits patiently, holding up a biscuit and licking his lips.

The young man at the wheel leans out of the window. No gunfire for a full minute. Is that the end of it, or will the whole shooting match start up again? Some of the roads may still be blocked, dangerous, but he's late with an urgent order and can't risk losing his job – not with his youngest child sick and another mouth to feed on the way. He cranks the gearstick. Better go for it. At least not much to get in the way.

He stomps his foot to the floor, roaring forward into the morning, and, as the van veers though the bakery gates, yellow sun blinds its side.

The grinning fox painted there seems to blink in the light.

第一章

TO GO IS TO DIE

Two miles away, Ruby is also impatient to get moving, listening hard as a fresh volley of gunshots echoes across the rooftops.

It's difficult to tell where the fighting's coming from now: the Chinese City? Could be even closer, the French Concession maybe, or even not far from home. From the veranda of White Cloud all she can see is confused smoke shapeshifting behind the trees that loom over the old temple.

She turns to Charlie. 'What do you think?'

'Still too dangerous. Give it another twenty minutes.'

'But Moonface will be getting away. We should go after Fei now—'

'I *know* that. But there's no point getting gunned down before we've even started. He'll already be miles down the Huangpu. We need a real plan.'

'Well *I* think it's dying down. I'm *sure* it is.'

She turns back towards the smoke, counting seconds between the gunfire like she always counts the gap between lightning and thunder when storms come bludgeoning in off the sea.

Five, six, seven . . .

It's ages since they climbed exhausted from the well, and now she's revived and ready to go again, the impulsive, fearless part of herself – Shanghai Ruby – urging her to action.

. . . eight, nine, ten, eleven—

Another blast shakes the rooftops and she scuffs the boards in frustration.

'OK, five more minutes. But then we've got to do something.'

Charlie takes off his new spectacles, cleaning them carefully with shoulders hunched. 'Moonface said he was taking Fei to his ancestral home. I'm just not sure exactly where that is. Dad would know, but there's no way to ask him. If he's even *alive*.'

'What about his – friends?'

'They'll all be dead now. Or in hiding . . .'

She reaches out and rests a hand on his shoulder. The tension and anxiety is holding him rigid there, but it softens very slightly at the touch.

'I'm sure your dad's alive,' she says. 'And so is Fei. And we can go after her and save her, I know we can.'

'Dad didn't look good,' Charlie groans. 'And who knows what we'll face upriver if we do go.'

Ruby glances at Lao Jin's spirit sword lying on the step beside her. Its copper blade is dull now, all of its trembling fire gone, and it looks like nothing more than a prop from the crash and bang of Chinese Opera. But it did really happen, she thinks: the spectral Shadow Warriors, the flickering of the sword as it parried bullets, and sliced through their cold, black forms.

'If we could deal with those things in the tunnel, we can stop Moonface. *Mei wenti*, Charlie. No problem.'

Charlie puts the glasses back on and shakes his head. Hard to tell whether he's shaking away the black memories of the tunnel, or denying the whole thing happened. Sometimes it's so hard to work out what he's thinking as the cogwheels whirr away with that quiet intensity.

'We'll catch them, Charlie. Save Fei.'

'But don't you see? We might not come back.' He counts off the dangers on his fingers. 'Bandits and rogue armies. Gangsters. And there's a real anti-foreigner feeling again. You know what Confucius said?'

'What?'

'When you go on a journey of revenge, dig *two* graves.'

'I don't get it.'

'One for the person you want to get revenge on. One for yourself. I have to go, but you can stay here. Keep safe.'

'But it's not revenge. It's a rescue and I'm going with you. Just like in *Outlaws of the Marsh*. I'll be Hu San Niang, and you be Lin Chong.'

Charlie takes in a sharp breath. 'We're too old for all that stuff. To go might be to die. This isn't a game.'

'I know that, Charlie. I'm not a little kid any more.' She jumps to her feet and sweeps the spirit sword from the step. 'Of course it isn't a game. This is real.'

She steps down amongst the weeds and sweeps clear a patch of damp earth, scuffing the stones away with her school shoes, then scores a large X in it with the tip of the sword.

'*That's* real,' she says.

'What?'

'The place where we start our journey. And the place we'll come back to. With Fei. We'll be *real* warriors, risking everything. For real.'

And in that moment she feels it. Feels there's a good

chance they will stand here again, whatever happens, whatever it takes.

If only Lao Jin was still here to help. Then it would be easier, much easier.

But he isn't.

Behind her in the shadows of the main hall Jin's body lies crumpled under a blanket. For the umpteenth time she glances back at it. There has been no miraculous return to life, of course. Stupid to think there could be – despite what she saw him do with his *ch'i*, his Taoist magic. Before she gathered courage to cover his face, she had checked one more time for breath, but there was nothing. At least he seemed at peace, or rather like he was concentrating on something only he could see, a million miles away . . .

Jin's faithful dog Straw is still huddled beside him, his muzzle resting on his master's belly, eyes tight shut.

Still it was *weird* about that photo on the grave. It jolly well looked like Jin, at least last night it did. Now, try as hard as she can, she's been unable to find it again. Not a trace – nor its mysterious inscription. *Gone back to the mountain.* She grips the sword tighter, eyes scanning the gravestones beneath the scrubby trees again. Surely it was right there?

A crow calls loudly overhead, its shadow settling on the shadow of a branch above, setting it dancing.

The bird stays there a moment, and then a solitary gunshot, not far off, shocks it back into flight.

Ruby startles with it, but that has to be at least five minutes since the last gunfire. Time to get going.

She looks back at Charlie. 'It's too dangerous for you out there on the streets. Even if the worst has stopped, the Green Hand might try and nab you. But do you think Amah would know where Moonface comes from?'

'Auntie gets things all mixed up. And it's not safe yet for you either.'

'Nothing can happen to *me* in broad daylight, can it? Not in the International Settlement. I'll be fifteen minutes.'

Charlie seems on the verge of arguing, then gives in. 'Go on then, it's worth a try. But be quick!'

'Cross my heart and . . .'

Hope to die.

She grimaces, looks up at the smoke-streaked sky above, the disc of the sun punching through, lighting the courtyard. But somehow it doesn't lift the last of the night off the bamboo grove, the silent graves. Maybe it's just tiredness, the after-effects of all that squinting in the pitch-dark tunnel.

'I'll be two shakes. No longer, I promise.'

She plants the sword on the cross she's made on the

ground, throws Charlie a determined smile, and then dashes away across the compound. At the last second she checks back and tosses Jin's hat to him, before spinning on her heel again and running for home.

Time to play the good little English girl again, she thinks. Even if it's just for the next few minutes.

A quick pair of eyes watches her go . . .

. . . sees her dart for the hole in the gates, her pale, slim shadow keeping pace beneath her . . .

. . . sees Charlie pacing the veranda, his own eyes fixed on Ruby. From there the gaze travels to Jin's dead body, the scruffy dog beside it.

The spirit sword lying where she placed it.

The watcher focuses on the cross in the dirt. If you look really closely, even that casts a shadow, the furrowed soil making another cross fractionally to one side.

Everything has a shadow. Sometimes you can't see it, but it's always there, waiting for the light, the right moment, the right eyes. Every object – clouds, trees, people, mountains, telegraph wires, ants, flowers. Every moment, every journey. Every life has a shadow.

And every love too.

And sometimes, when the world's a complete mess and nothing makes sense, the shadow world is very close indeed. You can fail to notice the boundary between this world and the one beyond. Stray across a line.

The watcher turns and melts into the darkness under the trees.

第二章

NO MORE NOODLES

It feels like she's the only thing moving in the whole vast city.

The building site on the corner of the street is deserted, holes filled with frothed, muddy water and wheelbarrows and shovels abandoned. Beyond that a car stands motionless on the glittering tram tracks, one door wrenched open, passengers and driver nowhere to be seen. No trams rumbling, no Sikh policemen whistling frantically, nothing.

A fresh burst of gunfire shatters the silence and stops her dead in her tracks. Ruby tilts her head. How far away was that, and which direction? And is it better to keep to the main streets or dodge across the Wilderness?

Take the old short cut, she thinks. No way of really knowing which is better and every second could count.

At the corner she cuts onto the path across the waste ground, sweat breaking as she runs full tilt for the Mansions. There's another sound now, a growling in the air above her, and a moment later an aeroplane's shadow flits across her own. Shielding her eyes against the brightness, she glances up to see a biplane wobbling away towards Nantao like some disorientated bumblebee, the silhouettes of the pilot and passenger clearly visible in the open cockpit.

Must be someone taking a look at the aftermath of last night's battles, she thinks. Journalists, or maybe one of the foreign air forces. What must the city look like from up there? Probably you'd see *everything* more clearly, see where the checkpoints are shut or open, spot which streets are safe and which ones the Green Hand are still blocking. Perhaps you'd even be able to see Moonface's launch out on the river. Track it all the way . . .

Fat chance!

Down here it feels more like a maze this morning. You don't know what's around even the next corner.

She runs on, prickly weeds flicking her shins. It's good Dad tried to help in the end, but how could he have *done* it? How could he have betrayed Fei to the Green Hand in the first place? Now look what's happened. And God only knows where Mother is.

12

Well, it can wait. The single most urgent thing is to rescue Fei. Nothing else matters, except that – and keeping close to Charlie, and helping *him*.

In the distance the plane turns, blurring into the smoke. She squints to follow its course and jogs on – and virtually stumbles straight over a body lying sprawled on the rough track.

Oh God.

It's a young man, his head wrenched to one side amongst the yellowing grass and weeds, the back of his jacket soaked dark with blood. One hand is reaching out stiffly, and shiny bluebottle flies already fidgeting the air over the body.

Cautiously she circles to get a better look. The man's eyes are wide open and the drops of morning dew on his eyelashes shiver in the breeze. Knotted around his neck is a blood-red kerchief. Must be one of the Communists, she thinks, tricked into the open and then hacked down by the Green Hand.

Curiosity nudges the fear to one side, and she crouches down beside him. There's something familiar in the slope of those eyebrows, the hollowed cheeks, but it takes a long moment for the penny to drop.

That's it! The noodle seller – the one who passed the package to Charlie before that mess of a journey into the old city. He had looked up and down the street, fear pulsing in those quick, dark eyes.

And now he's stone cold dead.

Ruby rocks back on her heels. She can't just leave him like that, it's not right, especially if he's a friend of the Tang family. That's what I always used to do, she thinks, take care of things. Like the dead baby in Hankow. She reaches out with trembling fingertips to close his eyelids, but the rigor mortis has set in and they won't budge. Grimacing, she fumbles the tight knot of the kerchief undone and then lays it over his face. The ink has leached out of the cheap material, leaving a blotchy red ring marked around his neck.

She straightens, mutters half a quick prayer, then turns and hares away along the track, eager now for the safety of the Mansions.

There's always death here, she knows that: the bodies of tramps frosted on the pavements in the morning after long winter's nights, the awful stories in the paper about gangsters, overheard gossip about atrocities further afield.

But now it feels so close. Just a whisker away and lurking in wait for you if you take the wrong turn, whether you're a Taoist martial-arts master or a schoolchild or even just a humble noodle seller.

If the city is quiet, the stillness in Riverside Mansions

14

is unearthly. Even the dust motes have stopped moving in the sunlit entrance lobby. Nobody in sight at all, staff and residents all hidden away behind closed doors.

If I see Mother I'll just bolt for it, she thinks as the lift hums its way to the top floor. There's no way I'm backing out of helping Fei, and no way she's going to stop me.

And if I see Dad?

In those last moments in the Chinese City, with bullets flying, there was a glimpse of the father she once knew: the one whose smile occasionally filled his face, who showed Tom and her the moon's craters through his telescope. The one who seemed to have disappeared for good when Tom died. There are so many questions she's bursting to ask, anger too. But there's just no way the conversation will end with him waving her off on the rescue mission with words of encouragement when the air has been cleared. *If* it can ever be cleared . . .

I'm as good as on my own for now, she thinks. At least as far as my stupid family goes.

And what about the ghosts?

There's not a hint of the pins and needles prickling, the goosebumps lying flat and smooth on her skin. And there's no sign of Tom either.

There wasn't even a *glimpse* of him the whole way

back through the tunnel . . . and nothing more this morning. Maybe he's gone for good, she thinks, maybe I won't see him again. But I *did* see him, I'm sure of that.

She takes a deep breath to steady herself, and then climbs the backstairs to the servants' quarters two at a time, desperate not to lose another minute.

When she sees Ruby, Amah hesitates a second and then throws a fierce hug around her, squeezing tight.

'Thank Heaven,' she mutters. 'I was worried, Ruby. So worried.'

'I'm fine. I need to ask you something—'

'Did you find Fei? What happened to you last night?'

'I – well, we . . .'

How to explain everything that's happened since the last time she was here? Best to keep it as simple as possible. Just the vital bits of the story.

'I went with Charlie to the Chinese City.'

Amah's papery forehead wrinkles. 'In that chaos? You must both be *absolutely crazy*. And how could you have done that anyway? The barriers were all shut.'

'That man I told you about at the temple – Lao Jin – he showed us a secret way and we went to one of Moonface's houses and tried to rescue Fei. Mister Tang was there – and Dad too. But he was injured

16

badly, Mister Tang that is, and Moonface got away and took Fei with him—'

Amah groans. 'Slow down, girl! You're babbling.' She lets go of Ruby's shoulders and sinks down on the little bed, shaking her head. 'I knew it. I knew it.'

'Knew what?'

'That my brother would end up in trouble like this. He gets starry-eyed and thinks he can make the world a better place. But you can't really, can you? You can only take care of the things around you. Your family for example.'

'I need to know something important.'

But Amah's not listening. 'Where did they go? Hospital? Or have the Green Hand got him?'

'I don't know,' Ruby moans, feet twitching restlessly beneath her. 'Amah, I need to know something about Moonface.'

The old lady shakes her head again. 'What a mess. My poor brother – and then there's your mother in hospital again—'

'Hospital?'

'Saint Luke's. Mister Harkner says it's her nerves. But if you ask me it's her *shen*, her spirit – it's all over the place. She needs a priest, not a doctor. Kept muttering away about seeing things that couldn't be there.'

Now the shivers start coming hard again all over. Somewhere far away across town a train whistle shrieks.

'*Things?*'

Amah reaches out to squeeze her hand. 'Oh, you poor girl. You look white as a sheet. Your mother will be fine—'

'I know she will. It's *Fei* I'm worried about, Amah!'

'We must notify the authorities. Your father will know what to do . . .'

'But we need to do something now!'

In the silence that follows, Ruby's gaze roams the room – and locks on to the tiny photograph on the dresser, the one of the young Mister Tang and Amah standing on the main street of that distant village. Twenty years ago? Maybe more. She crosses the floor and picks up the framed print.

'At least you're safe,' Amah sighs.

'Is this Plum Blossom Village? Where you and Mister Tang grew up?'

'*Peach* Blossom,' Amah corrects. 'We were born there. Before the bandits ransacked it. It's where Moonface started. Running a pack of thugs and lording it over everyone. Can't believe he's *still* plaguing our lives—'

'Where is it?'

'Fifty li or so downriver from Hankow. On the north bank.'

'Do you think he still goes there?'

'They say his old home is a big place somewhere upriver so I suppose so. Why?'

'I need to get going,' Ruby says. 'Can you lend me some money?'

'Go where, for Heaven's sake?'

'We're going after Fei. We're heading upriver.'

Amah jumps to her feet, eyes flashing. 'Out of the question. The night porter told me the Nationalists are attacking Hankow and there's something really bad going on up beyond the Gorges. Your parents will *kill* me if I let you out of here.'

'I'm sorry, Amah.'

The old lady grabs Ruby by the shoulders, shaking her fiercely. 'You're talking nonsense. Mister Harkner's in Customs. He can pull strings, find out where Moonface has taken Fei. It'll be ransom he's after. Think of your parents, Ruby—'

'I can look after myself,' Ruby says impatiently, tugging her arms free of Amah's grip. 'And besides, they don't care about *me*.'

'Of course they do, you silly girl. They love you.'

'I've promised Charlie we'll go—'

Amah moves to block her exit, but Ruby ducks under her flailing arm. By the door there's a pot containing some cash – Amah's housekeeping – and as she bundles through the door she snatches a handful of coins, then turns and runs hard down the darkened corridor.

'Rubyyyyy!' Amah calls, her voice desperate. 'Don't go! That part of the country is thick with foxes. I've *seen* what they can do.'

I'm sorry. Really sorry, Ruby thinks, banging through the door into the stairwell, her old guardian's voice still pleading for her to stop, as she tries to follow, but unable to run on her crippled, bound feet.

'It'll be suicide . . . !'

I can do it, Amah, Ruby thinks as she bounds down the steps. I'll find Fei. And I'll come back, safe and sound.

Cross my heart and . . .

Half a mile away the Liska Bakery van is hurtling towards the river, the driver peering anxiously over his steering wheel, dodging the remains of a smoking barricade and turning off Nanking Road down a side street. As the tyres rumble over some smouldering debris the painted fox on the side shakes violently.

Damn it. Never going to make it on time, he thinks. Faster.

第三章

GHOSTS ON RED FLOWER STREET

At last the city is coming back to some kind of life. Bareheaded coolies are starting to load boats on the Bund, rickshaw men clattering out to find their first fares of the day. A group of jittery bankers order an early round of drinks in the Shanghai Club where they've been taking shelter all night. *Just to steady the old nerves.*

At the North Station a black loco is hissing pent-up steam. Anxiously the fireman taps the pressure gauge and then lets out a long blast of the whistle, hoping it will somehow hurry *someone* into making a decision.

A mile away Ruby hears the shrill wail and it quickens her pace, dropping an idea straight into her head. Moonface must be miles down the Huangpu, she thinks. Maybe onto the Yangtze already. But if we hop a train towards Nanking maybe we can cut him off. Dad took us there once to do something for work. It doesn't take long and then maybe we'd be further up the Yangtze than Moonface's boat. Got to tell Charlie, convince him we can do it. We've got to get going, that's for sure . . .

Amah's cash jangles in her pocket as she bowls past Fratelli's Ices and then, at the corner of Canton and Kiangse Road, she comes to a skidding halt. Two long black cars are parked across the junction, Green Hand men fanned out across the road waving anyone passing to a stop, inspecting papers. On the back of an open truck, three young men and a woman sit disconsolately with their hands tied, gazes fixed to the floor as if an immense weight has been placed on the back of their necks.

I could do the good little English girl routine, Ruby thinks. But what if they've got my description from last night? From Moonface even? And there was that man who came to our flat. Better play safe.

There's a narrow cut-through by the library and she takes that now, running as fast as she can, taking the next left, then right, then right again. Not a way she normally goes. She turns onto a long street that leads back towards White Cloud, a memory struggling to come to the surface – something about this street, but what is it? The sunny side of the alley looks inviting and she jags across the road suddenly, eyes searching for whatever the half memory is stirring—

She doesn't hear the van approaching at all.

Doesn't see the pale green Liska Bakery colours, or the painted logo on the side – or the driver staring wide-eyed in alarm at the young girl dashing across the road right in front of him.

His gloved hands grip the wheel and then he wrenches it to one side, stamping the brake, tyres skidding.

There's a thump on the wing as the van comes shuddering to a stop, and he glances in his mirror, feeling sick to his stomach and expecting to see the foreign girl laid out cold on the tarmac.

It'll be prison. Worse. The family will starve . . .

But no. Thank Heaven for that! Somehow the girl's standing on the pavement, an old man in scruffy clothes steadying her by one shoulder, looking her over. The driver is about to get out and double check, but the pedestrian looks his way, gives a wave and shouts that it's *OK and no harm done.*

And maybe it's better not to get involved. The boss hates things to get messy. The driver cranks the gear lever into place and heads off – just that bit slower – towards Astor House, heart pounding and mouth dry.

* * *

But that's not how the whole thing seems to Ruby.

One minute she's running, feeling chilled in the shadows, and the sun-warmed pavement across the road looks so inviting. She *feels* the van bearing down on her before she sees or hears it, all so sudden there is no time to be scared. Head whipping round she has a clear view of the driver wrestling the wheel, then she braces for impact, frozen to the tarmac, eyes tight shut. Then it's all very muddled: she's flying through the air, spinning, an image of a fox – a ridiculous cartoon fox with a big grin – stamped on her retina, her scream stopped up in her mouth. As if strong hands have grabbed hold of her, she is lifted high, twisted through the air and then set down on her feet. And then she's leaning against a lamp post, blinking in the sunlight, the driver of the van getting back into his cab and roaring away.

She straightens up. Did the van hit her? Surely it must have done, but there's no pain, just a funny, aching sensation high up on both arms, where Amah gripped her . . .

She looks around the empty street, disorientated, reaching out for the support of the lamp post.

Wasn't there a man here – a moment ago? An old man, helping me to my feet? He said I was OK . . .

24

But there's no one, not a soul on either the sunny or shadowed side of the street. Hardly going to rescue Fei if I can't even cross the stupid street safely, she thinks, rubbing her shoulders and looking around, the shock still pumping.

Disorientated, Ruby glances up at the house beside her. A flight of steps leads up to a heavy black door painted with the number 354. To its right there's a darkened window with a silver candelabra and a peculiar painting of a hand traced in white on the glass – and the memory falls into place. It's the house Mother left in tears with that wild horsey look on her face and then lied about to Dad. Ruby's about to turn away when the door opens, and a woman dressed head to toe in white materialises against the darkened hall beyond. Her hair is bound in a kind of turban, a long dress flowing around her in waves.

'Young lady!' she calls. 'Are you all right? I seenk you are hurt?'

The accent is heavy – the familiar White Russian intonation a bit like Andrei's – but it's the woman's startled gaze that grabs her attention.

'No. No, I'm fine.' Ruby rubs her arms again, watching as the peculiar woman hurries down the steps towards her. But a yard or two short the Russian stops midstride, and her eyes pop open even wider.

25

Her face pales, as white as the turban, as she peers past Ruby into the space just beyond her aching shoulders, as if looking at something truly horrific there. Ruby shudders and looks round wildly, panicked to see what the woman has seen behind her. Maybe a gun-toting gangster, a ghost, a fox spirit even . . .

But there's nothing. Just the empty street, the skid marks from the van's tyres on the road like black exclamation marks.

'*Bozhe moy!*' the woman gasps. 'Oh. *Bozhe moy.* You poor girl!'

That familiar electric shocking twitches all over Ruby's skin again, as if something ghastly *is* standing right behind her, just out of sight.

The woman takes a breath, composing herself. 'You are Madame Harkner's leettle girl, aren't you?'

The fear is holding Ruby so tight now she can hardly breathe.

'What is it? Tell me!'

'You come in, please. Come in at once to Madame Zsa Zsa's.'

'But I've got to go . . .'

'You must come in, young lady.'

'No, really . . .' Ruby mumbles, but the woman's reaction and her hypnotic eyes are so strong that they are holding her to the spot.

26

'You *must*. I need to give you advice. You are in terrible danger. You are surrounded – completely *surrounded* I say to you – by spirits of dead.' The white lady shakes her head. 'Zsa Zsa has never, ever seen anything like eet. You poor, poor child.'

第四章

THE LINE OF FATE

The woman turns and strides into the house in a flurry of white linen.

As if hypnotised Ruby follows her, pulled into the space she's vacated, up the steps and then on into the hushed hallway beyond. A heavy oriental rug silences the school shoes, and thick red drapes muffle the walls.

'Thees way. Don't be shy . . .' the woman's voice calls from ahead, drawing Ruby further and through an open doorway into a kind of sitting room, the space stuffed full of polished furniture and ornaments. From a wing-backed armchair a plump white cat gazes at Ruby with acidic eyes, unblinking. Next to it on a sideboard a pile of wax fruit sits under a glass dome, never to ripen, never to rot.

The Russian lady's composure has returned, and

she studies Ruby now with a mix of concern and something more like pity. She motions her to a seat at a gleaming mahogany table.

'So. You are sure you feel well? I sink that lorry heet you,' she purrs in her deep, accented voice.

'It only brushed me,' Ruby says, looking round the room again, trying to control the furious prickling on her skin. An unseen clock is ticking heavily somewhere, the gaps between the seconds dragging. Through a forest of candles she can see that big white hand traced on the front window, the dotted lines crawling across its surface, fingertips marked with strange squiggles. Underneath, in reverse, she deciphers:

MADAME ZSA ZSA
RUSSIAN CLAIRVOYANT AND PALMIST
TO ROYALTY

'You are safe here. Sit down for a moment. Please,' the woman says. A few strands of hair snake from the turban, the heavy make-up on her face intensifying the whites of her eyes, the gaze of her big black pupils.

'How do you know who I am?'

Madame Zsa Zsa laughs. 'Some theengs are obvious. You are very like your mama. Now, sit.'

Ruby perches on a straight-backed chair. Charlie

29

will be wondering where I've got to, she thinks. I should get going, otherwise he'll come looking for me. It's still really dangerous out there.

But something about the room, about the White Russian, is holding her. Zsa Zsa leans forward, her eyes reaching out for Ruby's. 'So. Why you come? What do you want to know?'

'Nothing – I . . .'

'Don't be silly. Everyone has much they want to know from Zsa Zsa. But maybe too afraid to ask.'

'I didn't mean to come here, it was an accident—'

'You *flew*, my girl.' Zsa Zsa wiggles her fingers through the air, rings twinkling silver on her long fingers. 'The lorry it heet and you fly through air. And then you land on feet.'

She pauses, drops her voice to a whisper. 'And there are no accidents. When I come down I see ALL ghosts around you. Just for second. You must be very scared. So what do you want to know from Madame Zsa Zsa?'

Ruby returns her gaze, biting her lip. 'I'm not afraid.'

'Ask me a question.'

'Well – what was Mother doing here?'

'That is between her and me. But I theenk you are a *sensitive*. You have seen things most people do not see. I expect you have seen your *leetle* brother too?'

Ruby sits bolt upright.

'Of course you have. So let Zsa Zsa help. Give me your hand.'

'Why?'

'Our lives are in our hands, young lady.'

'My friend says foreign fortune tellers can't get things right here.'

'Then your friend is eegnorant. Are you not little bit interested?'

Under the table Ruby wipes her clammy palm on her dress. Maybe a few minutes won't hurt. After all, this strange Russian lady is taking her *seriously* about the ghosts. About Tom.

'What did you mean about ghosts around me?'

'Give me your hand. Don't be afraid.'

'I said I'm not afraid . . .'

She rubs her hand again and then slides it across the polished wood. Zsa Zsa reaches out and takes it gently, spreading the fingers, studying the back, then turning it over, smoothing the oval palm and gazing at it as if staring into a deep pond.

'Eenteresting.'

She peers closer, tracing a line around the fleshy part of Ruby's thumb. Her touch feels reassuring and Ruby leans closer to peer at her own hand.

'Is that – my life line? Is it a long one?'

The woman laughs. 'Not simple as that. Not seemple at all.'

Her face darkens, fine lines corrugating around her eyes as she looks closer. 'You have a water hand. Like mine. We are the ones who *see*, Miss Harkner.'

'See what?'

The fat cat on the sofa starts to purr rhythmically.

'Shhh. Just relax. Listen to old Cheiro the cat. Relax your eyes. Sometimes we look *too* hard, you know?'

The cat's purring gets louder, buzzing in Ruby's ears. Its gaze is intense, unsettling. A slice of sun spills through the window, but the room seems to be getting darker somehow, the tick of the clock sounding slower and slower.

'I can see *love* in your life. But it is troubled.'

A blush warms Ruby's cheeks and her mind flicks back to Charlie. 'What do you mean? Troubled?'

'All love carries shadow. But this one *verrrry* strong. You are going on a long and very dangerous journey—'

Ruby's mouth drops open.

'The most dangerous part of your life is coming. If you survive, you will live a long, long life, Ruby. Very long. You must make this journey. Is very eemportant.'

'What must I do?'

'Shhh. Look at your hand,' Zsa Zsa murmurs.

'Just relax. Can you see something? Something around your leettle finger?' Like a conjuror she wafts her hand over Ruby's outstretched palm. 'There. I theenk you see it now.'

Ruby gasps.

Tied around the base of her little finger is a fine, red thread. It's very faint, almost too dim to see – but definitely there, like a single strand of cotton knotted to make a loop and then running away across the table and dropping out of sight to the swirl of the Oriental carpets on the floor.

'What is it?'

'Chinese magic,' Zsa Zsa whispers. 'Very bee-yoo-tee-ful Chinese magic. This thread matters very much, young lady. If you are lost, if hope gone, look for this thread and follow it. It will guide you.'

Ruby stares at the thread. It seems to hover on the edge of visibility, disappearing when she tries to focus on it, and glowing again when she looks away.

'What is it?' she whispers, spellbound. 'What's it doing there?'

'You tied it there, Ruby.'

A loud bang on the street startles them both. There's the rumble of a motorcycle and then silence again. When Ruby looks at her hand the thread is barely visible.

'Now you must go,' Zsa Zsa says. 'Go quickly.'

Ruby's eyes still linger on her hand.

'But—'

'You must go. Now.'

The cat moves then, rearing up and opening its mouth wide, the fur rippling all over. He hisses, staring at Ruby.

'Cheiro sees them too,' Zsa Zsa says. 'The ghosts.'

Glancing around her, Ruby gets to her feet, moving uncertainly towards the door.

'Do you know a boy called Andrei?'

Zsa Zsa inclines her head. Shrugs.

'He told me about a Russian fortune teller who said something about a White Terror coming to the city. Was that you?'

The cat's still making a steady hissing at Ruby, those lemony eyes gleaming.

'You must go, young lady.'

'But what does it mean?'

'It was a dream,' Zsa Zsa says quietly – so softly her words are almost lost in the noise the Persian cat is making. 'A dream of future. A pale revenant.'

Ruby's hand is already on the door, but she has to know. 'Revenant?'

'One who comes back. Who won't keep still.'

'A ghost – a fox spirit?'

'Something wonderful,' the woman says, 'or something *terrifying*. It is not clear to me. Not yet. Now please go.'

The chills and tingling have taken complete hold. Head spinning, Ruby nods, takes one last glance at the cat, the turbaned woman's hypnotic eyes, and then blunders down the hall. On her finger the red line is still pulsing as if her own heartbeat is fluttering the blood through it, but fading fast as she makes for the front door.

The thread leads out to the street, is visible a moment longer and then is obliterated by the sun.

第五章

THE ROAR OF THE DISTANT SEA

Dad would say it was just her imagination running riot. That fortune tellers were nothing but *bunkum*, taking advantage of *gullible fools*. The Dad of old would say it with a lopsided smile, the one of recent months with a stormy look on his face – but both would agree that what she's just heard is rot. Ruby stops, squints, runs her left index finger around where the thread was tied: there's nothing to see except her pale skin, nothing to feel.

A vague memory stirs, a piece of folklore or something. Amah would know . . . but I can't return to the Mansions, she thinks. We've got to get going.

Around her the city is cranking up its usual beat: rickshaws cluttering the streets, a tram clanking along, even a few shoppers heading towards Nanking Road. The gaggles of Green Hand men, their black cars and helpless prisoners seem to have melted away with the thread in the morning light.

If it still *is* morning.

How long has she been gone? It feels like she has been *hours* in that strange room on Red Flower Street, and before that the thing with the van, the argument with Amah . . .

The sun is much, much higher overhead now. Eager for warmth, desperate to check Charlie is OK, she keeps to the brightness where she can and sprints the rest of the way to White Cloud, rehearsing arguments in her head to convince Charlie to take her with him.

But at the temple there's no sign of him on the veranda, or in the pooled shadows of the main hall. Surely he hasn't ventured out to look for her? I've been much longer than I said I'd be, Ruby thinks, breathing hard, her eyes scouring the temple grounds from the gates. Maybe he's gone. Or maybe Andrei came back with the police. Or the Green Hand.

Oh God! Shouldn't have got sidetracked . . .

Cautiously she crosses the courtyard. Jin's body still lies where it fell, covered by the blanket. If anyone has been here surely they would have removed the body? But there's no sign of Straw next to him.

Maybe he went off with Charlie, or maybe the temple was raided?

She steps up onto the veranda, panic mounting, and is about to start shouting out Charlie's name when she hears a low whistle come from right beneath her feet. She drops to her knees, tilting her head towards the boards.

'Charlie? Is that you?'

'Yes. Where on earth have you *been*?'

'I had a sort of accident,' she says.

'Accident? Are you OK?'

'Doesn't matter. What are you doing down there?'

'There were Green Hand here. About quarter of an hour ago, maybe less. That dog of Jin's barked at them at the gate and it gave me enough time to get under here. Hang on . . .'

A second later Charlie's scrambling out, brushing dust from his clothes. He's trying to look calm but his movements are jumpy. The spirit sword is grasped in one hand, Jin's hat in the other.

'You were gone *ages*, Ruby. I was about to come and look for you—'

'Have they gone? The Green Hand?'

He nods. 'Think so. I looked after the sword. And your hat.' He holds them out to her, nodding in that earnest way of his. 'I thought you'd want them.'

'Thanks.' She takes the Fedora in one hand, the spirit blade in the other, her fingers wrapping snugly round the worn hilt.

'What do you mean about an accident?'

'Just a close shave. I'm fine.'

'Did you find Auntie?'

Ruby nods. 'I'll tell you on the way.'

'On the way where?'

'I thought we could go to the North Station. Try and get a ticket for Nanking.'

'That's just what I was thinking! As long as the trains are running.'

'They are. I heard them.'

She glances again at Jin, and feels the grief tug at her. 'What did they do, the Green Hand men?'

'They just poked around for ages, looking for something I think. They went through the back rooms and all over the main hall. When they got fed up they tried to beat Straw with a stick, but he gave them the runaround. One of them took a pot shot at him, but he scarpered through the gate.'

'And what about Jin?'

'They just checked he was dead, swore at him, then scurried off in their cars. I'll tell you a weird thing though: before they got here I had a look for that Almanac of yours. It's gone from the hiding place.'

Ruby looks at him, eyebrows raised. 'You said it was all rubbish.'

'I just thought it might help. Somehow . . . I don't know . . .'

'Maybe Andrei took it? Or Yu Lan?'

Charlie shrugs. 'Who knows? Can't imagine that chicken Yu sneaking back here last night. He's just a spoilt rich kid. Anyway, it's gone.'

He looks helpless for a moment, shuffling a foot in the dust, peering at the 'X' Ruby has drawn there.

'Listen, it could be hundreds of miles, Ruby. Hundreds. I have to go after Fei but you don't have to—'

'I want to go. I want to go with you, Charlie. Two of us will stand a better chance than one. We did so well last night.' She wants to tell him about the fortune teller, wants to tell him about the look on Zsa Zsa's face and what she said about the journey. But it can keep. Mustn't risk making him think I'm being stupid. Not up to the task ahead. 'Don't you want me to come with you?'

Charlie frowns, unable to meet her gaze for a moment. 'Of course I want you to come. I just – don't want you to get mixed up in all this trouble.'

'I already am mixed up in it.' She looks away towards the North Station, her mood lifted by what he's just said. *Of course, I want you to come.* She turns back again with half a smile on her face. 'Hey. Thursday's child. Remember the rhyme? Thursday's child has far to go. *Mei wenti*.'

She jams the battered Fedora back down on her head and Charlie stifles a hint of a grin back.

'So let's go.'

They scramble over the back wall of the temple, throw quick glances up and down the street and then merge into the returning crowds. Lao Jin's pack is bouncing on Charlie's shoulders, the spirit sword wrapped in Ruby's Cardigan inside. There wasn't much else to pack, just Jin's dented cups and fire-blackened kettle, a second threadbare blanket.

At the last minute, with Charlie's back turned, Ruby had thrown in Tom's old wind-up monkey. Something about it must be important, otherwise why would Jin have brought it here? For that matter, Ruby thinks as they wheel onto Fukien Road, how did Jin find it in the first place? At least it feels right to have the thing with them – a link to Tom. They hurry on towards the bridge across Soochow Creek, the spot where Fei always swore she'd seen a hopping vampire on the mud one winter evening years ago.

41

The train whistle shrills over the sound of the passing traffic.

'Faster,' she pants. The trains just tend to go when they're full these days and it would be too awful to miss one by a few minutes and have to wait hours for the next. But Charlie's slowing, turning to her and pointing. They're approaching Uchiyama's, and the old Japanese bookseller has his door open. Nothing panics him into shutting up shop for long.

'Hang on a mo.'

Charlie ducks through the doorway and by the time Ruby has joined him, he's already rummaging a shelf of maps near the counter.

The bookseller looks up, squinting. 'Miss Harkner. Good afternoon. Lovely hat you have there.'

Ruby nods a greeting, rather thrown she's been recognised so easily.

'And how did that old ghost book work out for you?'

'It was – interesting. Thank you.'

'Thought it might be. Going on a trip?'

'Just a hike,' she says, trying to brighten her smile.

'Take care, won't you,' Uchiyama says, shuffling the papers on his desk. 'Bad weather coming they say. By the way, your father was here, a little earlier. Looking for you. He seemed a bit upset.'

Ruby looks at the bookseller sharply. 'Was he – I mean, did he say where he was going?'

'No. He looked pale, I thought.'

'If he comes back again, tell him I'll be home as soon as I can,' Ruby says.

Charlie has opened up a map with a blue cloth cover, and comes back over to the counter fighting it back into shape. 'This might help,' he whispers in Chinese. 'It's in English. Drawn up by your lot, but you can read it.'

He points at the title stamped in gold letters on the cover.

ADMIRALTY LARGE CHART
YANGTZE: NANKING TO HANKOW

'They're not *my lot*,' Ruby mutters, then turns to Uchiyama. 'How much?'

'I'd rather you steal,' the bookseller sighs. 'Then I will not be included in whatever foolish scheme you two are hatching. Going upriver then?'

'No,' Ruby says firmly. 'We're just heading out into the countryside. For some fresh air.'

'We could all do with that,' Uchiyama murmurs. He glances out of the window and pulls a face, as if he's just tasted something very bitter. 'There were

43

some other people looking for you, Miss Harkner. Not that long ago. *Very* unpleasant types indeed.'

On full alert, Ruby edges back into the sunlight blinding the shop front.

Very unpleasant types can only mean Green Hand. Maybe they've even got the bookshop under surveillance. After all Dad comes here all the time so they might well be watching it. But the pair of eyes that *are* trained on her belong to a much more familiar and friendly face. Straw is sitting resolutely in the middle of the pavement, ignoring the other passers-by, eyes raised to greet them. He gets to his feet and rakes his front legs in a long stretch, as if bowing.

Ruby crouches down to hug the dog's slim shoulders.

'Of course you found us,' she murmurs, feeling the reassuring softness there. 'You clever boy. Have you got anything to tell us, then?'

Straw's tail wags harder, but none of that guttural growling comes from his mouth, nothing that could be mangled-up Chinese. Instead his tongue lolls out of the corner of his mouth, panting a bit. Yesterday, the day before, he seemed so knowing, so aware. Now he just has that same half-hopeful, half-wary look in his amber eyes that so many of the city's strays have. Just a dog, nothing more.

'We can't take him with us, Ruby. He belongs here—'

'I don't think *we* get to choose. We might be his only friends now Lao Jin's gone. Let's take him with us, Charlie. Please.'

At the mention of Jin's name Straw gives a single solitary bark and then turns and trots resolutely away towards the bridge over the Creek, his claws ticking rhythmically on the paving stones. Charlie watches him for a moment, shrugs and then sets off after him.

'OK. But let's get out of here before those Green Hand boys come back,' he calls over his shoulder. 'Or your dad in case he tries to stop us.'

Ruby moves to follow, but for a second her feet drag. Beyond the creek there's only a few hundred yards to Boundary Road and the edge of the Settlement, but she can still turn back. Dad looked pale, Uchiyama said. Maybe it's wrong just to leave him in the lurch, in trouble. It *is* wrong . . . But it would be just as wrong not to help Fei, to help Charlie.

She remembers again that day of cold, blue waves at the beach – the day she swam out, the Ruby who knew no fear, who thought she could beat anything – remembers the tug of the current taking hold of her, the sudden clear thought that she'd made a *big* mistake – nothingness below her, the beach lost behind a wall of rolling sea. And then miraculously Dad had come thrashing through the waves and found her in a furrow about to go under, and dragged her back to the gritty sand, his eyes a mixture of triumph and alarm. On the beach Mother had flapped around like a demented seagull, cross and relieved all at once, Tom gazing at Ruby in astonishment, trying to take in what had happened. But Dad had just flopped down and gazed out at the waves, silent for a long five minutes while Mother fussed on and Tom's laughter gradually subsided. He saved me, she thinks, maybe I shouldn't just abandon him now.

'Ruby!'

Charlie's shout brings her back with a start. He's already a good fifty paces down the street.

'I heard a train whistle. There must be one about to go!'

'Coming!' she shouts and sets off down the street in pursuit, her mind still full of the dark blue sea. Feels like she's swimming out again, towards the horizon, into the tug of the cold hungry water.

They're only just out of sight across the bridge, when a black car pulls up outside Uchiyama's. Two men in Chinese robes jump from the running boards, eyes raking the street. One of them bangs on the car roof and a tall, rangy man springs from the back seat. He glowers at the shop in front of him, and when he turns to bark an order his mouth is crammed full of sharp teeth. He lifts his head like an animal picking up a scent and turns towards the bookshop.

Behind his counter Mister Uchiyama peers through the dusty window and feels his stomach twist as he recognises the figure: One Ball Lu.

Moonface's feared right-hand man. He normally just concentrates on running the city's opium racket, not bothered with shaking down small traders for squeeze money. What on earth does he want here then? At least the young girl got away, Uchiyama thinks.

He takes a deep breath. Time to act really stupid and hope for the best. They say Lu made mincemeat of a man who crossed him once. Literally.

The old Japanese man clears his throat, plants a bright but blank smile on his face and braces himself.

第六章

NIGHT TRAIN TO NANKING

The station is rammed with people. Now the fighting's died down everyone is in a hurry to get somewhere other than where they are: families from inland carrying as many possessions as they can, ragged soldiers either on their way to, or from, some battle they'd rather not think about. A knot of men in Western suits, gripping suitcases, gathered round a blackboard trying to decipher a list of times scrawled there. No one seems at ease.

Not a single Foreign Devil in sight this afternoon, Ruby thinks. Not even a missionary. Her arms feel really sore now, and she rubs them again, wondering how Amah managed to hurt her so much. Forget it, she thinks. Pull yourself together. Shanghai Ruby never cries! Midday has long since passed and they've been hanging around trying to find out what's happening for a good three hours. Either people don't know, or they don't want to talk, and even the uniformed staff don't seem to have a clue.

She jams the hat down harder, eyes straining for Charlie who's got fed up waiting and gone to see if he can *make something happen*. Overhead the long hand of the station clock shudders another minute forward. Half past five. That makes more than twenty minutes since he waded into the scrum leaving her with the pack and Straw. Can't lose him at the first hurdle, she thinks. What if he's been grabbed? What if the Green Hand are watching the stations?

No, that's ridiculous. Even if they are looking for us, they won't expect a couple of kids to head *out* of the safety of Shanghai. And besides, in all this muddle, it would be impossible to spot us, wouldn't it?

A finger raps her shoulder and she wheels round, alarmed, then relieved to see that it's Charlie, slightly out of breath but eyes brighter than they've been all day.

'There's one – about to go. There's a train on the far platform – waiting hours' apparently. They've just got the signal. We've got to be really quick.'

With Straw glued to their heels they weave through the station, past queues, simmering arguments, gaggles of people moving in opposite directions. Scraps of conversation and gossip fill the air, Shanghai dialect mixed with accents from far-off provinces, voices all charged, all darkly ominous.

'They've taken Hankow—'

'Rubbish. The Communists won't allow it . . .'

'. . . bodies in the river. And you can't get beyond . . .'

'. . . my uncle heard the English are shelling right now. Hundreds dead.'

A whistle sounds, hollowing the air.

'Hurry,' Charlie gasps. 'I need a dollar.'

'What for? That's way too much, isn't it?' Ruby hisses.

'Bad times, higher prices,' Charlie pants back over the ruckus in the hall. 'This is the last train for days. The warlord's going to close the line. So we're going to travel "pidgin".'

Beyond the covered platforms, other dormant locomotives and wagons, there's a long train waiting on a distant platform, its engine snorting steam and black smoke. As they hurry it starts to grind into motion, edging away from the station. Frustrated passengers are trying to make their way towards it, but a group of Chinese soldiers holds them back, jabbing the air with bayonets fixed.

'Get back. It's full!' one of them growls.

'We're too late,' Ruby gasps.

'Not yet.' Charlie veers away to a small hut at the far end of the platform. 'Give me that silver dollar now. Keep your head down.'

Ruby fumbles the heavy coin from her pocket and plants it in Charlie's palm. He lifts his head and whistles sharply through his teeth and a moment later a guard emerges from the hut, a heavyset man with fat rippling his neck. He beckons them over, snaps the dollar from Charlie's hand and then quickly puts it between his teeth and gives it a bite.

He nods, then sees Straw. 'Didn't say anything about mutts.'

'Please,' Charlie says. 'My dad will kill me if my sister and me don't bring our dog home.'

'Half a dollar more.'

The whistle screeches again.

'Last chance.'

Anxiously Ruby fishes out another coin. That's almost all their money gone already, but there's no choice. The fat-necked man leads them round the back of his hut at a jog, away from the soldiers, and then down two steps onto the rails, picking his way across sleepers and the next set of tracks. Behind the black locomotive are three overcrowded carriages, a few passengers still scrambling up to

51

'fresh air' seats on the roof, and after them clank a string of boxcars, the doors to the first few wide open, dozens of soldiers packed tight like fish in a tin.

As they come alongside, the train is still only at walking pace, the loco hissing as it gathers its burden and strains forwards. Fat Neck puts his whistle to his lips and gives a short peep, and a soldier appears at the door of the wooden van at the back. He holds out his hand to Charlie, beckons urgently, and then helps him up onto the steps. Trying to keep her head down, Ruby follows, feels the soldier's rough palm grip her own, and then she's lifted up and standing beside Charlie.

In the dim light of the guard's van, the soldier and his companion gaze silently at the children.

'What about Straw?' Ruby gasps to Charlie, keeping the brim of her hat shielding her face.

But Fat Neck has already swept the dog up in one meaty arm and hopped, with surprising agility, onto the metal steps as the train picks up speed, rails clacking beneath them as the station slips away.

He sets Straw down and ruffles his head, then turns to Charlie. 'He's a nice old boy, I can see why you want him. And now I just need a few copper cash to pay these gentlemen,' he nods at the soldiers, 'and no one need know how many company rules we're breaking. How's that?'

'Pay him,' Charlie whispers. 'Or they'll throw us off at the next stop.'

Heart sinking, Ruby drops a few more coins in the man's paw of a hand and turns away.

'Your sister seems a bit shy,' the guard laughs, nodding to the darkened interior of the main part of the wagon. 'But you've bought yourselves the best seats in the house. Bunk in there, with the mail sacks. If you hear any trouble, just bury yourself and wait for the all clear. There's Communists on the line with their home-made bombs. Might not be plain sailing this evening. And put your dog on a damn string, will you?'

The wheels beneath are clicking a rhythm from the track, the speed increasing. Ruby glances back through the open guard's door and sees the grand buildings of the city falling behind, already small – and getting smaller.

By some trick of the light or movement, or incline of the rail, it's as though they are sinking slowly, but steadily, into the ground.

第七章

FLAMING FOX

An hour later the train is overtaken by cloud-laden dusk.

It's even darker in the guard's van where Ruby and Charlie have snuggled down as best they can amongst the mail sacks. Each hessian bag is stamped with names of cities inland: NANKING, CHANGSHA, HANKOW, ICHANG. Charlie spreads out the Admiralty map and peers at it by the light of a match. His face is warmed by the flame, his eyes glinting as they rove the twisting river on the chart.

'And you're sure about what Amah said about Peach Blossom Village?'

'Yes. She said Moonface still goes there. Or near there.'

'It's not on the map.'

'Of course not. It's just some insignificant village.'

The match snuffs out against his fingers. 'Ouch.

Peach Blossom might be insignificant to you, but—'

'It's not insignificant to *me*,' Ruby says quickly. 'I didn't mean that. It's where Amah and your dad came from. Your mum.' She pauses. 'So really it's where you come from too.'

Charlie's face is a blur in the gloom. 'I've never been there. Not sure I can find it.'

'So we'll get close and then ask. Amah said it was fifty li short of Hankow. What about asking the guard?'

'He won't know,' Charlie says. 'And the fewer who know where we're going the better. Old Uchiyama already knows we're heading upriver.'

'He wouldn't tell anyone bad.'

'Not unless he had to. And he might tell your dad when he sees him again.'

Ruby shifts her weight, trying to get comfortable. Maybe I should have waited to tell Dad, she thinks, see if he could help . . .

Straw is lying close against her, snoring on the end of the piece of parcel twine they've found and used to improvise a lead. The bite of the twisted string makes her think again of the red thread wound around her little finger this morning.

Not a sign of it since, but she can't help looking for it now and then. Even in the muddle at the station when she was waiting. How weird that was, and yet how important it felt.

In the open doorway one of the soldiers is silhouetted against a block of fading sky, sparks from the engine twinkling by in the dusk. She wonders if he or the others have guessed she's not Chinese. Maybe they don't care though. The guard has taken a big chunk of 'squeeze' and he'll share that out. That's how China works. Dad's always going on about squeeze and how it *keeps the whole damn machine running*. More than they'll earn in a week probably, and that and the food it'll guarantee will be more important than turfing us off at some distant station.

Charlie's voice comes again. 'Best plan is to catch Moonface on the river. Maybe in Nanking.'

'I reckon we must be going way faster than a boat. We'll be there before him.'

'But what then? It'll be like trying to pick a needle from the bottom of the ocean. And even then Moonface is hardly just going to give Fei up to us.'

Ruby nods. Charlie's right of course, this is the man who drowned his own mother in a barrel, whose men have drained people of their blood.

'At least we're on the way,' she says, trying to put strength into the words. 'And we've got a plan.'

'Half a plan at most.' Charlie sighs. 'I think we're only just through Soochow Station.'

'I'm going to have a look.'

High above there's an air vent. Ruby clambers up the mail bags and parcels, bracing for support as the train rocks, and presses her eye to the slots. The landscape beyond is almost dark now, small fields and paddies stitched together by waterways that glint as they reflect the very last of the daylight. An occasional ox and cart nothing but shadow on an embankment, the smoke and smuts from the loco filling the cooling, early autumn air. A silent village. A black sampan on a darkening canal.

It all looks so lonely, desolate.

The line curves to the left, and briefly the loco is visible piling steam over its shoulder. Beyond it something flickers, like the lightning of a distant storm fluttering just over the horizon. She squints through the grille for a better look but smut from the engine flies into her eye, hot, sharp, making it water furiously, and she staggers back clumsily onto the sacks.

Blinking hard to clear her vision, bright light spills on her face and through her tears she sees the taller of the soldiers bending over her.

'A foreign devil,' he says, nodding to himself. Then, in Pidgin: 'Melican girl?'

'English.'

'Engliss girl b'long Shanghai side. Not Nanking

side now. Plenty bad.'

'I do belong here,' she answers in Chinese. 'This is my country too.'

The soldier takes a long pull at his cigarette, then flicks it away through the open wagon door in a fiery arc.

'Plenty years ago I fight with England and US,' he says, sticking to Pidgin. 'Dig plenty tunnel for English soldiers. Then long boat home.'

He mimes the action of digging, then the bobbing of a ship on rough seas.

'Where?'

'*Faguo*,' he says quietly. France. And in his face is that same look that used to pass across Dad's face whenever she and Tom nagged about the Great War and the trenches, eager to hear about the clanking tanks, or fighter aces in the skies. But Dad would just fall silent, eyes focusing on something else.

The soldier takes a breath, pulls out a packet of cigarettes, hesitates, and then offers her one. 'You likee smoke, Missee?'

Ruby shakes her head. 'No, thanks. No likee.'

Her watering eyes have fallen on the crude image printed in solid red and black on the box: a beautiful flame-red fox, his huge paintbrush of a tail writing the brand name above.

The animal's face glints in the lamplight, big piercing eyes staring at her. In her watering vision those eyes seem almost to be moving, alive. And really familiar too somehow.

She wipes her eyes, staring at the packet as it shakes in the soldier's hand. It makes her think again of the fox spirit in White Cloud, that drooling mouth. Her hands and legs start to tingle as she watches it, but somehow it's also oddly reassuring. Like seeing the face of someone you know miles and miles from home, amongst strangers. Straw yawns and gets to his feet and then sniffs at the outstretched packet, nosing it eagerly.

'Not for you, old boy,' the soldier laughs and goes back to the compartment at the end of the van and his vigil at the doorway.

Night rolls around the train. Small halts and stations flash by, some burning a light, some veiled in darkness. At times the train slows to walking pace, as if uncertain of what lies ahead, frustratingly long minutes before the steady click click of the rail beats faster again. The fifth or sixth time it happens, the engine crawls snail speed for a good quarter of an hour before slowly grinding to a stop. In the silence that follows a distant but distinct rumble rolls through the darkness. Charlie scrambles to his feet, lifting himself up to the vent.

'Trouble,' he says. 'There's a fight going on, some big guns firing. Small stuff as well.'

'These soldiers don't seem so bad,' Ruby whispers. 'They'll protect us.'

'You know what they say, bandits and soldiers all breathe from the same nostril. No difference really – they'll just be looking out for number one.'

The two soldiers are leaning out of the open door of the van, peering into the oncoming night, faces tense in the lamplight as the train jolts forward again.

'Keep your heads down,' the tall one calls. 'We'll probably just steam clear through it.'

He snaps the bolt of his rifle and tucks the packet of cigarettes away in a trouser pocket.

'If we can just get as far as Chenkiang,' Charlie mutters, 'we'll be back on the river. We might need to change sides fast though.'

'What do you mean?'

'We can show our colours if we have to . . .'

He nods at his jacket pocket, and from it pulls a long red strip of cloth.

'But we're not Communists,' Ruby hisses.

'We – we might need to be.'

'But aren't they dangerous? Dad always says—'

'My dad knows them better than yours does, Ruby. He says they're OK. Most of them.'

There's a renewed urgency to the train's momentum, the wheels rumbling faster beneath, and gunfire – the steady pounding of something big and heavy – is much louder now. Ruby edges closer to Charlie, nudging into him, but as her shoulder brushes his it feels *really* sore. She catches her breath.

'Ow.'

'You OK?'

'Just a bit bruised. That's all—'

An explosion rocks the van, cutting Ruby short. She steadies herself with one hand, gripping Straw with the other, imagining the loco and all its carriages rolling from severed rails, tumbling over and over down an embankment to some blackened canal. But, after a shudder that convulses the entire length of the train, it settles back to its rhythm.

'Keep down, you two,' Fat Neck shouts. 'They're trying to blow the line.'

The two soldiers are aiming their rifles through the open doorway, squinting down their sights for enemies on the rails ahead – and both suddenly tense, firing almost simultaneously. A reek of gunsmoke fills the darkened wagon. The train's whistle blows long and loud, and then the train shakes again and starts to lose speed. Mouth set in a determined line, the taller soldier steadies himself, then fires off three more rounds.

'Whatever happens,' Ruby says, 'I'm glad we're trying to do this, Charlie. I'm glad – I'm with you.'

She wants to ask him to hold her hand, but, at the same time, wants to show how brave she can be, that she really is Shanghai Ruby again, and can play her part.

Perhaps Charlie feels the need, though. He reaches out, his own hand steady even though everything in the carriage is shaking like mad as the train brakes hard, wheels squealing on the rails. He rests his palm on her shoulder.

'Keep your face hidden if anything happens. Don't let them see you're a foreigner. Or a girl.'

The train grinds to a halt as shouts and bellowed orders ring through the night. Before Ruby can argue Charlie has scrambled to join the guard and the soldiers, all of them jumping down to the ground below.

'Stay here!' she calls, but he's gone.

More sporadic firing filters through the wall, then a splintering sound close by, like someone's taken a hatchet to the roof of the next carriage. She pushes her ear to the wood and hears a scream – a long way off, but ragged and horrible – and she burrows a bit deeper into the postal sacks, tugging Straw on his improvised leash.

'You stay here at least, boy. I don't want to lose you now.'

She holds the scruffy dog close, feels his wet nose nuzzle her neck, and then an almighty boom shakes the night behind them. A bomb? If they blow the line behind we'll be trapped, she thinks. They might take hostages. A foreigner like me would be a prize possession. She's heard tales of missionaries and steamship captains kept prisoner for weeks, months, moved from one hideaway to another while ransom negotiations drag on and on, the captives getting thinner and more desperate. And everyone knows about the beastly things that happened to passengers on the Peking-Shanghai Express at Lincheng . . .

Another thunderous roar sounds from very close by, and a moment later, Charlie's head reappears in the doorway.

'Come and see this,' he shouts, eyes charged with adrenaline.

She scrambles to join him, down the metal steps and onto an overgrown siding where their train has come to rest. Weeds poke through the gravel at her feet, the vast, low-lying countryside unfolding wide around them. But Charlie's eyes are fixed on the line back towards Shanghai, the soldiers and guards all peering in the same direction. Another train is approaching fast from behind, pluming white smoke, the ground beneath their feet starting to shake as it approaches.

The soldiers are beaming, slapping each other on the back. But Charlie's face is grim. 'It's the warlord's armoured train. It's coming to clear the line.'

'What's happening?'

'Communists ahead.' Charlie leans close, whispering now. 'But they won't stand a chance against this thing.'

The ground is trembling harder now as the engine heaves into view, snorting steam from every pore. From the cab roof a heavy-duty searchlight is swinging across the landscape, seeking prey.

Charlie pulls a face. 'You can see why people thought trains were bad magic,' he shouts over the engine's sound.

The train thunders past. Armoured plates are bolted to every surface, swivelling gun turrets and slit-sighted observation posts mounted on top. Three carriages back a hefty cannon is elevating, pointing down the line. As the carriage passes it detonates, the muzzle flashing as it spews a shell towards the distant firefight.

'That'll do for those swine,' the taller soldier says,

grimacing. 'Chase those Reds back into the swamp or wipe them out where they stand.'

Charlie nods, but doesn't answer, and climbs slowly back up into the van, hand thrust deep into his pocket.

Ruby hesitates a moment. There's cheering from the soldiers on their train, people waving caps out of windows and doors as an intense burst of new flashes light the horizon. She looks away across the fields and ditches below them. The moon has risen, painting pale light on the countryside: a little way off a line of willows blow peacefully in the breeze. It's hard to believe a few miles to her right a battle is raging. People are dying there, she thinks. It just seems so stupid, Chinese fighting Chinese.

There's a crescendo of explosions and small arms fire up the line – and then silence.

A shiver grips her. She takes a last glance at the darkened countryside and then clambers back into the van to find Charlie.

When the great armoured train clunks past on the mainline some twenty minutes later there's still not a soul visible on-board, just the blind slits of the gun turrets, the armoured shields all down and fire blackened in places. It trundles back towards Shanghai and as soon as it clears the points they're moving again.

Ruby climbs to the vent to take a look as they approach the scene of the battle.

'Best not,' Charlie says. He's been quiet ever since the arrival of the gun train, his face sombre.

'I want to see.'

Cool air flows through the slots as she presses her face to them. At first she can see nothing, then a smouldering fire flickers into view, the skeletal remains of an open-backed lorry, slewed across a dirt road, its bones still burning. Around it, bodies – some dozen or so – lie strewn, a few face down, others lying on their backs staring up at the stars above. A white horse lies dead beside the rails.

Ruby's gaze follows the eerie sight as it slides past, and then she sinks back down beside Charlie.

'At least we got through,' she says.

Charlie frowns. He turns away and rummages in Jin's old pack, pulling out the blanket. 'At what price?'

'We have to keep going, to get Fei,' Ruby says. 'It would've been hopeless to get stopped there.'

Charlie goes to say something, then checks himself and pulls the blanket over them both. It's decidedly cool now, the van's door still open to the night chill. Ruby tries to push the image of the flaming truck and the bodies from her head, but as soon as she manages that, other – darker – thoughts creep back.

'Charlie?'

'What?'

'About that accident this morning. A van nearly hit me – I thought he was going to run me down. I thought it was going to kill me.'

'But it didn't. What about it?'

The train roars across a bridge beneath them, the note of the wheels and engine deepening.

'I keep seeing foxes too.'

'What do you mean?'

'On the cigarette packet that soldier's got – it was like it was looking at me, Charlie. And when the van nearly hit me this morning I'm sure I saw one then. But I can't have done, can I?'

Charlie's hand reaches towards hers under the blanket and she's glad to feel its warmth enclose hers and even squeeze gently, the contact between their palms pulsing.

She squeezes back.

'Do you think it means anything?'

'You're seeing foxes because you're thinking about them. It's like someone says a place you've never heard of and the next thing you know you're reading about it in the newspaper. That kind of thing.'

'OK. If you say so.'

Another five long minutes pass, sleep at last

67

gathering in Ruby's eyes. She keeps seeing that fox face though, keeps remembering the day in the temple when they trapped the *huli jing* and chucked it down the well.

'Charlie,' she whispers.

'What now?'

'Nothing. It's just . . .'

'What?'

'It doesn't matter. Sleep well.'

Lulled by the train's motion, she drifts towards sleep, and then briefly – as so often before on the edge of sleeping or waking – sees that river shining, snaking into darkness below her. She's flying higher and higher this time though, hundreds of miles of shining, beaten silver spooling beneath her. Higher and higher . . .

When the guard decides to check up on his pidgin cargo, he sees half a smile on Ruby's sleeping face. And good luck to them both, he thinks, turning back to the soldiers and their card game, the smile reflected briefly on his own tired and drawn face.

第八章

ELEPHANTS ON PURPLE MOUNTAIN

She wakes to her shoulder being shaken hard, Charlie crouching over her, dawn light already spilling into the van.

'We're just passing Chenkiang, Ruby. Have a look.'

She rubs her eyes. The guard and soldiers are fast asleep on bed rolls and she steadies herself to pick past them to the open door, the cold morning rush of the air. Below, there's a tumble of low roofs, a knot of dark greenery above the tiles, a wooded hill topped by an elegant, seven-storeyed pagoda.

And then beyond that she sees the Yangtze.

It's partly obscured by the trees, but it looks vast in the early morning light, far bigger than she remembers, dotted with junks and boats of all sizes, all of them dwarfed by the river. They look like insects, waterboatmen and pond-skaters on a huge pond.

Either side of it the countryside has started to roll, the flatlands rearing into low sweeping hills, mist clinging like some Chinese brush painting.

Charlie screws up his face. 'We could jump for it here . . . Maybe we could find help near the river. From some of our—' He hesitates. 'From friends.'

'We don't know Chenkiang,' Ruby says, shaking the last of the sleep from her head. 'At least I've been to Nanking before. And we can get help at the British Consulate. Maybe even the Navy – or the River Patrol.'

'We should keep them out of it. Stick to friends.'

'What do you mean "friends"?'

Charlie's hand is thrust deep in his pocket again. 'You know what I mean. *Friends*, of Dad's.'

It's too late anyway. Already Chenkiang has slipped away in the train's smoky wake.

'We're going to need help to find that boat,' Ruby says. 'We should try whatever – *whoever* we can.'

She looks at Charlie for agreement, but he's dropped back into his own thoughts, gazing at the river. Presumably by 'friends' he means Communists, people linked to Mister Tang.

'Are you OK, Charlie?'

He turns and nods his head briefly and then gazes back out at the dawn. 'Yep. Fine.'

'Maybe we shouldn't get involved with people like them.'

'They're just people,' Charlie says quickly, dropping his voice. 'People who want to make the country better, just like the *Outlaws of the Marsh* back in the old days.'

The guard and soldiers are stirring under their padded blankets.

'Let's not talk about it now.'

Fat Neck brews tea on a little stove and shares some of that and a mouthful or two of some cold, gluey rice with the soldiers and his 'pidgin cargo'. To their left, through the open door, a big mountain is rising its back to the lightening sky. Nanking not far off now, Ruby thinks. That's the hill above the tomb of the Great Ming Emperor. Dad took us there. Tom was still alive then, Dad on one of his good days after some meeting or other, spring sun shining as they strolled from the Customs House through the streets, across the lake with the artificial islands – turtles rolling in the blossom-strewn water – up onto the hillside and past those two elephant statues guarding the way to the tomb.

Let's have some fun, Dad had said, his limp as light as it could ever be. *We should try and throw stones onto the elephant's back. It's good luck apparently if they stick there.* He bent down to pick up a stone. *Utter rot of course.*

And yet, as they stood tossing small round pebbles up to the lofted, rounded backs of the animals, and Tom got his nowhere near, a strange kind of urgency had gripped Dad. As if it mattered more than he would allow.

'Come on, little chap, a bit harder, give it some air. Like this.'

Ruby got one to lodge on the fourth go, and Dad of course got one straight off. But Tom couldn't get anything high enough and pebble after pebble rolled down the stone elephant's rounded flanks and clunked to the stone below.

'*Bad* luck for you, Tom,' Ruby had taunted.

'I told you it's bloody nonsense,' Dad had snapped, his voice surprisingly fierce. She winces now at that teasing. What had happened in the end? Had Dad thrown one up for him – or lifted him high up to give him a boost? She just can't recall, but can still feel the cloud that then trailed them to the tomb itself. Dad's limp back with a vengeance as they climbed the steps. But that can't be why Tom had *such* bad luck, can it? Maybe if he'd just got his own stone to stick everything would have been OK?

Charlie nudges her in the ribs, as a platform and ticket office roll past.

'Taiping Station,' he whispers. 'We're nearly there.'

Ruby nods, but the memory still has her in its grip, emotion rising in her chest again. Silently she watches the waters of the lake slide below, the artificial, squared islands linked by causeways, dotted with cypress trees, a tiled roof or two poking through the trees. Beyond that the flanks of the city wall rise high, running away to right and left to enfold Nanking in their grip.

She swallows the grief back down as the train slips along the north side and, hissing out the last of its power, runs at last into the main station.

'As soon as we stop, you two scram,' Fat Neck growls. 'I'll be sacked if the station master finds I've been running Pidgin back here.'

The tall soldier taps Ruby on the shoulder as she gets ready to hop down onto the platform. 'I know there are good foreign devils,' he says, 'but not everyone else does. Take care.'

'Thank you,' she says. 'Come on, Straw.'

Charlie's already down onto the crowded platform and she hurries to join him amongst the yawning soldiers spilling from the box cars.

'So? What's the plan?'

'I don't want to argue, but I'm not going near

73

your consulate,' Charlie says. 'Do you know how to get there?'

'I think so. Why?'

'Then you head there. You'll be safe – and I'll go to a place I know. And look for my dad's contacts.'

'Which street?'

'I'm not going to tell you. Just in case.' And then his face softens and he smiles, maybe aware how self-important he's sounding. 'It's best you don't know.'

'But I don't want to split up, Charlie,' she whispers hoarsely. 'Bother the consulate. I'll come with you and we'll trust the Comm—'

'Shhh.' Charlie's eyes flare in alarm and he presses a finger to her lips. 'Keep it down. You said we should try *whoever*. You're right. You try your lot and I'll try mine. We've got to give Fei every chance.'

'But—'

'She's my sister, Ruby. My decision, OK? If I'm not back outside the consulate by dusk ask to be put on the first boat home. And if you find my dad tell him I went to see Big Uncle.'

'Big Uncle who?'

'Just Big Uncle. Got it?'

'We could try them both together and—'

'No, Ruby. This will be quicker. We'll cover twice the ground like this. See you later. *Zai jian*.'

And with that he turns on his heel and jogs away towards the heart of the city, Jin's pack bouncing on his back.

Ruby watches him go, breath held – and then turns away, tugging Straw close for comfort.

A mile away at that moment, on the wide river of morning light that is the Yangtze, a motorised cruiser is powering upstream. Its wake washes against the sampans and small boats clustered there, leaving them rocking and cursing. Oblivious, the burly figure standing by the helmsman on the bridge stares into the channel ahead, eyes devouring everything he can see: the junks, the wooded hills, the glitter of the sun.

'How good to be heading home,' he mutters through clenched teeth, each of the pockmarks cratering his big round face picked out by the light. 'Full speed! I want to get there. I need to be on home ground.'

The man at the wheel nods and eases the throttle forward.

'I'm going to chat to our lovely passenger.'

He makes his way down to the cabin below. Two of his thin henchmen jump to attention as he enters, but Moonface waves them away, and strides heavily to the luxurious state room at the back of the cruiser, humming under his breath.

'Knock, knock!'

'Go away!'

The young girl looks up at him from where she's tied to a heavy chair, trying to look strong, pigtails flying, eyes flashing. 'Let me go, you old bastard. I'm not scared of you, old fat face.'

Moonface smiles: a long, thin smile that stops Fei's words in her mouth. She is scared, he can see that. He's used to seeing it in people's faces. He's seen that look for years and years and years.

'I'm not going to hurt you, young lady,' he says. 'I'm after bigger fish to fry.'

'You can go to hell, you stinking piece of—'

'Shhh. Let me show you something.' The gangster boss reaches up then, sweeping his hand across his face like some Chinese opera villain. And as he pulls it away the features have changed completely, revealing an older, darker, thinner face – that is there for a moment and then gone in the next, a glimpse of a lean and hungry animal, its mouth full of sharp teeth and drooling tongue, and then the wide moony face is back.

'I've *been* to hell,' he whispers. 'I've been to hell and I've come back again. Do you understand?'

Fei's mouth drops open, but no words will come. What on earth was that? Some weird kind of a trick or something. His face is back to pockmarked normal, but the image of that thing still hovers in her vision like it's been burned there. Her mouth has gone dust dry, her knees weak. It's all she can do not to wet herself.

'I want you to be comfortable,' Moonface says. 'Really I do. Maybe you can even become Moonface's bride one day soon. Couple more years.'

The words send fresh fear through her veins and she screws her eyes tight.

'Leave me alone. Get lost.'

But even behind her lids all she can see is that strange, dark, twisted face. Like something out of a dream, or nightmare. Something right out of the pages of the *Strange Tales*, and it's got her!

She feels Moonface pinch her cheek. 'And what a very delicious piece of bait you are, young lady.'

第九章

NO DOGS (AND NO CHINESE)

The official stares at Ruby across his wide, mirror-polished desk. With his heavy eyebrows, clipped grey moustache and beard, he looks like a fierce playing-card King, his upper body and powerful head reflected on the surface in front of him.

'I told you, young lady. *No* dogs allowed. And you don't seem to understand that the consulate has more on its plate than some runaway Chinese waif and a wild story about gangster bosses. I can put out a wireless message for our captains to keep their eyes open, but have you any idea how big that river out there is?' He throws his hands as wide as the polished desk, hands slick over its surface.

'If anything happens to our dog, my father will have a fit. He's a big shot in the Customs Service—'

'Blast your damn dog,' the man thunders. 'There's

all hell breaking loose up at Wanhsien. We've got a full-scale diplomatic incident and the natives are what you might call restless. Jungle drums and all that – could be rioting here in the city by the end of the day. There are Communists right here in the city plotting to slit our throats, the Nationalists are at the walls of Hankow and God only knows what will happen when the warlord's troops realise the game's up for Nanking. Rape and pillage. That's the usual game. Do I make myself clear?'

He wipes his forehead.

Ruby looks around at the heavy dark wood panelling, the clock ticking away as oblivious to what she has said as the stupid man opposite.

'I need to get on the river, to head for Hankow—'

'It would be complete madness. You're an unaccompanied minor. I forbid it. Only the Chink boats are running. And you don't want to be on one of those.'

There's a knock on the door and a young man with slicked down hair comes in. He hands the official a telegram, then flashes an encouraging smile across the desk at Ruby.

'Hello, young lady. Fancy a brew?'

'No thank you. I don't need tea. I need someone to help me find my friend.'

The bearded man glares at the telegram then folds it thoughtfully, before looking back at her.

'You say your name is Ruby Harkner. Daughter of Mr Victor Harkner of Maritime Customs?'

She nods. The man's tone has changed suddenly. Perhaps his heart is softening a bit?

'Please help me.'

'Well. Something might be arranged, but I must attend to urgent business first.' He gets heavily to his feet. 'Let me make some enquiries, and you wait somewhere more comfortable.'

'If my friend shows up, will someone let me know?'

'Of course. James, will you show Miss Harkner to the Green Room?'

The young man hesitates then leads her out, down a corridor past an open door and cut-glass English voices, the chatter of a typewriter. China could be a thousand miles away right now.

James looks over his shoulder. 'My boss isn't a bad sort. He's just got a lot on his shoulders right now – he has to make sure people are safe. How about something to eat?'

'Will someone take care of my dog?'

The young man smiles again. 'Don't give it another thought.' He waves her through a door and into a gloomy room. The shutters are closed and in the

80

lamplight a dark green patterned wallpaper gives the room a sombre air. 'I'll rustle you up some breakfast while you have a rest.'

Ruby nods. Two mouthfuls of rice in twenty-four hours has left a void and the hunger is knocking at her now. She looks around the room. On one wall, hanging against the awful wallpaper, a series of framed prints draw her eye. Red-jacketed huntsmen on horses, galloping through a dull imitation of English countryside, a stream of hounds chasing a beautiful, swish-tailed fox along the banks of a river.

Another fox! Once you're looking for them, they *are* everywhere, just like Charlie said. But it looks like the hunt has got this one trapped. She scowls at the huntsmen with distaste. Just the types who throng the clubs along the Bund back home.

At least this young man, James, seems kind—

The sound of the key turning loudly in the lock makes her jump.

She turns back to the door, pumps the handle hard, and realises she's a prisoner.

The afternoon is fading as Charlie trudges on through Nanking's bustling streets. Here, as in Shanghai, day-to-day business is getting muddled up with rumour and gossip and there's a nervous edge to people's voices.

81

Charlie's hunt for a mystery man he's never met, for a 'friend of a friend of a friend' of Dad's, has been fruitless. No one seems to know Big Uncle Woo at the Flying Phoenix Tea House, but surely that was the name Dad had made him repeat and promise to keep tight to himself. The woman running the place didn't want to know, wrinkling her nose and shooing him away.

'I don't need any trouble today,' she had snapped. 'Beat it.' Then added in a loud voice, just that bit *too* loud: 'I never heard of anyone called Big Uncle Woo.'

As he moved back towards the door, an old man sitting on his own, white hair puffed in a cloud around his head, whistled softly to him.

'Who are you looking for?'

Charlie bit his lip, eyeing up the stranger. He seemed relaxed, not tense like the woman behind the counter, the kind of face you feel you've met before. Worth the risk.

'A man called Big Uncle.'

The man looked around quickly, judging the distance between him and a tangle of soldiers at a nearby table. 'Run for it, young man. That stupid old bag is trying to drop you in it. Try the Blue Turtle Inn, near the Red Cross Hospital. If he's not there, you might find his friends. Go!'

From there it had been a long and confused jog across the city to the hospital and a frustrating hunt to find the Blue Turtle. When at last someone pointed out the grubby signboard and he squeezed through the narrowest of doors, Charlie found himself in the kind of place that Dad always railed against: girls and young women propping up the bar in short, thin dresses, foreign sailors and scruffy-looking businessmen getting drunk. Hardly the place for a comrade. A tattooed giant of an American leaning against the stairway, shirtsleeves rolled to his powerful biceps, moved to block him. Surprisingly when he opened his mouth he came out with not half bad Chinese. 'Can I help you, kid? Think you've taken a wrong turn.'

'Someone said I might find my uncle here. Big Uncle Woo.'

The man scratched the back of his head vaguely. 'Why do you need to find him then?'

'I'm trying to find my sister. I need help to check boats going upriver.'

'Try one of the gin palaces up on Socony Hill. Be careful.'

And so the day dragged on, the figures passing on the street seeming to be casting more and more glances at him, the red kerchief in his pocket burning a hole there. At one point an open lorry, British, came scurrying past, the back of it loaded to the gills with naval ratings, bayonets reflecting slices of sunlight, faces tensed for trouble.

Now, worrying he should have long been back with Ruby, Charlie climbs the bluff overlooking the river. The buildings here are more Western in style, the company executives of Socony Oil and other firms huddled together for safety and the fresher air.

One more try and then I must get back to find Ruby, he thinks. We'll have missed Fei at this rate, damn it.

Cautiously he enters a raucous cave of a place near the city wall. It's jammed with sailors from the Yangtze Patrol knocking back as much as they can, the atmosphere jagged. At the back there's a table free and he makes his way to it, trying to judge who to approach, and slumps down in the gloom. Tiredness reaches out, and between ordering a bowl of noodles and their arrival, he tries to catch a bit of rest, his head slipping down onto his folded arms, the noise of the bar washing in his ears, his eyelids flickering open, closed, open.

He stares sideways at his hand, groggy with exhaustion – and then, one side or the other of sleep, Charlie sees, or thinks he sees, a thin trail of red twine tied around his little finger.

Confused, he waggles it, staring at the thing. He reaches out with the other hand to feel the string, but at that moment a shadow blocks out the light as a hand grips his wrist vice-like – and the thread vanishes.

A voice growls in Pidgin.

'You no b'long Melican side. And why you look-see man like Big Uncle? Tell me!'

Startled truly awake Charlie finds himself staring into the deepest, most intensely blue eyes he's ever seen. As blue as noonday midsummer sky, bluer even than Ruby's. The face surrounding them is beaten by the elements, the colour of old terracotta, the lines scored in it deep and furrowed. The man leans closer, his breath rich with the stink of alcohol.

'Speakee! Plenty quick, brother. Or else.'

A half mile away Ruby sits staring at the half eaten plate of sausage and congealed egg brought to her hours and hours ago. It wasn't bad then, but she was so angry at first she couldn't think about taking a bite. Now it's grim.

She sighs, then slices another mouthful and chews the gristly, cold meat before forcing it down, hunger winning out over pride.

How dare they lock her up like some stupid criminal? They're supposed to help people in distress.

Especially people their own shade of pinky white! But all her repetitive drumming on the door has done is bruised the sides of her hands – and eventually brought a hammering back on the other side and a gruff order to *put a sock in it* and wait until they've worked out how to get her back to Shanghai *as soon as bloody well possible*.

When young James looked in half an hour ago he smiled apologetically and blocked her from rushing the door. 'I'm sorry,' he said, 'but it really isn't up for discussion.'

She shook her head angrily and turned her back to the shuttered window. 'My father will be furious when he hears how you're treating me.'

The young man coughed, his voice calm. 'Well, firstly, he's the one who's asked us to detain you if you happened to pass this way. And lo and behold you walked *right* through our front door. And – secondly – his standing might not be that high now. I wouldn't throw his name around too much if I was you.'

'What do you mean?'

'There's a warrant out in Shanghai. For his arrest.'

The door snicked shut again, the lock turning as her heart sunk deeper to her shoes.

Arrest? Must be for getting in all this stupid mess with the Green Hand. So I really am on my own, she thought. No sign of Charlie either . . . And if I get shipped home, and Mother is incapable and Dad is on the run or locked up somewhere, then the worst could happen. I might get sent back to England. Some boarding school there.

Ruby had waited five minutes and then unlatched the window. The river breeze flowed through the heavy, metal-reinforced shutters bolted across, and despite her best attempts the padlock on the inside refused to let them budge one inch. Not even when she visualised the *ch'i* that Jin transferred to her, saw it burn in her belly and flow into her arms, could she get any sense that the thing would give way.

Now tears of frustration are filling her eyes as she chews the inedible sausage. What if Charlie doesn't come back? No one around here is going to care about him, not amongst all the other problems in the city, on the river. What if they don't let him in? Or tell him she's gone?

Damn it, I should have convinced him to stick together, she thinks. Gone to look for his 'friends' with him.

She gets up, paces the room, trying to work a strategy, the tears stinging. *Far to go?* That's a joke, she's only got as far as Nanking and been stopped in her tracks. *Full of woe* more like. The tears brim as her eyes fall on the fox-hunting pictures. It's a sequence, the wild-eyed fox tiring and the hounds closing. In the first image there's a field between him and the pack, but by the last of the five he's almost caught, tongue lolling desperately, the jaws of the pack about to rip him limb from limb.

She looks closer at the poor animal, the tears bubbling, feeling as sorry for him as for herself – and through the distortion of those tears – very slowly, but definitely – she sees the fox start to *move*.

Blood swooshes in her ears, the hairs rippling on the back of her neck as she stares at the image. Like a Felix the Cat animation in the picture house, he's *moving*! The red tail flickers, then sweeps a great, slow arc, and the fox's head turns, away from the chasing pack.

Ruby blinks furiously, wiping her eyes clear. He's stopped moving now, that's for sure – but isn't he facing the other way? Like he's doubled back and thrown the hounds. It looks like they'll miss him now that he can charge along that river bank. She waits, willing the creature to move again, but he doesn't – and instead she retraces her own steps. And in *each* ghastly print he's facing the other way, weaving through the undergrowth. Viewed in this order he's now evading capture, the pack falling further and further off.

In the last one the fox is nowhere to be seen. Just green fields, a big bright sky towering over everything. The fox has vanished.

Maybe I'm just going quite mad, she thinks. It's in the blood after all, look at Mother. After all, the fortune teller said *you're just like her* . . . Or did I just remember it wrong?

She leans closer, tingling rippling her skin – and then hears an insistent, loud rap on the shutter.

第十章

CAPTAIN MARLAIS

Through the slit between the armoured shutters she can see a lamplit figure, and relief washes through her.

'Charlie!' she shouts, 'Charlie, I'm here!'

'Shhh,' he hisses. 'We're going to get you out.'

'We?'

'Me and the Captain here. And your silly old dog.'

And yes, she can hear Straw now, scratching away at the wall beneath with his claws, whining frantically.

'What Captain?' Ruby says, confused. 'Be quick. They want to ship me back to Shanghai.'

'Can't have that now, can we?' a deep, American voice rumbles. 'We're going to bust ya out, little lady. Step back and get ready to jump through this thing.'

She backs away, the tears still wet on her eyelashes. Presumably they're going to saw through the lock or pick it or something. Like in some adventure story when—

The detonation of the gunshot is stunningly loud. Before she's had a chance to regather her senses the shutters have been yanked back, the broken padlock clattering to the paving stones below, and Charlie is at the window, stretching out his hand.

'Let's go!' he shouts.

Quickly she grabs Jin's hat from the table, and scrambles up onto the ledge, scraping her shin on the metal sill, and then half falls, half jumps to the ground below. A pair of strong hands catch her, steadying her back to her feet as Straw barks madly.

'Run, landlubbers,' the blue-eyed man shouts. 'Follow old Marlais and kiss Nanking goodbye.'

It's dark outside but she can see they're in a small courtyard, the city wall towering above. Already cries of alarm are spreading through the consulate. Charlie tugs her by the hand, leads her at a run across the courtyard and through a small door. The tall figure of the Captain lumbers ahead of them in the gloom, his pistol briefly visible in a meaty hand, Straw scampering along beside. They turn abrupt right, down a narrow alley stuffed with darkness that twists towards the wall.

More shouting from behind now. A whistle blowing

frantically and someone shouting 'Intruders!' at the top of his lungs.

'Quickly,' the Captain shouts, 'up here.'

A steep flight of steps climbs the rampart, and Ruby takes them as fast as she can, gaining on their guide. On top of the wall the breeze is strong, flowing with the river, and looking over the serrated battlements she sees the scruffy bank, wooden jetties and mud flats between them and the vast darkness of the Yangtze beyond.

A gunshot rings out.

'Short cut!' the man grunts and leads them to the wall's edge.

Below, a clear thirty feet or more, a wide, open wagon loaded with hay is parked tight to the wall. The man turns and looks at her with those dizzyingly blue eyes, the shadow of his dark, peaked cap unable to extinguish their gleam.

'I hear you're a brave and very capable young lady,' he says, firing her a playful look. 'If you want to sail with old Marlais you'd better prove it.' He nods at the waiting cart below. 'We're gonna jump. Or the soldiers at the gate will get us. Or the bloody Brits. So off you go!'

Ruby takes a breath, stares back at the man and those dazzling eyes of his, looks for Charlie who nods reassuringly, hears the boots behind them drumming on the steps, and then hurls herself clear of the outward sloping wall, hoping against hope that she's judged the trajectory right.

The rush of the cold night air is fierce and then she whumps into the hay, legs folding up beneath, knees jabbing her ribs and knocking the breath from her. She rolls to the edge and a fraction later Charlie lands hard beside her, sending up another cloud of hay and dust. But that is nothing to compare with the force that the Captain makes as his heavy form slams into the trailer.

But what about Straw? Dogs can't jump like that.

She looks back up at the wall, hears him barking away and then silence. Charlie reads her mind, grabbing her by the arm, urging her over the side of the cart. 'Straw will find us! Or take care of himself.'

The American has dropped a couple of coins into the palm of the waiting cart driver and then beckons them on across the ground towards the river, down a muddy track between two big oil tanks.

'I'll lose my licence for this,' he grins. 'Again!'

As he runs he pulls a torch from his pocket and starts flashing the light towards the silent river. Another light flickers back in answer, and in the gloom Ruby can just make out a chunky steamship silhouetted against the emptiness beyond, black smoke boiling up from its funnel.

More gunshots detonate behind, a loudhailer crackling into life, sparking the night with a stern Chinese voice. 'Stop! Stop or we shoot.'

A volley of firing blasts through the darkness, and Ruby flinches, legs stuttering beneath her mid stride.

'Don't worry,' the Captain says, reaching out to steady her on the uneven ground. 'They're chasing shadows.'

The man leads them at a dash onto a long jetty, over the stinking mud exposed by the low level of the river, across a gangplank and onto the deck of the ship. Then he climbs fast to the bridge above, voice booming. 'Cast off forrad! Cast off aft! Full steam ahead. Full steam a-bloody-head!'

He leans down to where Ruby is standing breathless on the deck. 'Welcome aboard the *Lu Haitun*. Captain Marlais Jones at your humble service. Pull in that gangplank someone, for God's sake!'

Ruby looks at the ship's name, printed in bold letters on a life ring fastened to the railing beside them. *Lu Haitun*.

Green Dolphin, she translates to herself.

Still getting his own breath back, Charlie nudges her in the ribs and points back towards the city, the crack of the gunshots. From out of the murk a figure appears, Straw sprinting across the mud, skittering up and onto the gangway just as a crew member is about to pull it in.

'Stoke up!' Marlais bellows.

The *Haitun* pushes into the river's current and the entire boat, every fixture and fitting, every bolt and nut, shakes like mad. As Ruby bends to give Straw a hug, she hears a great whoosh overhead. She looks up to see a shower of sparks belch from the black funnel. They rush up, tumbling and churning in the sky like agitated stars, and then – for the briefest of moments – those dots of light form a rough image of a huge and fiery fox against the dark heavens above. It blazes brilliant orange and then an instant later the sparks blink out and the giant figure is gone.

She turns to Charlie, to ask if he has seen it too, but he's already clambering up the steep stair to the bridge.

Mouth open, she stares back at the emptiness, the picture of the fox still stamped on her vision. It should be scary seeing that, she thinks, but instead all she can feel chasing through her is a wild excitement.

第十一章

OLD LADIES AND WALKING STICKS

The *Haitun* shudders upstream curling white wake from its bows, the darkened river and the night engulfing it.

Deep beneath Ruby's feet the engines throb, shaking loose flakes of rust that sizzle red-orange in the ship's flickering electric light. The lamps of Nanking fall swiftly away, dwindle to pinpricks, and as the river bends, one by one they wink out of existence. Buoyed by their escape, at being on the river at last, Ruby runs forward. The moon has slipped from the clouds to show the full width of the Yangtze ahead: a wide, shimmering path between low black hills, an occasional dot of light showing the position of a junk or a distant moored boat.

She finds Captain Marlais leaning on the rail, eyes scouring the river. Even in this gloom his eyes shine blue. Beside him, silently, an elderly Chinese man in a gown stands perfectly straight, long white beard twitching as he moves his head, his eyes also fixed on the water. He holds his index finger erect, the nail there some two or three inches long, catching the moonlight. A younger Chinese man grips the spoked wheel with both hands and glances repeatedly to the older man and back. A slight twitch of the nail one way and the wheel changes their course just slightly. The concentration from all three men is intense, wordless, and Ruby is afraid to break the silence.

At last Captain Marlais takes a deep breath and seems to relax a bit. He reaches for the speaking tube.

'OK, Mister McQueen. Engines slow ahead. Let me know about the pumps.'

He turns to Ruby.

'That's put some water between us and Nanking. There's a British Naval cruiser there and a US Yangtze River Patrol somewhere not far behind. Have to be careful though. Just enough moonlight for me and Old Lee here' – he jerks a thumb in the direction of the man with the fingernail – 'to find our way without a local pilot. Sandbanks keep shifting ya see, and the water's low for September. Always different every time you pass. Don't want to end up stuck fast.'

He holds out a hand, and in the tough, hardened

shake her own hand almost disappears.

'I'm Ruby. Ruby Harkner. Pleased to meet you.'

'Very polite! Marlais Jones. But everyone just calls me the Captain. This is Old Lee, my eyes and ears on the river. We've been up and down it more times than you've been to the . . . had dinner, young lady. And Young Chen here is my steersman. You are on a ship of the Yangtze Rapid line heading upriver. An unscheduled voyage! Destination, who knows?'

He peers into her eyes, a long and disconcerting look that reminds her of how Doctor Sprick used to examine her during check-ups, then nods at Charlie.

'Your friend here told me a bit. How far you want to go then?'

'We're looking for someone—'

'I know,' Marlais says. 'It seems your gang boss came through, just a few hours ago. Mister Lee here had our rowboat out ferrying to the north bank and they saw a white-topped cruiser go right past. Nearly overturned them in their wash. Isn't that right, Lee?'

The white-bearded man nods slowly, looking at Ruby.

'But how do you know it was Moonface?'

Marlais frowns. 'Has to be, doesn't it? There's nothing else like that on the river right now. And you get an eye for this kind of thing when you've

98

been at it as long as me.'

'Then let's get after him!'

'Steady, young lady. There's a bad stretch of the river ahead and the moon's not going to last long. We need to wait until first light and then we can get some decent steam on again. He'll have a much shallower draft than us—'

'But we'll lose him. We'll lose Fei.'

'Lee here could find a duck on this river, young lady. You'll have to trust us. There's bandits and soldiers commandeering boats and shooting at anything that moves.' He raps his knuckles on the steel shutters flapped back over their heads. 'We've got armour plating for that – but there are other dangers out there at the moment.'

He sighs and when he speaks again his voice is deeper, a low murmur against the engines. 'Things armour's no good against.'

Ruby gulps. 'Like what?'

Marlais' right hand is squeezing something in his strong palm, a muffled clickety-click coming from it as he weighs up his words. Rubbing walnuts together, Ruby thinks. She's seen old Chinese men doing that, wearing their rough shells down to a smooth sheen as they worry away their tension.

'Like what?' she repeats.

'This is the Yangtze, Miss Harkner. What the Chinese call "The Long River". I've sailed the world and *all* the waters of this little green pea of a planet are strange. But there's nothing stranger than this one: sandbanks that appear and disappear, a water level that rises and falls forty feet in a day, villages that are thriving one year and ghost towns the next, rapids and rocks and whirlpools that want to smash you to bits. And further up there are dragons waiting for us in whirlpools the size of houses and monkey spirits that throw rocks at you in the gorges because they don't want people like us there.'

Ruby listens, spellbound. 'I keep seeing weird things too,' she whispers. 'Everywhere. And a fortune teller told me—'

Captain Marlais holds up a stubby finger, then touches it to his lips. 'Let's not talk about it now. Wait for daylight. Go and find a cabin to bunk in. We're running virtually empty passenger-wise what with the fuss up at Wanhsien. Choose any you like on the top deck, probably best to keep forrad in case you need to take cover on the bridge. And keep away from the last one on the port side aft. Number nine. Special passenger in there who doesn't wanna be disturbed. He's making a very special journey.'

'A special journey?'

'Secret.'

Marlais smiles at her, at Straw. His fist stops contracting and opens, and briefly she sees the dark walnuts he's working there.

'Feed that dog of yours, Miss Harkner. And then get some sleep. Nothing'll trouble you. Not tonight at any rate.'

He turns away to Old Lee and whispers something to him and the old Chinese pilot goes to the starboard rail, leans out and squints into the darkness.

'Is everything OK?' Ruby asks. There's something tense in Old Lee's actions, the quick shake of the head that he throws Marlais now.

'River's short of water for the season. It's going to take at least one more big drink from the Heavens before winter.'

The Captain peers upriver, into the distance. 'As my Welsh grandmother – God rest her eternal soul – used to say, it's raining old ladies and walking sticks up there. River will be in spate before we know it.' And he starts grinding the walnuts in his hand again, double speed.

Along the covered walkway on the upper deck a couple of Chinese deckhands are coiling ropes. They ignore the new passengers, muttering away in a thick dialect

Ruby doesn't recognise. Another, his face and hands coal blackened, emerges from a doorway and throws them a quick scowl, then looks away. Not exactly welcoming. The cold wind snaps at Ruby and she pulls the cardigan tight around her, feeling her arms ache again.

She reaches out to snag Charlie on the shoulder. 'So what *did* happen in Nanking. Did you find the people you were looking for? Is Captain Marlais a Communist?'

'No he isn't. And keep your voice down, for Heaven's sake. We can't trust anyone until we're sure.'

'Not even him?'

'Something's not right. Could be smuggling stuff. Pidgin cargo. Maybe he's running guns or something.'

He takes a quick glance at the deckhands and then steps into a dimly lit corridor. Another cold breeze comes trembling down the river. Over the fug of coal smoke and oil you can smell rain, like when a typhoon's coming in off the sea. The moon slips away behind cloud and for a moment, on all the river, across the wide horizon of the north bank and the chunk of China beyond, there's nothing visible, not a scrap of light. The *Haitun*'s flickering bulbs suddenly seem very bright, like they're on some pleasure steamer floating on an immense dark sea.

This is the real thing, she thinks. Heading into the Interior, night sailing on the Yangtze. The last time we were on this water we were heading the other way on a Royal Navy boat with Tom's coffin, having that ridiculous meal in the officers' mess – but that was all fake. Like they were pretending we weren't even *in* China any more. Now we're heading back into the *real* country, on the real river. She's always hoped for a moment like this – out in the middle of China, with Charlie, just the two of them.

As she turns to follow him her eyes fall on a series of small neat holes punched into the metal doorway, and her excitement is checked.

She touches the cold metal of one of the wounds: real bullet holes made by real bullets.

Rain starts to fall as the night deepens, gentle at first, then a hard steady downpour that soaks the river and the countryside around.

Half a mile behind them a small white sampan cuts through the last ripples of their wake. Not a soul to be seen on the bamboo matting on the foredeck, no sign of life under the arched canopy that takes up the middle half of the low-lying boat. But on the back a figure hunches over a long bladed oar. Impassive under the pouring rain he works the oar slowly, ever so slowly, the water cascading off the brim of a wide straw hat, the sampan moving unusually quickly, effortlessly, as it follows the *Haitun* into the cloudburst.

第十二章

WHAT HAPPENED IN NANKING

Charlie looks at her bared shoulder and whistles through his teeth.

The look on his face is alarming, the kind of reaction people give when they don't want to show you they're worried, but the thing you've told them – or shown them – forces it out.

'It can't be that bad,' she says, hastily pulling a sheet over her shoulder.

'You should take a look,' Charlie says. 'Is the other one as painful?'

'Pretty much.'

If she was feeling on edge before, then that look on Charlie's face has made her all the more so. In the corridor there was an awkward moment as they looked at the row of dark wooden cabin doors. A choice to be made.

'I think we should share,' Charlie declared. 'For safety. We should keep close to each other.'

Ruby felt the warmth rise to her cheeks, the familiar rush that made the girls at school call her Beetroot Girl. Much better to keep together, much more comforting – but something held her back for a moment. Maybe Mother's voice at the back of her head banging on about *girls who should know better*.

'I don't know—'

'What about last night? On the train?'

'Yes, but, there was nowhere else to sleep—'

Charlie frowned. 'I just mean be in the same room,' he added hastily. 'We're blood brother and sister! We used to go skinny-dipping, remember?'

She nodded, glad the decision was made, but now the intimacy of baring her injury, and Charlie's reaction to it, are all a bit overwhelming.

There's a mirror above the washbasin in the cabin and cautiously she slips the sheet back off again and turns her right shoulder to the glass to get a proper look.

She gasps. Stamped on her skin are three long bruises, mottled purple and black, and one on the inside of the arm that looks even worse.

'Oh God!'

'The other side's the same,' he murmurs.

Hurriedly Ruby covers up the bruising. The blood's burning in her cheeks, but the rest of her body feels cold and she puts the cardigan back on too, before wrapping the edge of a wool blanket over that.

Charlie looks at her thoughtfully.

'You say Amah did it?'

'She tried to stop me leaving—'

'She wouldn't hurt you, not like that.'

'Maybe it was when the van nearly brushed me.'

'But they look like finger marks.'

'I don't know. It's all a muddle in my head. I can remember an old man picking me up. Maybe it was that.'

Charlie waits for more, but she shakes her head.

'What, Ruby?'

'You were going to tell me about Nanking.'

He sighs. 'Wild goose chase. I walked miles and miles. Everyone looked like they hadn't got a clue what I was on about – or looked terrified.'

'And Big Uncle? Is he a Communist?'

'An important one, I think.'

'And your dad too?'

Charlie nods. 'Sort of. It's complicated.'

'And after that? How did you know where I was?'

'Your friend Straw, of course. He's brighter than he looks, I'll grant you that! And the Captain helped of course.'

Charlie hesitates, as though on the verge of blurting something out, but checking himself.

Ruby pulls the blanket tighter. 'Well, go on. How did you find *him*?'

'I think *he* found *me*. He was really grumpy, threatening he was going to turn me over to the American Military Police – or even the local magistrate. He wanted to know what I was doing chasing a man like Big Uncle. Then I mentioned Fei and, I don't know, your name, your dad's – anything that came to mind – and he changed. Shook my hand like he wanted to pull it off.'

The engines thump away below deck setting the single bulb above them flickering.

'What do you mean?'

'He got all excited. Said I should follow him. We slipped out of the bar by a back door, followed some tiny lanes and came out near your consulate. I was still in two minds about whether to trust him. I thought maybe you'd be safer there, especially if he was up to no good. But then Straw came rushing up to us and growling away—'

'What did he say?'

'He didn't *say* anything. But he definitely wanted us to follow. I said, *Where's Ruby?* and he tore off round the back of the building, through a gateway and we were in the yard. Then the Captain shot the padlock off and you know the rest.'

'Why didn't you think you could trust him?'

'These foreign captains of the Yangtze Rapid are a real bunch of rogues. They don't listen to anyone, not the Americans, not the Yangtze Patrol. They just do what's best for them, Dad says. Whoever pays the most.'

Ruby nods thoughtfully. There's something a bit wild about Marlais, maybe even something a bit dangerous. You can feel it when those eyes of his spark. 'Maybe he's smuggling something or someone in that cabin?'

'I dunno,' Charlie shrugs. 'Could be a general for one tinpot army or another. Or opium.'

The engines change note beneath, dropping to a gentler rhythm, and the *Haitun* sways for a moment before a long roar resounds the length of the boat, making Ruby startle.

Charlie's shoulders sag. 'That's the anchor chain. We're not going any further tonight, damn it.'

'How long will it take to get to Hankow?'

'Old Lee says maybe just a few days. It depends on the weather and the bandits. And on what's happening at Wanhsien. Everything's being ordered off the river.'

'But not this boat?'

'I told you, the Yangtze Rapid don't play by the rules. They sneak up and down when they're not supposed to.'

He pauses, about to pull himself up to the top bunk, and flashes her a grin, the rain loud on the roof above.

'You know what people call them sometimes?'

'What?'

'Ghost ships.'

第十三章

DARK STRANGER, FLYING BULLETS

The crackle of gunfire wakes her abruptly.

Just single shots, separated by ten, fifteen, twenty seconds, but definitely gunshots between the steady chatter of the rain. She strains to listen to the shooting, and rolls over, wincing as the bruises throb, and the groan that comes with it stops in her mouth.

By the door there's a dark figure.

It's indistinct, but someone is standing there, watching her.

'Charlieeee?' she whispers softly.

The shadow doesn't answer, but seems to solidify, to grow just a bit taller. For one dread-filled moment she thinks it's the Black Thing from her room again, the figure who stalked her in the Mansions and stifled the breath in her chest. Jin had pretty much dismissed it as a figment of her imagination, but it had petrified her. Could it be back again, out to get me? she thinks, panic rising.

But no, this is different, for one thing she can breathe OK. And for another she manages to sit up without the paralysis that had held her tight that night. Straw is curled at the foot of her bunk, snoring hard, oblivious to the shadow by the door.

'Charlie?' she hisses again.

She can make out the figure's head now, inclined slightly to one side as if about to ask a question.

'What is it?' Charlie's voice mumbles from overhead, mouth full of sleep. She looks up and sees his face float over the edge of the bunk. 'What's up?'

Her gaze swings back to the door, but the thing – whatever it was – has gone. Evaporated. No tingling running under her skin. No goosebumps.

Just the end of a dream perhaps? And yet – and yet. There's a feeling of presence that lingers where it stood. Like when she gets in the lift at the Mansions and can still sense its last passenger.

'What?' Charlie's voice comes again, impatiently this time.

'Nothing. I mean – there's gunfire. Listen!'

Between the peppering of the rain it comes again, a sharp retort, then a pause and then two more chasing it. Feet go thumping along the deck outside the cabin window and a shadow flicks across the curtained porthole. Deep beneath them the engines are shuddering into life and a moment later a heavy rap shakes their door in its frame.

Captain Marlais sticks his head through without waiting for an answer.

'Shift your bones, you two. We're under attack from the bank. And in this weather!' His face is flush with excitement. 'Bridge-side, plenty quick,' he adds in Pidgin, and is gone.

A metallic ricochet sounds overhead, the bullet glancing off something very close by and whining past their window, and they both scramble from their bunks without another word.

On the bridge the armour plating has been flapped down over the starboard windows and door. As they make safety there's a deafening bang on the shielding and they both duck instinctively.

Marlais snorts. 'Don't worry. That stuff's thick enough to stop anything but a cannon shell. Rest of the boat's more vulnerable – seen a bullet go clean through the whole thing once. Lost a deck coolie last year. And a travelling salesman. Blammo.'

A bell rings on the control panel in front of him. He turns to the young man at the wheel and nods, swinging the lever to HALF SPEED AHEAD.

'What about your other passenger?' Ruby says.

'I'm under strict orders not to disturb him. He knows his business.'

Charlie peers through a tiny slit in the armouring. 'Who's firing at us?'

'Haven't got a clue,' Marlais grins. 'Not Nationalists – not from the north bank. Could be Reds. Some nasty bandits on this stretch at the moment too, but they don't normally bother in the rain.'

Ruby rests a hand on the shaking bulwark and peers forwards, and the full glory of the Yangtze fills her vision properly for the first time. From the deck of the warship that brought the family home last year it had looked big enough, but from the bridge of the low-slung *Haitun* the river is colossal, as if it could swallow them and all the boats she's ever seen – and still look empty. For a moment all thought of gunfire is washed away by its sheer size, the weight of the water rolling past them. She feels as if she's been shrunk, as if she is facing something that is just *too* big. A tiny sampan ahead bobbing on the swell looks so ridiculously small that it makes her feel dizzy. The downpour is beating the water hard and making what looks like smoke on its surface, and to right and left the banks are barely visible, thin smudges in the dawn, yellow reeds running a line between river and sky. Everything else – low hills, countryside, boats further upstream – is blurred to nothing.

Marlais nudges her, shaking her from the mesmerising sight. 'Old ladies and walking sticks, I told you. And now bullets too!'

Ruby peers towards the distant north bank. 'Will they try and board?'

'I doubt it. But I've got two boys getting the Lewis gun ready just in case.'

Silent, and standing tall beside him, Old Lee stares into the swirl of the water. He lifts the finger with the long nail, then tips it slightly to starboard. A volley of shots hammer against the armour plating again, startling Charlie back from his vantage point.

Ruby looks anxiously at the Captain as the *Haitun* veers course. 'But now we're heading *towards* them.'

'Trust Mister Lee,' Marlais nods. 'Much worse if we jammed on that sandbank, wouldn't it? Then they could just come and finish us off. We'd be as dead as old Joe Munro, wouldn't we?'

'Who?'

But the Captain waves the question away, peering ahead again, blue eyes shining as if filled with sun, not rain. He works the walnuts in his hand again, then grabs the speaking tube. 'Engine room! How are those pumps, Mister McQueen?'

He pulls a face as he listens to the answer and turns back to Ruby. 'We'll slip past these idiots and we'll find your young hostage, don't worry. Old Marlais never let anyone down yet. As long as we dodge the sandbars, the storm that's coming, the Yangtze Patrol, the British Navy, any drifting junks or rafts, the bandits, the Reds and all the rest . . .'

The rain squalls in through the open port side, and Marlais moves to pull a bamboo screen down across it, shrouding the bridge in gloom. The *Haitun*'s engines throb rhythmically and over that drone he starts to sing beneath his breath.

'*Farewell and adieu to you fair Spanish ladies, farewell and adieu to you ladies of Spain . . .*'

He pauses. 'Not like that one? How about this? *Now when I was a little boy my mother said to me, that if I didn't kiss the girls my lips would grow mouldeeee, and I sailed the seas for many a year not knowing what I was missin' . . .*'

He grins mischievously, then finishes the verse. '*. . . so I set me sails before the gales and started to a'kissin' – I started to a'kissin' . . .*'

He turns, makes his way down the companionway into the bowels of the *Haitun* leaving the last words hanging in the air.

Ruby feels Charlie's gaze on her. Presumably he can't catch that kind of English, but still she feels flustered. Ever since they started their pursuit he's been more like his old self, more full of his usual vim and vigour, than the weeks before when he was obviously waiting for something bad to happen. Now the bad thing has happened, and the chase is on, he's come back to life. He smiles now, that lopsided smile that always makes her feel good, the smile she noticed when they met for the first time chucking mud bombs at each other in the Wilderness. She thinks about sharing a cabin, of how they huddled together for warmth on the rocking train.

Maybe it can happen, she thinks, as another volley of gunshots furrows the air overhead. Maybe we can be together one day, despite everything. When all this is done. Charlie and me.

She hears the distant, teasing laughter of the girls at school. A Chinese boy? Trust you, you stupid frecklehead. Your children would be mongrels and everyone would cut you dead—

Forget them – they haven't a clue about Shanghai Ruby and what she can do! She shuts the thought away and looks at Charlie again. He's talking quietly to the young man at the wheel, eyes flicking to the water, nodding urgently. He looks taller this morning, more than halfway towards being an adult, she thinks.

And so am I.

第十四章

GREEN GLOOP AND OILY SOUP

A last stray bullet zips the air overhead and then the *Haitun* has shivered its way out of range of the bandits in the reeds, and the rainy Yangtze and its mists engulf them again.

Ruby tugs Charlie by the sleeve.

'Want to take a look around the ship?'

He shakes his head and nods upriver. 'I'll stay up here for a bit. Chen thinks we must be making ground on that cruiser, especially if we can get up to full steam. I want to keep a lookout. Maybe we'll catch them even before Hankow.'

'And what if – what if we meet spirits, those Shadow Warriors again . . .'

She braces herself for argument, dismissal. Under her school shoes the metal deck is vibrating uncomfortably.

Charlie raises his eyebrows. 'You saw something this morning, didn't you? In the cabin?'

'How – how do you know?'

'Because you looked white. There was nothing there, Ruby—'

'You saw those things in the tunnel,' she says, on the defensive. 'You saw Tom.'

'Yes,' Charlie murmurs, looking away. 'I did.'

Her fingernail is banging her front teeth again. She pulls it away irritably, ready to argue.

But Charlie just shrugs. 'There was nothing there this morning, Ruby. Maybe just a dream.'

'But those Shadow Warriors . . .'

'If they come back you'll know what to do.' The lopsided smile is back. 'Why else do you think I kept your sword safe all the way round Nanking.'

The rain keeps falling, blown in squalls by a blustery wind. Spiralling columns of mist twist the water's surface and buffet the *Haitun* as the banks drift in and out of view.

Ruby heads for shelter on the leeward side, thinking hard. Is Charlie convinced about the spirit sword and what they saw, or does he *still* think they somehow dreamed those figures up in the tunnel? On the deck below two hands are busy wrapping a flapping black wraith of tarpaulin over the bulk of a mounted, ugly-looking machine gun. The river's moving faster now, or their own speed has increased, the water dashing along the side of the *Haitun*.

'Ahoyyyyyy!'

A long, drawn-out cry from someone on the prow rings out and then Marlais' unmistakeable voice is bellowing staccato Pidgin at someone.

Close by there's a loud groaning, the sharp snap of a sail taking the wind, and a second or two later a huge, black junk fills her vision, bowling downriver, not more than ten paces of choppy water separating them. The Chinese boat sits high, dwarfing the *Haitun*, a few figures on deck staring into the murk ahead, rigging and sail creaking again as the squalls bite. A great mass of heavy, dark wood charging downriver.

A man high on the raised rear looks across at them and lifts a hand, shouting something that is caught by wind and rain and falls lost in the water between.

Ruby follows it, making her way astern, watching the junk disappear rapidly into the mists. But at the last cabin window on the port side, the mystery passenger's berth, curiosity drags at her feet and she slows. Maybe she can get a glimpse in and see who, or what, is in there?

She softens her footsteps, wishing again she had

some of those cloth shoes so many Chinese wear instead of the clumpy school things that make such a racket. But as she creeps past the porthole she sees the curtain is drawn shut, and the glass shows just her own pale reflection hanging there, mouth open in anticipation.

You'll catch flies, Mother would say.

Disappointed, she moves on, under the rattling tin roof to the railing at the stern. The junk that was so big moments ago is now just a small speck on the rolling brown and bottle green Yangtze. Nothing else in sight. Just a lot of water and cloud.

Marlais appears at her shoulder and plants a hand on the wet, rusting rail, glaring at the disappearing junk.

'Big enough for you?' he growls.

Ruby nods.

'And yet you saw that numbskull, all this space and he nearly stoved us in. Way out of his channel. That's why we have to keep eyes sharp all the time. Or we'll be down there and the eels eating us for tea. You see anything else?'

'No. Nothing.'

The walnuts are cracking away in his other hand. 'This is one of the widest spots here. The banks are low and they've been left to go to ruin in places. If you get a really big load of water coming down, the river takes first chance it can get to have a wander. Miles wide then.'

He turns to look at her, eyes gleaming. 'You can see the darndest things then, Missee. The darndest things.'

Ruby swallows hard. 'Like what?'

'People see and hear things. I can tell you some strange stories. And I bet you can tell me some too.'

'Stories?'

He winks. 'Ghost stories. But first I want my cook to have a look at your bruises. He's good with things like that. His father was a decent doctor . . .'

'How do you know about them?'

'Young Charlie told me. He's very worried about you, you know. He said they looked awful?'

'No,' she stumbles. 'It's nothing really.'

'Nonsense. No arguing.'

He leads her down into the cramped kitchen quarters with its hot fug of sizzling green onion and steaming rice, the coal-smudged faces of the stokers hunkered down, chopsticks working fast.

'The black gang,' Marlais says, nodding at them. 'If they stoke themselves properly, they can build a fire like you wouldn't believe, these boys.' He claps one of the lean Chinese on his stained vest. 'Eatee plenty, chop chop. We b'long Hankow side. Catchee one

123

piece bad man! McQueen still down below?'

One of the men points and then bends back to his bowl.

Marlais sniffs the air. 'I pay 'em properly too. Lot of captains just rely on them taking squeeze, getting what they can. That's OK for some of your crew. But not its heart and soul.' He raises his voice. 'Cook! You takee look at this, please.'

A man emerges from the steam. He too has a stained white vest, but it's topped off rather ridiculously by an old chef's hat flopped on his shaved head like a melting ice cream.

'It's just a bruise,' Ruby repeats in Chinese.

The man doesn't say anything but leads her back to a recessed bunk, motioning her to sit down.

'You can trust Cook,' Marlais says. 'I need to see my chief engineer about something.'

The chef draws a grubby curtain to shield them from the stokers and motions Ruby to take off her cardigan.

'Are you really a doctor?' she says in Chinese.

He smiles. 'Better doctor than cook. My old man trained me. I can see you're hurt badly.'

'How?'

'Some things are obvious. Just relax.'

His rough-looking hands are surprisingly gentle,

reassuring as he turns her shoulder and side to the light. But his lined face reacts like Charlie's when he sees the the purpling bruises emerge.

'*Very* strong grip someone had on you.'

Carefully he palpates the area, watching her face for reaction. Despite his caution, Ruby winces, her eyes watering.

The cook nods. 'I need to put something on it. A poultice my dad used to make. You rest there.'

He leaves her on the bunk and she leans back, feeling the rocking of the boat, trying to avoid looking at the bruising herself.

She listens to the chatter of the stokers, breathes the galley's rich aroma. Everything's so different from that last passage downriver on the gunboat. They had sat – Dad, Mother and her – in the officer's mess, being offered soup and pork cutlet as if dining in a posh hotel rather than fleeing a riot-torn city. She remembers holding back the smarting tears as she forced some of the food down. Trying to avoid Dad's gaze and his own reddened eyes. Trying not to think about Tom in his little coffin somewhere below. The Naval Captain wittered on about the weather and the races in Shanghai as if nothing had happened, and Mother suddenly sicked up the oily soup and bolted from the table.

The curtain swishes back and the cook leans over

her, a steaming bowl of green sludge in one hand, a loosely rolled bandage in the other.

'This will help.'

She sniffs suspiciously at the bowl, but it can't be worse than drinking the stuff Jin made.

'What's in it?'

'Mugwort,' he smiles. 'And a lot of other herbs. Secret recipe.'

He starts to gloop the mixture onto her skin. It feels warm and reassuring as it covers the angry marks, but the cook's face is looking thoughtful again.

'So how did you get these bruises then?'

'My aunt was trying to stop me running off.'

He screws his face up tight.

'Really? I've only seen marks like this once before, young lady, years ago. My old dad was called to help a woman who'd just escaped something much worse than an angry auntie . . . looked a bit like this.'

'Something much worse?' Ruby stutters, the look in the cook's eyes triggering the chills through her again.

'A nasty bandit,' the cook mutters, as he winds a bandage into place over the poultice. 'Mind you, some aunts can be pretty fierce. Forget it—'

His words are cut short as a siren blasts the tight confines of the galley and he looks up sharply.

'It's the all-hands warning. Something serious.'

Quickly he ties off the bandages both sides and nods. 'That should help you—'

The Captain's voice can be heard now, his voice made metallic by a loud hailer as he rattles out the orders.

'All hands on deck! Prepare to repel boarders! Fire hoses ready! Get that Lewis gun up, boys!! And be plenty quick about it! We're under attack for real, not just pot shots!'

第十五章

BANDITS AND LANTERNS

Chaos on the *Haitun*. Crew come scrambling from their quarters, pulling braces over sinewy shoulders, some running aft, others breaking out rifles. Everywhere feet drum metal steps, hands grab railings, as Marlais' voice thunders again: 'Port side! Fire when ready!'

The rain is still dropping in buckets, the ship veering hard to starboard, deck tipping as Ruby runs for the wheelhouse. She's on the wrong side of the boat and can't see the threat, but glancing down a corridor that cuts across the ship, she sees a big shadow block the river beyond. A young crewman bangs into her and curses – but his face isn't angry, just scared.

'Bandits, bad ones,' he hisses, then hurtles down to the lower level.

Away to the right, something catches the corner of her eye then and she turns to see a sampan bobbing on the water, its deck jammed with half a dozen figures. A red banner is fluttering from a staff held by the figure perched on the bow. Surely that's not the threat? She hesitates, peering through the veil of the rain, and sees that it's a young woman waving the flag, one foot planted on the bowsprit, as if about to leap into the river. Or clear across it.

'Ruby!'

Charlie is tugging her by the arm.

'We've got to take shelter in the wheelhouse.'

She points at the little boat. 'Who do you think they are?'

'No idea.' Charlie shakes his head. 'We've got bigger problems—'

A heavy impact slams the *Haitun*'s port side and shakes the ship, throwing Ruby off balance. A few seconds later a second, even heavier blow tips the whole boat to starboard, tumbling them both against the railing. Charlie trips over a coiled rope and jackknifes over the side, hands flailing frantically for some kind of a hold, fingers gripping emptiness – and for a God-awful second Ruby thinks he's lost into the water. But Charlie's always stronger than people think, more skilful. He twists in midair and somehow grabs the lower railing, and then he's dangling over the river, feet skimming the choppy surface, hauling himself up. Ruby takes hold of his free hand and drags him back onto the deck.

'Thanks,' he stutters, glancing back shocked at the roiling water, then pushes her towards the bridge.

As they make the safety of the wheelhouse Ruby glances back to starboard. The overloaded sampan with the young woman is closing, lying so low between the waves that it looks as though she is striding across the water, and then armour plating bangs down into place, and the vision is cut off dead.

On the bridge Young Chen is braced with both hands on the wheel, feet planted as he fights the shove of the attacking boat. There's another thud, followed by the clanking of metal on metal from the port side, followed by ragged cheering from what sounds like a small army.

Marlais scowls. 'Grappling hook.'

He squints through the armour.

'Now what?' Ruby pants.

'Now we're going to have to fight, damn it,' Marlais snarls. 'Last resort.' He's already unfastening a long rifle from the roof of the wheelhouse, ratcheting the bolt back and forth as he mutters under his breath. 'This mob are taking advantage of the fact that with all the fuss up at Wanhsien there won't be any dammed help for miles.'

Gunshots bang along the port side of the *Haitun* and then the din is intensified by a great whooshing sound. Marlais turns, a grim smile on his face. 'At least our fire hose's working.'

'There's another boat,' Ruby says. 'On the right side.'

Marlais looks puzzled and steps across the wheelhouse, peering through the slit in the armoured shutters. 'God only knows,' he says. 'They look like a bunch of kids.'

Outside the bridge there's fresh shouting and screaming, another burst of gunfire. Through the gaps in the shutters that side, Ruby can make out the size of the boat that's jammed up against them – at least as big as the junk that gave them a narrow squeak just minutes ago. Its bulk is blocking out what light there is, throwing shadow across them.

Without warning her left side fires into volleys of pins and needles, every single fine hair on her arm sticking upright. Not the cold this time, not even the fear, though that's definitely working hard. No, this is *exactly* like in the Mansions, like the day they caught the fox.

Something's here, she thinks. Something that belongs somewhere else. I need the sword.

She skips back across the bridge, unbolts the central

131

door that leads to the cabins and darts through it.

'Get back at once!' Marlais barks. 'Close that hatch.'

'I've got to get something,' she shouts over the racket as the door bangs shut behind her.

Gunfire raps the hull of the boat as she runs. There's another scream, cut abruptly short. All the while the tingling is getting harder, both arms now, like someone's jabbing away at her with dressmaking pins, hundreds of them pressing her flesh. All she can think of is grabbing the sword, feeling Jin's gift in her hands. Can't just stand still and do nothing . . .

She ducks into their cabin, thrusts shaky hands into the pack and grabs the hilt of the sword.

In the faint light the blade looks dull, flimsy. Maybe just a tiny hint of green shimmering in the characters around the stars etched there. She stares at it hard – if there are any spirits close by wouldn't it be glowing like in the tunnel? Maybe its magic is all used up, or her own *ch'i* too weak. So long since Jin transferred that energy to her . . .

Still, it feels good to hold it at least. As she runs back to the bridge she hears Charlie calling her name – and then the drumming of heavy footsteps behind her.

The door to the wheelhouse is open and Charlie is leaning out, beckoning wildly.

'For Heaven's sake, run!'

The footsteps thumping behind are closing and Ruby glances back to see a gaunt-faced man, his two-handed sword raised, ready to strike. Almost on her.

Instinctively she raises the spirit sword in both hands, hoping maybe to parry the man's blow, desperately willing the blade to come to life and make her hands move, to turn her into the warrior again.

But nothing comes. The sword looks and feels feeble.

The bandit's face cracks into a horrid leer and he lunges forward. Ruby braces – and simultaneously a deafening bang rings in her ears. The man spins as if someone's grabbed him by the shoulder and he slams into the wall.

Ruby turns to see Marlais lowering his smoking rifle.

'No disobeying orders,' he grunts, then his eyes fall on the slim sword in Ruby's hands.

'And what the hell is that?'

'It's . . . it's—'

'Never mind.'

Marlais pulls her roughly over the threshold, banging the door behind. 'If it all goes belly up, jump in the ship's dinghy and cast yourselves loose. Don't try and swim, you'll never make it.'

'What about you? And the rest?'

'We'll defend the *Haitun* to the last if needs—'

The splintering of wood cuts him short as the other door to the bridge rips from its frame, tumbling inwards, two wild-eyed bandits falling with it. Old Lee snaps into life with a snarl, pulling an antique pistol from the folds of his gown and firing. The first man screams, blood gouting onto the cabin wall, and suddenly the confined space is full of bodies, the noise intense, blades flashing, the stench of smoke from pistols and rifles as more bandits surge forward. Charlie pulls Ruby back by the crook of her arm, retreating into the far corner as Old Lee shoots again.

Young Chen is still trying to keep one hand on the wheel, parrying blows from a knife-wielding attacker with the other. A muscle-bound bandit gets him in a headlock, wrenches him away from the spokes of the wheel, and then, with a horribly clear view, Ruby sees another attacker run him clean through with a sword. Chen's face goes white, his hands reaching down to try and grab the blade, rolling and falling as the *Haitun* swings on the current, the wheel spinning free. Chen stumbles towards Ruby, a look of incomprehension on his face, and slumps at her feet.

第十六章

THE BLOOD IN THE SHOE

Marlais swears blackly, raises his rifle and starts repeatedly to fire into the melee.

But Ruby's eyes are fixed on the young man dying at her feet. She feels something warm and wet on her socked foot now, seeping into her shoe. With horror she sees the blood flowing from Chen and backs away, stumbling out of the starboard door and into the confusion of battle. Below, there's hand-to-hand fighting between a dozen or more bandits and the *Haitun*'s crew. A fire hose is powering through the rain, soaking everything. Her foot feels gloopy and warm and she can't think straight, but glancing round, she sees something else: the smaller boat has drawn alongside the *Haitun*, and the young woman is leaping onto their deck, pulling two short swords from behind her back. She's wearing a blood-red Chinese jacket tied tight at the waist, strands of black hair flying loose from the bun on her head as she runs to attack, screaming something at the top of her lungs, the blades flashing.

She's really quite young, not much older than sixteen, seventeen at most. Scrambling behind, three young men follow with fighting sticks, maybe a little older, and another girl with her hair tied up in a plum-coloured scarf.

The first girl is almost on her.

'Who are you?' Ruby shouts. Charlie is by her side now, his eyes also glued to the extraordinary girl.

But she ignores them both, hurtling past and charging into the skirmish on the front deck, her high voice clear over the sounds of battle.

'Red Lantern Defence Force! Defend China!'

Transfixed, Ruby watches as the girl plants a foot on a capstan and jumps – no, *flies* – through the air. She lands in the middle of the melee, ducks a blow, then strikes at speed, first one blade then the other. A bandit wheels away, clutching his face as if fighting off a wasp, and a fraction later another doubles up, gripping his stomach. The boys are with her now, their staves blurring in the rain as they unleash a flurry of whip-crack martial arts' moves.

The other girl is standing beside Ruby now. She

peers into Ruby's eyes, frowns, then thumps Charlie in the chest, rattling out a question.

'Who are you? Identify yourself to the Red Lantern Defence Force!'

She's a bit older than the first, trying to look as fierce, but there's a gleam in her eyes, something almost playful.

'My name's Charlie. Charlie Tang.'

Any hint of mirth drops away. 'What's your real name? Chinese name?'

'Tang Jia Li,' Charlie stutters. 'But everyone calls—'

'The foreign will be swept away,' the girl snaps. 'China will belong to the Chinese.'

She throws another look at Ruby, hostile, suspicious.

'And foreign devil,' she whispers. 'Who are you?'

'I'm not a foreign devil,' Ruby says, meeting her gaze. 'I was born here—'

The girl snorts and shakes her head. 'Don't answer like that to Tian Lan when she asks you! Have you heard what's happening upriver?'

'That's not my fault—'

A hammering of gun shots breaks in the wheelhouse and Marlais comes stumbling out, followed by Old Lee.

'They've got the wheelhouse,' he shouts. 'They'll put us on the sandbar . . .'

He sees the newcomers now.

'You what people?' he says gruffly to Plum Scarf in Pidgin.

The girl turns to Charlie, firing staccato Chinese. 'Tell this man we will get rid of bandits and in return he must take us up river. We need to get to Ichang—'

'Tell them, Charlie,' Marlais interrupts, 'nobody orders me around on my ship.'

But the red-jacketed girl and the boys are already pushing past into the wheelhouse, undeterred by the intensity of battle inside. Old Lee is crouched by the door, trying to aim at a target and avoid hitting his own men, or the newcomers. He sees Ruby and glances down at the blade hanging forgotten in her hands, his eyes narrowing as he reaches out that long fingernail to tap it.

'Where did you get this, girl?' he whispers, his voice hoarse.

'A – friend gave it to me. A Taoist priest.'

Old Lee grunts, then turns back to aim again. 'Powerful. Hope you know what you're doing.'

He discharges his weapon, squints through the smoke, fires again.

'We are winning,' he whispers. 'Thanks to these youngsters . . .'

The tingling has died away, but suddenly it surges

again across her neck – and then every square inch of her back prickles like fury. Whatever she felt before is definitely close now!

Ruby whips around, and sees a fleeting, grey smudge at the corner of her eye, far away at the end of the starboard deck. It's a tall, thin figure, slipping around the corner, gone before she's even really seen it, but the void it leaves behind sucks her forward.

The sword twitches in her clammy hands, moving her arms and distinctly pulling her away down the deck.

OK. *Mei wenti. Mei wenti.*

On the blade a faint gleam is starting to pulse in the copper, and she jogs forward, watching it, the blood in her shoe forgotten now. The rain is lashing harder again, thickening the air, the smoke billowing down in black swirls. She takes a breath and runs straight into it, the sword snapping up in her hands – and sees the figure at the stern.

A Shadow Warrior.

Or a fainter version of one, hard to see in the swirling smoke, almost the colour of the dark water beyond, but there, right there in front of her.

It raises an arm, then lurches forward, grabbing for her chest. Fear snags her limbs, but then the sword twists again, and she swishes it at the thing's head.

The Shadow sways back, eyes two dim points, mouth gaping open, hissing.

'Go home,' it gurgles. 'Go hooooome, little girl. Or die.'

The green glow is gathering in the copper blade and it steadies her nerves just a bit. The shape solidifies against the river, but doesn't attack again. Instead its gaze seems held by the spirit sword.

'Who are you? What do you want with me?'

'Go back,' it whispers. 'To go further is to die.'

'Who are you?'

'We protect our master,' the thing hisses, voice fading as it backs towards the rail. You can see the water right through it now. 'You – cannot stop – him. Not in the Otherworld and he – isssss almost there nowwwwww.'

The shape trembles on the edge of visibility, then smudges away into nothing, disappearing into the driving rain and smoke.

Gone.

Ruby waits, her fingers jittery and shaking, the sword vibrating its pale green light.

Nothing more to be seen. No voice hissing away into her ears, just the churning of the props as the *Haitun* veers across the water, and slowly the tingling eases . . .

Something comes snicking across the deck behind her, and she spins round expecting to see the Shadow again, or a bandit – but it's just Straw, wagging his tail and looking bedraggled in the downpour. Behind him the curtain to the mystery passenger's cabin twitches, as if someone's just drawn it rapidly shut.

A cheer erupts from the front of the ship and seconds later the huge bandit junk comes drifting past, bumping the Haitun one last time as she goes, a severed rope trailing into the water as its crew scrambles to leap aboard. Some are limping, others clutching bleeding wounds as they retreat. At least one mistimes his jump and disappears instantly into the thickly churning waters between the boats.

The very last of them is pursued by the girl in the crimson jacket, her twin blades raised threateningly overhead as she chases him all the way to the stern and then kicks the man over the rail like a deflated football. She glowers at the defeated ship and shouts at the top of her voice.

'Tell *everyone* the Red Lantern Defence Force is taking back the river!'

She turns to Ruby, cheekbones slick with rain, and tucks her stray hair back into place, poised, utterly sure of herself. A face without fear, a face that seems unmoved by what has just happened.

A real fighter. A mixture of envy and admiration floods through Ruby. She's *really* like Hu San Niang. Like she's stepped straight out of the pages of the *Water Margin* . . .

The girl is staring at her. 'You got one piece radio?' she asks then in Pidgin. 'Need radio. Talk Hankow side plenty quick.'

'I can speak Chinese,' Ruby says. 'You don't need to use Pidgin.'

'Oh.' The girl's eyebrows steeple as she switches back to Chinese. 'Aren't you a clever girl then? Well, get a move on and take me to whoever's in charge of this rust bucket.'

Ruby shifts her weight and feels that awful hot squidge of blood in her shoe again – and before she knows it, she's doubled at the rail and heaving up what little food she's had in the last twenty-four hours, the sight of Chen skewered, the reappearance of a Shadow Warrior suddenly too much. The sick burns her throat as she shuts her eyes tight.

If only Jin was here to set this girl straight . . .

Oh God. More. Got to get rid of this shoe . . .

At last the spasms ease and she bends down, hurriedly unbuckling the shoe with shaking fingers, and then hurls the stupid thing as hard as she can into the sodden Yangtze.

There's laughter behind her, a mocking laughter that stings her ears. Ruby rips off the sock and chucks that over the side to join it. There's blood smudged on her pale foot.

Behind her the girl in the red jacket is laughing even harder.

'This is the real China, little girl. Real blood. No use waving your toy sword around.'

Ruby turns, sees Charlie has come to join them and waits – hopes – that he will speak up for her. But instead he remains silent, biting his lip, and when Ruby tries to seek out his eyes, he avoids her gaze and looks away again to where the bandit junk is being swallowed by mist and cloud. Like he's really ill at ease, she thinks, heart sinking. Almost like he's embarrassed.

第十七章

HOW TO TIE A KNOT

At last the rain eases and watery sunshine drops on the river. Ruby sits in her cabin, one hand resting absentmindedly on Straw's head, the other still clutching the worn hilt of the spirit sword. Its glow has faded, and so has the tingling sensation, and now she just feels drained, exhausted. At a loss.

Charlie led her back to the haven of the cabin, away from the harsh stares of the Red Lanterns, then muttered something about *being sorry* and left in a hurry. That must be an hour ago, or more.

What's keeping him?

She looks at her cold, bare foot. She's washed it three times but still it feels like some of that blood's there – even though it looks clean. How awful the way Chen looked as he realised what had happened: a look of absolute disbelief and terror. Even the new sighting of a Shadow can't chase that away.

The girl in the red jacket looked at me like I was a kind of joke, she thinks, feeling the heat rise in her face. And Charlie hardly stood up for me, he just stood there with that confused look. Didn't want to hear about what I'd just seen . . .

Straw nudges against her arm and instinctively she goes to protect it, but then realises it's starting to feel a bit better. Maybe that old cook knew what he was doing after all.

'And at least I've got you, boy,' she mutters, bending down to ruffle the dog's head.

Straw makes a low grumbling in his throat, rolling the sounds like pebbles in a river. Maybe he's going to talk again? If there was a Shadow on the boat, then maybe it's *all* starting to happen again.

She looks him in the eyes. 'Do you need to tell me something?'

But Straw just drops his jaw, flaps out his tongue and yawns a huge yawn, gazing back at her with his amber eyes. He lets his front paws slide on the wooden floor and settles down.

Below, the engines are thrumming away, pushing them further upriver towards Hankow – who knows, maybe even beyond that, towards the Gorges even? Further than I've ever been . . .

The hissing voice of the Shadow is in her ears again, at least the memory of it.

Qu shi si, it said. To go is to die.

Maybe it *would* be best to turn around . . .

But no, she thinks. That's not possible. Fei needs me and I've given Charlie my word. And the Russian fortune teller said I *have* to make the journey. And more than that, more important, Lao Jin believed in me. He said I could do more than I thought I could, and he knew more than that girl with her red jacket and fancy footwork.

Where on *earth* has Charlie got to?

She wraps the sword carefully and slips it into Jin's sack and heads out onto the side deck. The river breeze caresses her bare foot, like it's wiping away the last trace of the blood. Suddenly she grabs the remaining shoe from the other one and tosses it far out into their white wake, the pale sunshine.

Mother would have a fit and a half!

She stifles a grin at the act of rebellion. Shanghai Ruby smiling again as the shoe and school and the last of the 'normal' world slip beneath the surface.

Further along, crew members are washing down the decks with buckets of sudsy water. A stoker sits on a wooden bench at the stern, having a nasty gash in his thigh sewn up by the cook.

He grimaces at her, motions with his head towards the wheelhouse. 'If you're looking for your friend, he's up there, talking to those Red Lantern types.'

'Who are they? The Red Lanterns?'

'One of these local defence forces that are springing up everywhere,' he grunts. 'At least this lot seem to know what they're doing.'

Ruby heads forward, her feet slapping the cool wet boards as sun slides through the clouds. With the chucking of the shoes some of the horror has eased – but as she glances into the wheelhouse she sees a deckhand mopping swirls of pale red on the ridged floor. A tall, dark-haired Westerner is at the helm, hands gripping the spokes, with Old Lee and Marlais in their usual positions, all eyes trained forward.

'Weather's clearing,' Marlais grunts, without taking his eyes off the river ahead. 'But not for long, there's a wall of water up there, believe me. And whatever's fallen on Yunan and Szechuan is coming our way.'

Ruby watches the hypnotic swirl of the mop as it struggles to clean the last of the blood.

'Is everything else OK now?'

'Not quite,' he mutters. 'Channel's wandering a bit. Not where it should be! And I don't trust that lot.' He nods at the foredeck below.

Ruby edges forward. The armoured shields are bolted back again and she sees Charlie talking animatedly with the two girls from the defence force. The boys are lounging on their backs on coiled ropes nearby, faces turned to the sky and passing a pipe from hand to hand. One of them is busy with a length of hemp, working an elaborate knot of some kind.

Marlais pulls a face. 'I owe them some thanks, I guess – but they don't want to hear it from the likes of you and me, young lady. We don't count, I'm afraid.'

Something flutters uncomfortably in her stomach and she hurries out.

'Charlie? Charlie!'

By the time she's dropping down the stairway to the foredeck that fluttering has become something stronger: irritation, anger even. Charlie is listening eagerly as the sword girl talks a streak into the morning, nodding agreement, his own face reflecting her excitement. He's oblivious to Ruby's approach until the last moment, doesn't hear her calling, all attention focused on Red Jacket and the words she's spinning.

'. . . every time we stand up for ourselves we're crushed again,' the girl says stridently, thumping the palm of one hand with the other to emphasise her words. 'The Taiping revolt, the Boxers, the revolution of 1911 – it all comes down to foreigners telling us what to do. And bandits and bloodthirsty warlords taking what they want from the land, from the people.'

Charlie nods eagerly again. 'So who are you with?'

'Nobody. We're standing up for ourselves.' She sweeps a hand at the country beyond. 'Until we've decided who to join. My father was a Boxer, and my great-grandfather fought with the Taiping revolt.'

Charlie's hanging on her every word. 'Did your father teach you to fight like that? You were – amazing!'

Ruby steps up and taps him smartly on the shoulder. 'Charlie. I need to talk to you!' Her words come a bit awkwardly, a bit too abrupt.

Charlie turns, refocusing, his face colouring a little bit. 'Ah, Ruby. Did you hear that? Tian Lan learnt that sword stuff from her father. He was a Boxer in the uprising against the missionaries and – the rest.'

Tian Lan turns full square to Ruby. 'Until they were crushed by the foreign devils.'

Ruby's pulse quickens, curiosity and irritation fighting each other. 'But the Boxers killed *innocent* people – missionary wives and children.'

Tian Lan shakes her head. 'There are *no* innocent people in times like that. My father was a brave man. He stood up to you foreign devils and the traitors. The local magistrate,' she spits vigorously on the deck, 'was going to execute him in a cage – *starve* him to death. But he escaped.'

Ruby goes to argue, but checks herself. The truth is she doesn't really know enough about the Boxers. They were so cruel to missionary families (even though Dad says the missionaries asked for it!), but at least they stood up for themselves. For China. The girl is looking at her defiantly, nostrils flared slightly, scrapping for a fight.

'Anyway,' she rattles on. 'I don't need to explain myself to the likes of you. Have you heard what your lot are doing up the river? Hundreds of innocent people killed!'

There's a silence on the deck. Ruby pushes her tongue hard against her cheek wall and turns to Charlie.

Come on, she thinks, come on, Charlie, speak up for me! *You* know I'm not like the rest.

But he lowers his eyes, looks down at the deck and keeps an uncomfortable silence.

Ruby hesitates, then turns back to the girl. 'It was good of you to help us. Thank you.'

'We weren't helping YOU! We were trying to rid this stretch of the river of those bandit scum. Besides, we needed a lift up towards Hankow.'

Maybe flattery will work. 'Could you help teach me some of those fighting moves? I had a *ba gua* teacher in

Shanghai, but he died—'

'No,' the girl says flatly, and turns away to her comrades, talking under her breath. 'Don't make me laugh.'

Ruby spins back to Charlie, feeling her indignation rise. 'Why does she have to be so rude?' she hisses. 'What have I done to *her*?'

'It's not you, Ruby—'

'But it's *stupid* to think I'm like the rest.'

Charlie shakes his head. 'Don't *annoy* her. I think they can help us.'

'We don't *need* her beastly help—'

'We do,' Charlie cuts back. 'We do need her, and her gang. They know what they're doing. They're real fighters, you saw them. And it's MY little sister in danger, isn't it? Not *yours*.'

Ruby holds his eyes, knows she's getting this all wrong. But it's hard to say the right thing.

Charlie nods again. 'And guess what they saw? That cruiser of Moonface's came through just a few hours ago. We're not far behind Fei! Tian Lan can help us!'

Ruby looks away from the Red Lantern group, trying to recover her composure. Sunlight is sifting down through the departing clouds, insects rising in columns above the warm, brown surface of the Yangtze. Out of nowhere a swallow forks down and skims the surface before hurling itself up again into the huge sky.

'So where are we now?' she says.

'Not far below Kiukiang I think,' Charlie says. 'Maybe we'll get Moonface before Hankow even. And we know what his boat's called now. The *Sea Witch*.'

Ruby screws up her eyes, as if trying to follow the bird in the huge sky overhead, but it's gone.

'Come and talk in the cabin. I need to tell you something—'

'Hey, Tang *Jia Li*,' the girl calls, stressing Charlie's Chinese name, 'come and tell us more about your sister. And your dad.'

'Jia Li?' Ruby parrots under her breath.

Charlie shrugs. 'It *is* my name—'

'Since when!'

'Give me ten minutes.'

His eyes flick a sheepish look of apology, and then he turns and walks over to the girl. Ruby hesitates, wondering whether to argue more with the girl, to ask Charlie again to come away. But he's deep in conversation again, gesticulating upriver to the dark skies ahead. She bites her lip hard and turns and climbs the metal steps back towards the cabin.

It feels like someone or something is tying knots in her intestines. Complicated ones at that.

第十八章

GHOSTS OF CHINA

The arguments keep playing in her head. Ruby lies on her bunk staring at the ceiling, running imaginary conversations, first her own voice, then what Charlie says back, then something else she should have said. But listening to the imagined dialogue she hears herself sounding *too* young, too *stupid*.

You like her more than me . . .

I thought we were sticking together . . .

What's so great about her *anyway . . . ?*

That look in Charlie's eyes though when he was talking to the girl . . . she had him on a hook, reeling him in like a fish. I should have said something to Charlie earlier, damn it, she thinks. Something about how I feel, maybe on the train, or in the tunnel. Or months ago! But he always sees me as a friend, or another sister, not anything *special*.

No good ever came of love across the races, Mother said, your life would be quite *simply dreadful*. But *some* people have managed it . . . and surely Charlie won't just drop me like that?

She jumps up from the bunk, frustrated, pacing. Maybe I should do some of those exercises we learnt from the Almanac, she thinks. Try and calm down a bit, regather some *ch'i*.

She tries to picture the book in her head, to see the diagrams on its faded pages, and loosen the tangle of thoughts about Charlie. Weird how the Almanac disappeared, she thinks, and a shame too. Even if Jin said you had to have the right eyes to read it properly, it might be *some* help now to mug up more about Green Frontiers and Shadows and Revenants and all that. To do the exercises right.

Straw gets up, whining uneasily as he watches her pace, his pale fur shivering with the throb of the engines.

There are voices in the corridor now, the sharp give and take of a real humdinger of an argument. Marlais and the Scottish engineer bickering about something. As if on cue the *Haitun* gives a shudder and a moment later the engines cut out midstroke, McQueen's voice suddenly loud and clear right outside the door.

'. . . damn lousy useless Jap pumps. I told you this

was a doomed trip, Marlais.'

'Some trips have got to be made,' the Captain rumbles back. 'You'll get your cut – and I've made a deal. Now shut your moaning up and see what you can do.'

Ruby bends down, trying to calm Straw and listen for more from either man – but there's nothing but the sound of departing footsteps, followed moments later by the roar of anchor chain rattling to the depths. The noise makes the slim dog jump, and Ruby wraps him tight in her bruised arms, as much for herself as for him.

The afternoon is a dead loss. The *Haitun* sits marooned midstream, the air muggy and buzzed by insects. Everyone else – Marlais, Old Lee, McQueen – is preoccupied with the engines, or other vital tasks that don't involve her. And *still* Charlie is locked in a huddle with the Red Lanterns.

Ruby collapses on the lower bunk and closes her eyes, listening to the drone of the flies, the tremor of the water rippling past the stricken boat.

When, at long last, Charlie does return, he seems distant and shunts her questions aside with single syllable answers, foot tapping impatiently as he listens to the clank of spanners and hammers below. It's as if he's really pulling away from her. But why? Because of this girl?

After the fourth stilted silence, Ruby stands up and looks at him, arms crossed.

'Well? What's going on? Did she say she'll help or not?'

'Huh?'

'That girl. Did she say she'd help?'

'It's not that simple,' Charlie sighs.

'But you asked her? You always keep things to yourself. Why won't you tell me?'

'There's no point anyway if they can't get the boat going,' Charlie huffs. 'Some *dolphin*! She's just a rusty old tub. Moonface will be putting miles between us.'

'They'll get the engines going again. The Captain wants to help.'

Charlie slumps down on the bunk, voice flat. 'What was it you wanted to tell me anyway?'

'You'll think it's silly.'

'I won't. Tell me.'

Ruby hesitates, trying to judge the words just right. 'At the end of the battle with the bandits I saw something. It was very faint, but there was a Shadow Warrior on the deck. I chased him to the back and he said some horrid things. And then he just disappeared.'

Charlie looks at her, his expression hard to read in the half-light of the cabin.

'Honest, Charlie. He looked just like the ones in the tunnel.'

'Ruby—'

'It said we'd die if we went any further.'

'Well, we're not going anywhere right now!'

Silence falls again. It feels like Charlie's drifting out of reach, like her concerns aren't the same as his, and she rushes to say what's on her mind, while she has the chance.

'Can you remember what the Almanac said about Green Frontiers? Where they are, how you know when you see them. That kind of thing?'

Charlie shakes his head. 'I don't know. All I can think about is getting after Fei and now we're stuck and going nowhere.' He thumps the bed with a fist.

Then his voice softens. 'I'm sorry. But we need to keep our heads and Tian Lan knows—'

A sharp knock on the door cuts him short and a fraction later Captain Marlais' head pokes into the cabin.

'Seeing as we're going absolutely bloody nowhere, I wonder if I might invite you two to dine with me. Captain's table. It's time we had a bit of a chat, you and me.'

Charlie gets up, half understanding, half not.

'When we move? Need go plenty quick.'

The Captain's cool, blue eyes seek out Charlie's. 'We move soon. Marlais will help you find little sister. Just keep an eye on those Red Lanterns for me. Savvy?'

Charlie nods, but Ruby can feel he's holding something back. Like he's guarding something he doesn't want to share with Marlais.

Or with her.

She goes to the porthole and gazes out, feeling the river flow shifting the *Haitun* about beneath her feet. On a low hill about a mile away a brightly lit pagoda pricks dark clouds beyond. A long minute or two later she hears Charlie leave the cabin and the door snick quietly shut – and distantly thunder comes rolling down and across the simmering river.

At last, as light fades, the gong sounds for dinner. The atmosphere is still close, clouds thickening again as dozens of moths batter themselves senseless against the fizzing light bulbs strung along the upper rail.

Charlie meets her in the corridor, locked up in his own thoughts. His shoulders have taken on that tension again, like a clothes hanger is wedged in the back of his jacket.

'Are you OK?' she whispers, trying to sound calmer

158

than she feels.

'I'd rather eat with the others.'

'Who?' she fires back, slightly too quickly.

'The crew. It'll all be in English in here and I won't be able to keep up.'

'I'll tell you what's happening. I promise. We need Captain Marlais just as much as you – as *we* – need those Red Lanterns.'

Charlie glances back, peering at her through his glasses, and then nods solemnly.

'You're right. Sorry.'

The table is set for five, with wine glasses and napkins and silver cutlery. Marlais has put on a dark jacket and tie, but only succeeds in looking like a pirate trying to scrub up for court. He motions them to sit and two crew members pull out their chairs.

'This feels wrong,' Charlie mutters, tugging at his sleeves as McQueen stomps in, wiping his hands on a rag, the oil and grease still graining his fingers.

Marlais pulls a face. 'That the best you can do, Mister McQueen? Got to keep up appearances.'

'If you want the rotten pumps changed, it's the best I can do.'

Ruby looks at the remaining empty place, curiosity pricking again. Maybe it's for the mystery passenger. But Charlie's mind is obviously elsewhere. 'Where is

Miss Tian Lan?' he asks, in stilted English.

'She declined my offer,' Marlais says with a shake of the head, just as Old Lee sweeps in silently and sits in the empty chair.

'What about the other passenger?' Ruby says, disappointed.

'Sadly not,' Marlais says. 'I am told he's off his food.'

'Is he ill?'

'He has to keep himself to himself,' Marlais says, raising his shaggy eyebrows. 'Isn't that right, Lee?'

'It is so.'

Charlie fumbles his napkin, looking sharply at the Captain. 'When we go? We need find sister!'

'Ask him,' Marlais nods, glancing at McQueen.

'First light,' the Scotsman says. 'As long as I get a good supper and then work half the night.'

'And when we Hankow-side?' Charlie presses.

Marlais reaches over and slaps Charlie's shoulder with his paw. 'Soon, chief. Soon. But now let's eat. And then what do you say? I rather fancy a ghost story to pass the time.'

He opens his eyes very wide, the blue dazzle of them reaching for Ruby's. 'A proper one, hey, Mister Lee?'

At the other end of the table Old Lee closes his eyes and nods solemnly.

'Good time for ghost stories. Between day and night.'

The bread that Ruby's hungrily bitten off sticks in her mouth. Thunder crackles away to the west and the gathering darkness around them seems to deepen as Marlais turns back to her.

'I bet you know some awful good ones, young lady.'

Ruby swallows the chewy bread with some difficulty and nods, and then concentrates on the bowl of fish chowder that's been set before her.

Marlais drains a glass of some kind of liquor and then two more, his eyes getting brighter all the time as they move on to plates of chicken stew and sweet potato. The silence is awkward, but at least we're getting some proper food at last, Ruby thinks. She looks round the table. The engineer eats fast, his mind clearly still on pistons and pumps. As he sops up the last of the chicken fat with his bread, he nods towards the galley. 'Not bad, old cook. For a bloody Chink.'

Charlie hears the word and stiffens in his chair, and Ruby feels her own hackles rise. She bites back a reply and tries to give Charlie a warning tap with her foot under the table, but he's just too far to reach. Need McQueen to help us too, she thinks and tries to change tack quickly.

'I'm really sorry about Mister Chen.'

'So am I,' Marlais growls. 'He was decent. Clever. For a Chinese.' He glances at McQueen, and then at Charlie.

Ruby frowns. Now the Captain's at it! It's the kind of thing Dad's awful club friends say without thinking twice. Bigoted.

And yet Marlais hasn't said *slopehead* or *chink*. He turns to look at her now, eyes twinkling. 'But then I'm decent. For a *Yank*. And you're decent, for a damn *Brit*. Even old McQueen here's not so bad given he's a *damn* Scotchman! All dancing around with a haggis in a kilt? Good and bad everywhere, Missee Harkner, wouldn't you say, regardless of creed, regardless of colour?' He fixes McQueen a stare.

Ruby nods, relieved that Marlais hasn't let her down.

'The Captain here's gone native,' McQueen grumbles into his rice. 'He's married one of 'em, can you believe? Upriver, isn't she, Marlais? Caught up in all that mess at Wanhsien.'

'You have a Chinese wife?' Ruby says, looking sharply at the Captain.

'Shut up, McQueen,' Marlais snaps, his mood changing in a flash, thumping the table hard making the cutlery clink together. 'And mind your Ps and bloody Qs.'

The engineer wipes his mouth with the back of his hand, then shoves back his chair and stalks towards the engine room. 'Please yourself. I'll get back to my work.'

Marlais leans back and starts cranking the walnuts in his right fist again, his breathing coming hard through his nostrils as he calms his anger.

'Let's forget McQueen and his manners, shall we? So, you know any ghost stories then, *Misseeee* Harkner?'

Ruby pulls a face.

'I bet you do. Children always do. Specially in this country.'

'My sister likes,' Charlie says quietly. 'Very much.'

'Then let's tell one for her,' Marlais grins. 'You first, young lady.'

'I don't really—'

'As part of your passage. Tell Marlais a story.' His eyes spark again in the gloom. 'I insist.'

Charlie's followed the gist. He leans forward and whispers in Chinese. 'We want him on our side, remember?'

Ruby's fingernail snakes up to tap her front teeth. She's not in the mood for telling ghost stories, not with the night falling and the memory of the Shadow Warrior still raw and the air hot and the stupid moths knocking themselves out in the lamp.

163

'It's your fee,' Marlais says firmly. 'A *rite of passage* if you like.'

She pulls the tapping fingernail away, and glances at Charlie who nods earnestly, encouraging her.

'OK. Well, this is one of Fei's favourites . . . it's from the *Strange Tales*. And it starts like this . . . *Henjiu, henjiu yiqian . . .*'

The strange tale of the painted skin

Henjiu, henjiu yiqian . . . Once upon a time there was a rich man called Wang who was out walking one morning when a woman passed him carrying a heavy bundle. He caught up and offered to help, and saw at once that she was young and very beautiful. Wang fell in love with her on the spot.

'What are you doing out so early?' he asked.

'I have run away,' she said, stifling a sob. 'I've got nowhere to go.'

'My own humble house is close by,' Wang said. 'I can give you shelter.'

'And what about your family, won't they mind?'

'You can hide in my study,' the man said. 'It's a hut in the grounds and nobody will know you are there.'

'That's wonderful,' the young woman said, wiping her tears. 'But I must ask you keep my presence there a secret. My life depends on it.'

The man agreed and swore not to tell a soul.

For several days they met each morning and Wang

fell more deeply in love than ever. But each time he left, the girl insisted she remain a secret.

'And you must only visit when I tell you to,' she said, and kissed him again.

After a week Wang started to feel uneasy, and confided the secret to his mother. She was worried they were harbouring a fugitive or worse, and told her son to get rid of the girl. But he paid no attention and kept his secret love.

A few days later Wang bumped into a Taoist priest who took one look at him and went pale.

'What have you been up to?' the priest gasped. 'Your whole being is wrapped in an evil aura.'

Wang ignored him and hurried away. How could a beautiful young girl like that work bad magic on anyone? Maybe the priest was just trying to demand a fat fee for exorcising a spirit. But something in the Taoist's words rang true. He didn't feel well, and there was something odd about the girl . . .

Wang hurried home and went straight to his study. The door was bolted tight - he was locked out! Suspicion growing, he clambered over a wall into the courtyard, crept up to the study window, and peered in.

A terrible sight greeted him: a green-skinned demon with glittering eyes and teeth like sawblades was leaning over something on the desk, carefully working a paint brush. No sign at all of the girl. Horrified Wang leaned closer, and saw that the monster was actually touching up details on a human skin - the young girl's! As soon as it was done, the thing shook out the skin, wrapped it around its body and immediately became again his young love.

Wang scrambled away as fast as his legs would carry him, all the way to the Taoist priest. He begged for help and the priest gave him a talisman to hang above his bedroom door for protection.

'Whatever happens, don't let her into your bedroom,' the priest said.

That night Wang placed the talisman over his locked door and tried to get to sleep. But just after midnight there was a tapping at his door.

'It's me, your love,' the 'girl' called.

'Go away. I have a talisman. Be gone!' Wang shouted, but the 'girl' broke the door to pieces and stood there, grinding her teeth, staring at the priest's charm.

'No. I won't be stopped,' she growled and leapt forward, ripping the thing to shreds - and then attacked Wang with fingers like iron, plucking the heart right from his chest. She fled into the night, leaving Wang dead on the floor.

Hearing a commotion the mother rushed in and found her son. Grief stricken she ran to the priest's house and demanded help.

'I cannot raise the dead,' the Taoist said. 'He should have listened to me in the first place. But we can deal with that foul ghoul. Follow me.'

Drawing his wooden sword they hurried back to Wang's village and after a long search found a house where a young woman had taken refuge. Gripping his sword tightly the priest called in a loud voice: 'Come out, vile spirit. And plague this district no longer. You touched my talisman so you are in my power.'

With a horrific scream the 'girl' materialised from out of the darkness and attacked, but the Taoist lifted his sword high and struck her a mighty blow. Instantly the skin fell from the monster, revealing its green skin, and with a second blow the priest lopped off its head. Black smoke gushed from the body and evaporated into the night, as calmly the priest rolled up the skin like a scroll and tucked it in his bag.

Ruby leans back and takes a sip of tea, her skin tingling all over. Marlais slaps the table hard, setting everything trembling in the lamplight. 'That's it! That's a story all right and well told too!' He takes a big swig from his tumbler. 'But you've left out the best bit. The happy ending!'

'Did I?'

'Yes!' he thunders, 'don't you remember? The mother goes to another wise man, a weird, scruffy old beggar – really smelly – and he coughs up a ball of phlegm into her hands and, pardon me at the meal table, tells her to eat it!'

The rest of it surges back into Ruby's head. As if she's flicking the pages of her beloved copy of the *Strange Tales* and the last sheet with the lurid woodblock prints is in front of her.

'Of course! And he tells her to run home and all the way back she can feel that phlegm stuck in her throat and it starts to pulse and get bigger and bigger, and just as she gets home she chokes it up again and it's a heart, a beating human heart, and she presses it into her dead son's chest and holds it there. And he comes back to life.'

'That's right,' Old Lee murmurs. 'Wang wakes up properly the next morning and says "I was drifting and drifting. It was like I was in a dream and all the time I felt this pain deep in my chest.'"

'I always loved the last line,' Ruby says excitedly, and she repeats it in Chinese. 'The wound formed a scar the size of a coin and no more, and in time even that disappeared.'

How on earth could I have forgotten that happy ending? she thinks, slumping back in the chair. The story has completely taken hold of her, made her forget, sent a thrill right through her. *Shanghai Ruby loves her Chinese folktales*, Dad always used to say. The thunder cracks again, closer now, prickling the night with electricity.

Marlais slaps her on the shoulder. 'In time, everything disappears! But now I'll tell you something to make your hearts beat even faster.'

He looks straight into Ruby's eyes. 'I'll tell you a real ghost story. Not something out of a writer's head – but something I've seen, and heard and felt. I'll tell you about old Joe Munro.'

'Who?' Ruby whispers.

'A rough old dog,' Marlais says, tipping more liquid into his glass. 'We went way back, me and Joe, seen our share of danger and fun up and down this river. Seen men drunk and seen men killed, seen the Yangtze snap boats in two. Heard strange stories, but nothing as strange as old Munro's death. And his ghost.'

'His ghost?' Ruby leans forward.

The Captain clears his throat. 'Well, old Joe . . . he sailed closer to the wind than the rest of us. Cargo he shouldn't have taken – both ways. We all do a bit of that now and then, but he always pushed too hard. One downriver trip he took a huge chunk of squeeze and shipped bundles and BUNDLES of opium. It was destined for people in Shanghai. For the Green Hand and Mister One Ball Lu – you heard of him?'

Charlie sits up straighter at that. The mention of Moonface's second in command cuts through Marlais' slurred English straight to his ears.

'He is bad man,' Charlie grunts through clenched teeth. 'Make China very bad.'

Marlais nods. 'Some say worse than old Moonface. He runs the opium racket and the business end of things.'

And Dad was mixed up with people like One Ball Lu, Ruby thinks, despairing inwardly at the reminder.

'Go on about Munro.'

'Well, he decided he'd swindle old Lu. He paid extra squeeze to customs inspectors at Ichang and Hankow and they looked the other way as his boat slipped past. Uninspected. But he got to thinking how he could make so much more money if he sold the opium directly to other contacts of his and not let Lu take the lion's share. So between Hankow and where we are right now he arranged for friends to take the opium off and spirit it away. He would blame it all on Hankow customs and then try and get extra squeeze from One Ball Lu to cover the imaginary fine. But it was all a lie. And what he didn't know was Lu had two spies on board to watch his cargo.'

Marlais pauses, moths battering the lamp again. 'Well, when those gentlemen learned of the scheme they did Munro in on the spot, cut his throat right from hairy ear to hairy ear and threw him down to the eels.'

He leans forward, drops his voice to a whisper. 'And that's when the *haunting* began.'

Ruby's mouth has gone dry. She takes another slurp of lukewarm tea.

'You've seen his ghost?'

'Heard him more like. Old Munro was cut and drowned five years ago but he won't lie still in his watery bed. If you're on a ship coming between Kiukiang and Hankow, at the right time of year, at the right spot on the water, he comes back.'

Vaguely Ruby's aware that Charlie is shifting restlessly, pushing his chair back, but she can't take her gaze from Marlais' blue, blue eyes.

'You're steaming along and all's fine and dandy.

And maybe nightfall's coming and you feel just how big and strange this country around you really is. But all's fine. And then it *happens*.'

He bangs the table lightly with his fist.

'Maybe a young deck coolie, or a passenger who five minutes ago was chatting rubbish at you, suddenly freezes, goes rigid. As rigid as only a corpse can be rigid, you know what I mean? And you shake them by the shoulder but they're not there, Ruby. They've gone somewhere else, and slowly – *slowly* – they turn their head toward you, your cabin boy or your missionary lady, and their eyes roll away back there in their sockets and all you can see is the whites, as white as egg white frying, and they open their mouth and – out – comes – old – Joe – Munro's – voice. Cursing and swearing and saying he'll get his revenge on everyone who crossed him and it sounds like his voice is coming from ten thousand miles away but it's loud too, it drowns out the river, and all around you your crew are shaking in their boots and trying not to show it. And you know why they're so scared?'

Ruby shakes her head, gripped tight.

'Because the person who old Joe uses as a voice box usually doesn't last long. Does he, Mister Lee?'

Ruby turns to look at Lee who's nodding quietly,

puffing up smoke from his long Chinese pipe.

'Have you seen it happen?' she whispers.

Marlais nods. 'Last year. Right around here.'

'You heard Munro speak?'

'As sure as I hear you. And you know who he chose to speak through?'

A dark cloud crosses Marlais' eyes.

'Who?' Ruby says, but she guesses the answer even as Marlais says it.

'Young Mister Chen. God rest his soul.'

The shivers chase through her again. Not thrill, just fear, remembering again the sensation of the blood in her shoe, the poor man dying before her.

'So you see, young lady. Whatever is happening to you right now, Old Marlais Jones at least will believe you.'

The thunder rolls through the *Haitun* again, shaking the Captain's glass on the polished table, followed a fraction later by the throb of the engines stirring into life below and a muffled whoop of triumph.

The Captain pushes back his chair and snaps to his feet. 'Good Lord, what do you know. Old McQueen must have charmed it.'

Ruby grabs hold of the Captain's arm.

'So you believe in ghosts?'

'Of course I do,' he sighs, the walnuts in his hand

scraping against each other. 'Every seaman does. Especially here. Especially now. You'll have to excuse me, Miss Harkner. I want to move the *Haitun* to a safer anchorage for the night.'

He stomps out with a wave of his hand, and it's only now as she digests what Marlais has said that she sees Charlie has slipped from the room. Old Lee studies her through his pipe smoke, nodding quietly to himself.

Nerves still jangled by the story of Munro and his disembodied spirit, Ruby makes her way out onto the top deck. The boards feel cold under her bare feet.

Where's Charlie got to?

The shadows beyond the feeble deck lights seem darker, deeper than last night. As she makes her way down to the foredeck she sees a constant flickering of brightness far upriver. A storm battering the hills, the Gorges beyond. And Fei out there amongst it all and God knows what else.

She hears voices in the gloom, and then close by sees figures. Charlie is talking with the Lanterns again, Tian Lan's jacket a red smear in the blackness, her voice and Charlie's pulsing against each other in turn, the words lost against the stuttering engine.

Ruby steps smartly towards them.

'Charlie?'

'What is it?'

175

His voice feels distant, his face only just visible.

'Why did you leave?'

'I wanted to listen to someone who was sober.'

Ruby looks at the girl and her gang who are standing silently now, arms folded, listening to their every word.

'I need to talk to you, about what Marlais said.'

'He's just an old drunk, Ruby. And I need to talk with Tian Lan.'

The girl laughs, and mutters something under her breath, too soft for Ruby to catch.

'Just give me ten minutes,' Charlie says. 'It'll be easier . . . and with the engines going again we need to make a proper plan.'

He gives Ruby an apologetic shrug.

'We have a plan, don't we?'

'We need a better one.'

She nods, tries to sound calm, but when she answers she hears her voice sounding brittle again. 'I'll be in the cabin. When you want me.'

It's stupid, Ruby thinks as she lies on her bunk. Stupid for that girl to be dismissive of me just because I'm a foreigner, just because my skin is this colour, thinks she knows me from that. Really stupid.

Time drags. She imagines Charlie laughing, or beaming in admiration at Tian Lan and the amazing stories she must have. Don't think about it, she groans, rolling over and closing her eyes. Think about something else. But it's hard, and when she does drag her mind elsewhere it only finds the chilling story of Munro or the reappearance of the Shadow and its hissed warning.

At last she hears footsteps. She keeps her eyes tight shut, feigning sleep, and moments later hears Charlie climbing into the top bunk. The carefully rehearsed, relaxed greeting she had been preparing disappears in a surge of irritation.

'Why were you so *long*?'

'What do you mean?'

'I said I needed to *talk*.'

Charlie turns restlessly on the bunk overhead. 'Tian Lan wanted to know about what's happening in Shanghai. I was telling her. She wants to take her band over to the Communists, but I want her to help—'

'But you've got *me*. How do you know you can trust her?'

'I don't yet. That's *why* I'm talking to them.'

His hand appears over the edge of the bunk, dangling down towards her, disembodied in the gloom.

'But you know you can trust me, Charlie and she's—'

'She's what?'

'It doesn't matter,' Ruby says, thinking better of arguing, just glad of Charlie's company. She reaches up, and feels her cold hand wrapped in Charlie's warm, smooth palm. He holds it for a full five seconds – and then lets go. In the silence they hear the engines churn the dark water outside.

'Thank Heaven we're moving again,' he grunts.

'I just don't understand why she was so rude to me.'

'Don't you see? Her family have suffered from the foreigners, Ruby – and not everybody is going to have the time to find out *your* life story. Or think you're different. I'm sorry. But it's the truth.'

'But I am different from the others.'

'I know. But she won't want to hear it.'

She bites back a reply and turns face down to the rough blankets. Drop by drop the rain has started to fall again. It gathers pace and in a few minutes has become a heavy, steady drumming over their heads. Charlie's words echo in her head for long minutes after she's heard his breathing shift from waking to the deeper rhythm of sleep.

'Goodnight,' she whispers at last as the ship's engines fall silent and the rain slams down harder . . .

. . . and rolls over into a tumble of dreams of green waters, fish and dolphins, eels in the slippery mud – and her swimming through it all. Crossing a threshold she sees shipwrecks, whitened bones and then a figure floating in the distance. Something snags her dreaming hands and looking down she sees the red thread again, tangling around her fingers, snaking off into the olive and bottle green waters, reaching out towards the distant spectral figure turning in the river's current . . .

第十九章

WHEN RIVERS DON'T BEHAVE

Ruby wakes with a jolt, dream forgotten in the rush from the depths of sleep.

The *Haitun* is moving again, the swell of the river rocking her bunk, but the engines are silent. She swings her feet to the cabin floor and looks to see if Charlie is awake yet. Heart sinking, she sees his bed is already empty.

Outside, feet are drumming along the deck, the ship's bell ringing and muffled shouting sounding from bow to stern. Groggily she glances at her watch to see it's only just past five thirty. Why on earth is Charlie up so early? Surely not to talk to that girl again. She recalls his last words before sleep and how they stung.

But the deep sleep has renewed her energy, her determination. No need to just take it from that girl! If there's a plan being hatched then I'm damn well going to be a part of it. Back in Shanghai it was always me who led the way, she thinks. And it still needs to be that way now!

She finds Charlie in the wheelhouse, staring at the river. He darts an anxious look at her and then turns to Marlais.

'Where are we?'

The Captain pulls a face.

'Yangtze's burst her damn banks,' he grunts. 'Never seen it come up that fast before. Take a look, Ruby, at a river that won't behave.'

His hand sweeps the wide view before them.

Water everywhere. A vast expanse, brimming with light as the rain clears, as if the ship has been picked up by some enormous hand and plonked down in the middle of an inland sea. The current is flowing, chaotically, curling around the ship, surging over hidden obstacles, frothing where it races. About a mile away a small island humps up out of the water, a pagoda perched on top like a ribbed lighthouse, and distant hills, still black with rain, crouch beyond.

Marlais grabs the speaking tube. 'Get that steam up, boys! McQueen, give me Slow Ahead as soon as you can. And all hands watch for sandbanks. Depth sounders to bow and stern! MOVE!'

Charlie's staring at the water, mouth agape. 'But we were so close!' He switches to English, raps Marlais on the shoulder. 'Where we now?'

'Not hundred per cent sure,' Marlais growls. 'River came up so fast it caught us off guard and the spar mooring slipped. We're off the main channel that's for sure. Could ground at any minute.'

His eyes are flicking across a chart stippled with depth markings, a larger map flapping in the breeze next to it. 'We could have gone a fair way in the night. I don't recognise that one out there,' he points at the pagoda, 'unless it's the last one before the Han river. But that doesn't make sense—'

A long shudder grips the *Haitun* as she slides on the flood, something clutching at the hull.

'Damn it!' Marlais whispers. 'We're on a bank. Where's the depth man?'

Black smoke swirls into the wheelhouse and a long, low growl roars along the *Haitun*'s hull. One of the armoured panels breaks loose and clangs down, blocking out the view of the pagoda as the engines come to life and the screws engage the current, vibration getting louder and louder. A young man dashes forward gripping a long bamboo pole and takes up position ready to test the depth, the Red

Lanterns gathering around him, peering down into the water. Tian Lan turns around and shouts back at the wheelhouse, her voice punching through the cacophony.

'What's that damn girl hollering about,' Marlais grumps to Old Lee.

'She say you number one bad Captain,' Lee mutters. 'She say you run over house below us.'

'Then we'll break loose. But we've got to find the channel again. Everything looks like it's in the wrong place, damn it.'

The juddering is worse now, the *Haitun* pushing against whatever they have struck below. Ruby sees the cook hurry forward carrying a steaming black pot. He runs to the bow, braces himself on the gunwale and then hurls the watery rice from it into the river where it turns the water the colour of milk.

Marlais' scowling face softens

'Well, quite right, Mister Cook,' he purrs.

'What's he doing?'

'Placating water dragons! Old Yangtze custom! They open their mouths for the rice and let us go.' A bell rings abruptly on the speed indicator and Marlais pushes the lever to SLOW AHEAD, and – after two extra big shakes – the *Haitun* lurches forward.

'Thank you, Mister McQueen,' Marlais calls. 'We'll

sound our way out of here and get back to the river. Must be *somewhere*!'

Ruby leans out and looks back at their churning wake. Where the *Haitun* was stuck there are dark shapes visible just below the surface, even a piece of thatch sticking up and loose straw floating on the surface.

'What happened?' she says.

'That girl was right. We're sailing down a village street.'

'So where are the people?'

'Drowned. Or had the sense to make higher land.' Marlais frowns, ratcheting the armoured shutter back into place. He points at the pagoda forward and to starboard. 'If that *is* the one near the mouth of the Han then we've somehow moved upriver without the engines running. Doesn't make sense, but it looks like it.'

Charlie taps the chart impatiently. 'What about Peach Blossom Village?'

'If I'm right about the Han then you're very close to it.' Marlais says as he peers forward, watching the depth sounder thrusting his pole into the water. 'Very close indeed.'

'But it's no use if it's all under water,' Charlie groans.

184

'It won't be,' Marlais says, pointing at the map. 'It's at least sixty feet above the mean water level. It'll be high and dry. We'll get you as close as we dare and then you and that girl and her crew can take the dinghy and have a look. Maybe McQueen will come with you, he's handy with a Winchester. Now let me concentrate, will ya?'

The burst river sweeps around them in great swirls and eddies and slow, spinning pools. Everybody's eyes are on the water, or the charts, or the boy with the pole calling out the depth.

'Seven . . . seven . . . six . . .'

'Engines slow,' Marlais orders.

'Six . . . five and a half . . . six . . .'

'Steady.'

They're moving towards the pagoda on the conical hill, Marlais' stubby finger keeping track on the chart, guiding them along a straight blue line.

'Canal,' he mutters as Ruby leans close to look. 'Water will be better here and it should take us through a break in the bank. Otherwise we may get marooned on some farmer's dung heap. Fitting end to my career!'

More than a mile away to port there's the sail of a junk black against the water, and a low-slung vessel further off. Marlais swings his binoculars towards it.

'Maybe it's Moonface's boat,' Charlie whispers, his

knuckles showing white as he grips the gunwale.

Marlais shakes his head. 'Not Moonface. British Navy boat heading downriver. Still in the main channel, clever boy.'

Ruby points at the radio mounted on the wall of the bridge. 'Can you call him? See if he's spotted Moonface?'

'Don't need their help,' the Captain snarls. 'It would only make things ten times worse.'

'But why?'

Marlais' face darkens beneath the shadow of his cap. 'Because I'm not meant to be out here,' he scowls. 'My licence was taken away. They could arrest me on the spot. I'm supposed to be confined to Shanghai.'

Ruby frowns. 'So why *are* you here?'

'Because I'm helping you. And I need to get to Wanhsien. If my girl's still alive that is—'

'But that doesn't make sense,' Ruby says, baffled. 'I mean you didn't know you were going to bump into us.'

Marlais' smile flickers back into life. 'Maybe I did, maybe I didn't. But really I was paid an absolute package to transport our passenger in cabin number nine. And once I've said I'll do something I keep to my word. Now hush a minute!'

* * *

The depth is sounded every few seconds as they creep forward along the drowned line of the canal. A stillness falls on the crew as the boy calls out the fathoms and they creep closer and closer to the low hill, Lee's fingernail tipping left, right, left again.

Silently Charlie slips down to the foredeck towards where Tian Lan and the other Lanterns are gathered, but as Ruby goes to follow him, Marlais puts a hand on her shoulder.

'You won't be able to persuade them you're anything else than a foreign devil, Miss Harkner. Don't waste your breath.'

'But Charlie knows I'm more than that. And—'

The Captain holds a finger to his lips.

'That boy's crazy about you. Can't you tell? But you need to back off now. Trust old Marlais on that.'

Ruby feels the blush spread up her neck to her face.

'Crazy?' she echoes, eyes seeking Charlie out.

'It's obvious.'

Charlie's smiling now, really smiling at something the girl's said. Tian Lan reaches out a long slender arm and drapes it over his slim shoulders. A shaft of sun breaks free of the cloud, lighting the moment like something out of the portrait studio on Nanking Road, a painted backcloth beyond of pagoda and scrolling blue and white clouds.

Marlais sighs. 'Don't worry yourself, girl. I've seen a lot of love in my time.'

Ruby pulls Jin's hat lower, looking away from the scene on the deck, from Marlais' searchlight gaze.

'It's not like that.'

'Ha! Isn't it?' Marlais laughs.

Something on the trembling surface of the flood catches Ruby's eye. Between the *Haitun* and the hillock there's a shape breaking the water, a long, low silhouette like a dragon boat, and a figure standing on it. Glad of the distraction, she grabs the binoculars hanging by the wheel. The image blurs, sharpens as she fumbles with the focus ring, and then she sees it clearly: a ridged temple roof standing clear of the water, chubby stylised dolphins rearing at either end, and perched precariously on the ridge is a young man in a monk's robe. He's seen them now, morning sun bright on his shaved head as he waves frantically for help. At the other end of the roof, as far as possible from the man is an animal of some kind. She squints and tightens the focus to get a better look, heart quickening.

A fox.

'What can you see then, my girl?' Marlais grunts, taking the binoculars from her gently. 'Ah. Another poor soul in need of rescue.'

'Can you see the animal next to him?' Ruby whispers.

Marlais shakes his head. 'Animal?'

When she grabs the binoculars again there's no sign of it.

'We're better off keeping clear,' Marlais says, 'they normally build temples on slightly higher land. We'll send the dinghy: I don't want to get stuck now.'

The monk's bare feet have barely touched deck before Charlie has raced up to him, hurling questions. He listens intently to the monk's answers and then runs to the bridge taking the steps two at a time, eyes bright.

'We're close,' he shouts. 'The monk says Peach Blossom Village is just over that ridge. Not more than four or five li beyond where the river's reached. See that line of willows on the ridge? And Tian Lan has agreed to come. We're going! We're going!'

Ruby turns to Marlais. 'Can we use the dinghy?'

'Of course. Take McQueen and a bunch of the tougher men with you too—'

Charlie shakes his head as he unpicks the English. 'The Lanterns won't take a foreigner,' he says in Chinese. 'It's me and them and any Chinese crew who can come along.'

Ruby's heart sinks. 'But what about *meeee*?'

'Can't be done. You must understand. You saw what Tian Lan and her lot can do! I need them now to help me fight Moonface. If he's there.'

Marlais watches the argument for a moment, then turns and slips away down the corridor.

'It's not right,' Ruby says, anger welling up. 'You and I have a pact. We're part of the Outlaws. All for one. We're meant to stick together at any price—'

'But this is the best strategy for rescuing Fei,' Charlie says, voice firm.

'But I want to go with you!'

'We'll just scout it out. And if we need help we'll signal. And then I promise we'll keep together.' And then, before she's had time to take that in, he leans forward and hugs her, hugs her really hard. 'I promise. But let me do this now.'

'Ouch,' she mutters, but holds him tightly back. 'Just keep safe. Please.'

Charlie unlocks his hug, looks a little flustered as he glances around to see if anyone has witnessed it.

'I'll be back,' Charlie says, and she scrunches her eyes shut as his footsteps bang away down the metal stairway.

He's right. The Lanterns won't take me, she thinks, and the most important thing is to get Fei. She steadies herself with a deep breath into the belly and when she opens her eyes again she's surprised to see the young monk standing beside her. He runs a hand over his egg smooth head, staring out at the water. The lower half of his robes are still wet, but he seems already recovered from his near drowning. He glances at her and tilts his head in greeting, a string of wooden beads clicking between the fingers of his other hand.

'Your friend says you speak Chinese.'

Ruby nods, trying not to look to where Charlie is already clambering into the *Haitun*'s rowboat.

'An old teacher of mine used to say: *sometimes acting like a tiger, sometimes like a mouse. Sometimes not acting at all.*'

'I don't understand.'

The monk points back at the roof of the submerged temple. 'The head monk and the others swam for it in the flood. Maybe they made it, maybe not. But I just climbed onto the roof to wait. Like a mouse. Sometimes it's better not to do too much. And sometimes it's better to do nothing.'

'What about the fox?'

He shakes his head. 'Poor thing. Jumped off and swam away, half drowned already.'

'Do you think he'll make it to the bank?'

The monk shrugs, then looks away at the roof again. 'Maybe. They're always stronger than they look. And who knows,' he raises his eyebrows, a smile breaking out, 'maybe it was a *huli jing*. Maybe it was a friendly one, looking out for me.'

Ruby watches silently as Charlie, the Lanterns and two crew members armed with rifles clamber into the dinghy. At the very last minute Straw – who has been restlessly pacing the deck – scampers down the stairway, along the lower deck and then jumps into the little boat. He pushes past the others and plants himself resolutely at the prow.

Charlie hesitates, glances up at Ruby and raises both arms apologetically, as the boat moves free of the *Haitun*.

'I'll take care of him. I promise!'

Slowly the little boat edges away, the gap widening to fifty yards, a hundred, its passengers blurring in the morning light.

She fetches the binoculars to bring the boat closer again. She can just make out Charlie amongst the others as they nose into the distant, waving reeds and then disembark, clambering onto the bank top by the willows, over it, and then gone.

The monk is still beside her, the beads edging through his fingers. 'It's always worse to be waiting,' he says at last. 'You should occupy yourself.'

'No thanks. I want to stay here.'

She keeps watching the watery landscape, trying to imagine the shore party walking slowly, cautiously to the village, seeing in her head the photograph from Amah's dresser, the old stories of bandits raiding the village, the well stuffed up with bodies flooding back. What if Moonface isn't there at all? What if they're all just gunned down on the spot? She kicks at the deck, her imagination quickly moving from bad to worse to worst. Maybe there will be Shadow Warriors there too.

Maybe that's the last time I'll see Charlie.

第二十章

SHORE PARTY ROUTED

The river haze is smudging the shapes in the binocular's lenses, making everything dreamlike. On the hill the pagoda seems to sway.

She scuffs the deck in frustration as the minutes drag and her imagination makes things worse and worse, killing Charlie first one way and then another.

I should have forced my way onto the boat, she thinks. Taken the sword. There's nothing to be seen where the shore party disappeared under the line of breeze-tossed willow, just the dot of the dinghy nudged into the reeds below. And you can see now that more of the submerged temple is clear of the debris-strewn water, a bigger chunk of glistening roof exposed.

Marlais brings her a bowl of rice and she wolfs it down without taking her eyes from the distant spot where the village must be.

'How do you know that's where your gangster's holed up?' he says.

'Moonface said he was taking Fei to his old home. And he used to live near here, my amah says.'

'We can give them another hour or so,' Marlais says, glancing at the water. 'No more.'

The monk clears his throat.

'I know that village,' he says quietly. 'Hardly anyone lives there any more. It's been sacked by bandits over and over again. Been twenty years since it thrived.'

'Do you know anything about Moonface? The gangster? He used to live nearby—'

'That was years ago,' the monk says. 'Before I was born. He was a vile bandit, my master said. But he's been gone years.'

'But he did live there?'

'So they say. If you can call a life like that living—'

A coughing of distant gunfire breaks across the water. There's silence for five full seconds and then another stuttering volley – much longer this time – and silence again.

Ruby grips the binoculars, trying to steady her hands enough to see clearly. Through the haze there's a hint of smoke coming from over the ridge as more shooting breaks the stillness, single shots and machine guns mixed.

Marlais fixes his gaze to the same point.

'We didn't send a machine gun. Must be someone else, your gangster, or the warlord's men. Not the usual bandits with their museum pieces.'

'I want to go. Now,' Ruby says, looking round at the Captain wildly.

But Marlais shakes his head. 'Nothing to go *in*, young lady. And we're going to have to move soon. If they can't manage then you won't. And I can't risk grounding us for good. I'll give them five minutes.'

He grimaces, face lined and drawn.

'Come on, dammit.'

More gunfire echoes across the water as those minutes tick by agonisingly, Ruby's eyes pressing harder and harder into the eyepieces of the binoculars, willing something to happen. It feels like she hasn't breathed for minutes, hours . . .

And then she sees figures moving below the trees. Three, four, five of them, hurrying down the bank, through the reeds – and a moment later the dinghy is edging out, wobbling, straightening, two crew members pulling hard on the oars, catching crabs as they try too hard.

Just behind there are other shapes on the bank now. Ten, fifteen, twenty silhouetted figures. There's a bright flash, and then another, and a moment later the sound of the gunshots chase the muzzle flashes.

Desperately Ruby scans the spectral figures on the little boat. Is Charlie on board? Is that him? There's no sign of the shorter figure of Fei, that's for sure. They must have been beaten off before they could get her.

'All hands!' Marlais bellows. 'Prepare to weigh anchor. And prepare to receive wounded.'

The dinghy is halfway to them, shifting angle to steer round some hidden object – and as it turns she at last sees Charlie in the binoculars, crouched in the front, three or four of the Lanterns ducked beside him while one of the *Haitun*'s men works both oars, rowing for all he's worth, and the other discharging his gun to try and give covering fire.

Ruby scampers down the stairway as the little boat's rope snakes over the rail and is tied fast. A moment later Charlie is tumbling onto the deck, face white, reaching back to help one of the wounded Lantern boys over after him. His arm is bloodied and face contorted in agony. Tian Lan jumps on board after him.

'I need a doctor!' she shouts.

Ruby grabs Charlie by the arm, desperate to hug him again. But his eyes are fixed somewhere else, and he just stares blankly past her, breathing hard.

'What is it? What is it, Charlie?'

'It was weird – really weird,' he says, the words stumbling in his mouth as he pulls the glasses from his face. He squints at the lenses, polishing them with the sleeve of his other arm. 'Maybe you were right all along. I think we're up against something – awful.'

'What do you mean? What happened?'

Charlie slumps to the deck, head bowed into his hands, muffling his words.

'What is it? Come on, tell me!'

'I saw this old man in the village. He seemed kind of familiar,' he mumbles. 'He knew who I was straight away. He called my name. He was sitting on the lip of the well and he told me he knew my folks.'

'An old man?' Ruby says. For some reason the prickling is firing all over again, making her shift uncomfortably as she strains to hear what Charlie's saying. 'What's so weird about that?'

'I got separated from the others and then Straw started barking like crazy and he led me straight to the man. He called my name and told me he used to know my mum and dad. How could he know who I was? And I asked about Moonface and the man said he doesn't come from here, Moonface I mean. His real home, his stronghold, is in the Gorges – somewhere called Hell's Throat. And then – then – he told me to run for my life and then . . .'

'What?'

'He just vanished right in front of me and the soldiers ambushed us.'

'Vanished?'

'I mean he was right there one minute and then the next he wasn't.' Charlie looks up, face still white with the shock. 'What on earth is happening?'

'What about Fei?'

Charlie's teeth are chattering now, chopping up the words. 'The man look-k-ked really familiar and he s-s-said something else. That M-m-moonface is out for revenge. And he's using Fei and he w-w-won't let her go. And then he d-d-disappeared and the soldiers attacked us.'

'Revenge?'

'You were right all along,' Charlie says. 'You were right.'

Beneath them the *Haitun*'s screws are churning the river as the boat shifts on the current. A few distant rifle shots are still echoing on the water. Ruby glances back at the ridge, the hidden village, and then groans.

'But what about Straw?'

Charlie shuts his eyes. 'I d-don't know. He ran off. Into the smoke, barking like mad . . . Listen, I think it's only going to get worse before it gets better. If you want to turn around – you could get a lift on a ship or junk going the other way – if you want to turn around that's OK with me.'

'No way,' Ruby says. 'We're staying together. No matter what.'

The depth sounder on the prow of the *Haitun* is reeling out the fathoms.

'Seven and a half . . . nine . . . eight . . . ten.'

Charlie looks back at her, eyes popping wide again. 'Maybe we can't do it.'

'We can do it,' Ruby says. 'We can do it if we stay together.'

The depth sounder keeps calling out numbers and the engines' throb grows stronger, as if the ship's more certain of itself. Regaining the main channel, picking up speed, moving upriver again.

Marlais comes back along the deck.

'So? No good on shore I take it?'

Ruby shakes her head. 'No. We have to go further. We have to go all the way to the Gorges.'

'It's not for the faint-hearted right now. You're sure?'

'I'm sure. We have to go.'

'Your friend here needs some warmth. He's in shock. And if we're going further together, then I need a private word with you, Ruby. An important one.'

He leads her to the far rail, points to a distant bend on the flooded river.

200

'See that? They call it Dead Man's Curve. Means we're back on the proper channel. At least I think we are. It's all so changed from last time we came through here.'

He looks at her intently.

'What *are* you doing out here on this strange old river, Ruby?'

'We're trying to rescue Charlie's sister.'

'There's more to it than that. Much more, I can tell. Did you know you were going to have to make this journey – I mean, a while ago?'

The Thursday's child rhyme sounds in her head and she thinks of the often-seen image of the snaking river glimpsed on the edge of sleep. 'I don't know. Maybe.'

Marlais frowns, the walnuts click-clacking away in his bronzed hand again.

'And you have no idea who our mystery passenger is?'

'No. How could I?'

'Dead Man is the last big bend before we make Hankow. The Nationalists might already have taken it and they might try to stop us, so we'll slip past very early tomorrow, try and keep our heads down.' He pauses, stops the creak of the walnuts and looks away. 'But before we do, someone wants a word with you.'

His tone sets Ruby's pulse racing. A second later the penny drops.

'It's your other passenger, isn't it?'

'Bingo. You're a smart one, aren't you?'

'But who is it? What do they want with me?'

'I don't know. But the man who booked our mysterious voyager's passage spoke of him very respectfully and gave me a lot of money. A lot, Ruby. So he must be *very* important indeed . . .'

The Captain's voice trails off and he nods at the rear cabin on the port side.

'Whoever it is, they'll only communicate by messages slipped under the door. Written in Chinese and read by Old Lee. And the last one said you're to wait for nightfall, Ruby, and go to cabin number nine and then knock twice. And do exactly what the person inside tells you to do.'

'But I don't understand. Why?'

The Captain shoves the woollen cap back on his head. 'That's all I know. Cross my heart and hope to die.'

第二十一章

MYSTERY VOYAGER

The sun drops fast to touch the rim of the hills and the light fades – and the door to cabin number nine stands before her.

Charlie is being cared for by the cook and the sounds of the engines and everything else have fallen away, the voices of the crew muffled and distant. She listens hard, but hears nothing above the wash of her heartbeat in her ears.

As a small girl, playing in the back garden on Bubbling Well Road, Ruby once found a nest of newly hatched spiders tumbled in a tight knot, each not much bigger than a pinhead, their brilliant green shining in a shaft of sun. She had crouched down over them, watching the furious movement, each driven by some tiny urge to move, to feed. Ignoring Mother's warning voice in her head, curiosity lifted her fingertip and she pushed it into the nest, and felt the tingle of tiny contacts, holding her finger there, feeling the spiders running all over it, over her hand, her wrist. Something intense, secretive, meant for her and no one else.

It feels just like that now: that this is something private, for her alone. But who on earth could this mystery passenger be? Someone with the money to get the *Haitun* moving when the river's meant to be closed to traffic. Someone who knows her – somehow.

She listens again and faintly above the rush of her blood comes a noise that sounds familiar, but that she can't place for now: like a loud cricket whirring in a metal can.

Her mouth feels dry. She steadies herself, then knocks softly, once. Twice.

There's no reply, just that metallic rattle – and then she hears footsteps on the other side of the door and the sound of the lock clicking. She takes the handle – and pushes the door open.

A slim, pale figure is sitting on the lower bunk, head turned towards her, but although the cabin light is burning overhead it doesn't seem to be working properly, doesn't seem able to illuminate the figure.

The passenger gets slowly to his feet and raises his arm, hand beckoning her to come in, and then, as if stage lights are coming up in the theatre, she sees his face and a single almighty shiver chases the length of her.

It's Tom.

More clearly, and more sharply now than she saw him in Shanghai: a perfect version of her little brother, smiling, just like he looked the day they went to the river and watched the cormorants, the day he got sick, with that expression that always came when they ventured that bit too far and strayed beyond what had been deemed safe and allowable. Excitement and apprehension in equal measure.

Where shall we go now, Ruby, what shall we do?

Dangling from his hand is the toy wind-up monkey, the last of its clockwork energy bashing the cymbals.

She hesitates for half a heartbeat, and then takes a step forward.

'Is it really you?' she manages to say at last, her voice trembling in her throat.

Tom nods, looks down at the monkey and winds the clockwork key, gripping the cymbals tight to let the charge build up and up. He cranks it harder and harder like he did when he was smaller.

Ruby reaches out a hand. 'Careful, you'll break it – again.'

The figure shakes his head, opens his fingers and

lets the cymbals batter each other again.

'He's fine, Ruby. He's as good as new. Thanks for bringing it.'

Ruby opens her mouth, struggling to find the right question, the right thing to say. She comes a step further, spellbound.

'I liked to wind it really hard,' Tom says. 'And I broke it in the end, but I remember you told me it would be mended. And now it is.'

'It got mended by itself somehow,' she stammers. 'I kept it when Mother wanted to chuck it. It seemed wrong just to throw it out with the rubbish.'

'I'm glad,' Tom says quietly, and then a worried look passes across his face. 'Close the door, will you? I don't want anyone to see me now.'

Glad of something to do, she turns and snicks the door shut, her shock still shaking her hard, but the questions pressing harder.

'What are you doing here on the boat?' she says. 'I mean, why aren't you – why are you here at all?'

'I couldn't rest,' he says, shrugging his shoulders. 'I've been roaming for a bit, trying to find the way to let go. To change. I ended up on this boat – someone told me I had to go back to Hankow.'

She takes another step closer. It feels cold in the cabin but not the kind of deathly chill she felt in the

Mansions, something more like the cool stillness they felt in the tunnel under the Wilderness.

'Can I sit down?' she says. 'My legs feel a bit shaky.'

He pats the bed beside him and then looks back to the monkey with a frown. 'I saw you in Shanghai. Lots of times, but you couldn't see me. It was sad. I even saw you in Hankow, after I – after it was too late. You were crying and I was trying to talk to you but you couldn't hear me, you couldn't see me.' He shakes his head. 'I wanted to say it was all OK, but you couldn't hear me.'

'But it wasn't OK!' Ruby says, shaking her head. 'You were – you were—'

Unable to finish the sentence, unable to take her eyes off Tom, she settles on the bunk, an arm's length away.

'I saw you in the Mansions, Tom. And I saw you in the tunnel under the city, but I thought maybe it was all in my imagination. It wasn't like you are now.'

'It wasn't the right time or the right place. I need to tell you something, but I couldn't tell you then.'

His voice is like she remembers, but it's not as if the sound is coming from him. More like it's forming inside her ear, or deeper than that. In her head.

Tom laughs suddenly.

'Ha! Did you see the wind chimes?'

She nods. 'It scared me.'

'I was trying to show you I was there, but I couldn't get across the Frontier properly. So I rang the bells to let you know I was coming back – and then I hid the monkey so you'd know it was me.'

For a moment she feels stupid – stupid not to have understood her little brother's message, but then she remembers the dark shadow in her room, the pain and fear as it crawled on her chest.

'There was something else – a kind of horrid black shadow. I thought it was going to kill me. Was that you too?'

He shakes his head. 'No. That must be something else . . . or nothing at all.'

Ruby keeps looking at her brother. He's so real now, so physically like the old Tom, but there's a kind of worldwise note to his voice. Like a grown up who's seen a lifetime or more of trouble. It reminds her of Dad somehow. Definitely something of Dad about him . . .

'Can I – touch you?'

He smiles. 'You can, but I won't feel it.'

Cautiously she stretches out her hand, half expecting her fingertips to pass straight through him like in some ghost story, but instead she just feels his skin on the back of his wrist, cool and resistant.

'You're cold.'

'Not really. I don't feel anything.'

It seems wrong to pull her hand away, so she leaves it there, her heart still trying to steady herself in her chest.

'Oh Tom, what's it like? I mean you're . . .'

The tears start to come now, stinging her eyelashes, one big drop blurring his face. She wipes it away, wanting to keep her sight clear.

'All I can say is it's OK. But I want to rest now. When I can go properly I think I'll just become something else. Or someone else. Or a bird. Or some cloud. Or a little spider.'

The tears won't stop replacing the ones she's busy wiping away, but the mention of spiders brings her up short.

'A spider?'

'Like the ones you showed me in the garden. Remember?'

A sob rocks up through her chest and she tries to hold it, eyes blurring. For a second or two more she fights it and then it comes, followed quickly by another, then another. The emotion releasing at last after all these months, lungs grabbing for air and letting it go in short, sharp bursts, tears tracing lines down her cheeks now, plopping onto the floor. She lets it all happen, lets the sadness come rushing out, one hand clenching then unclenching, the other still resting on Tom. It feels right, good, and long minutes pass as the grief tumbles out. At last she takes a deep sniff, trying to put on the brakes. I can't carry on like this, she thinks. It's not fair to Tom. Got to get a grip again. She takes another huge gulp of the cool air.

'But why – why are you here now?'

'I need you to help me leave. Ghosts are only meant to hang around for forty-nine days, but it seems I can't go yet.'

'I don't understand. Why can I see and hear you so clearly now?'

'Because we're getting near Hankow. And when I reach the place where I died I can leave. It'll be easier there. But I need you to help *let* me go.'

Her shoulders are still shaking a bit, the tears thick in her eyes. 'Oh Tom, I'm just so sorry, I'm so sorry,' she wails. 'It was all *my* fault. I took you to the river. You wouldn't have fallen in if I hadn't taken you there. And then I was slow to go and get the doctor. If I'd been quicker you would have . . . I'm sorry. I'm so sorrrryyyy . . .'

She shuts her eyes, her grief coughing out more tears, her nose running. And then she feels Tom put his arms around her and squeeze gently, ever so gently, his voice a whisper in the gloom of the cabin.

'Don't be stupid. It was just a thing that happened. It was probably something I ate anyway. You were amazing! I saw you jump out of the window into all the gunfire and you did your best. Shanghai Ruby always does her best, I know that. She always does the right thing.'

'But I miss you,' she sobs.

'I know.'

She cries steadily, but lighter now, like a storm passing and fading, and Tom keeps holding her. Is it imagination or can she feel he is getting a bit warmer? Slowly the quaking of her shoulders subsides and she puts her arms back around him.

'I can feel that you're holding me,' he says, his voice sparking like it always did when he felt excitement or surprise at something. 'But it's time for me to go.'

Anxiety rushes through Ruby. 'I don't want you to. I want to keep talking.'

'I have to go.'

'But we're not at Hankow yet.'

'We are,' Tom says quietly, 'it's dawn. We've been talking all night.'

'Don't be silly. It's only just got dark . . .'

'See for yourself.'

It can't be possible, she thinks, opening her eyes

211

to peer at the curtains. The engines are rumbling away now, she can feel that, and bleeding around the edge of the curtained porthole comes the faintest of morning light.

'I've got to go,' Tom says again, and she feels his arms letting go.

'Go?' she splutters. 'But go where? I don't understand.'

'Yes you do.'

She looks at him, so real, so solid, so present. And yet she knows he's right. This can't last.

'But I need your help. To rescue Fei and get home and—'

'There's always help when you need it,' he says, getting to his feet. 'And you're getting closer.'

She nods, gets unsteadily to her feet. A wave of tiredness weighs down on her as she does so, just like it feels when you've been up most of the night and your head feels empty, your feet like lead dragging you down. That image of the weighted coffin pops back into her head and she shoves it away as hard as she can.

'Perhaps you could stay a bit more?'

'No,' he says. 'Tell Mother and Dad I'm fine. Tell them it's all fine.'

'Will – will I see you again?'

'I don't think so.'

Then something shifts. The light dims in the cabin and Tom's suddenly hazy, indistinct. She reaches out again for him, but he slides right past her, through the door, right through the solid door like ghosts are supposed to do! Hurriedly she unbolts it and looks up and down the corridor. Not a trace of him, and no one else in sight. Something pulls her towards the stern of the ship, like her heart's being dragged that way. She hurries through the wooden door and on to the rear deck.

Dawn is indeed somehow seeping through the damp air, the mist suffused with early light, every droplet shining. Away to starboard she recognises the familiar smart buildings of the Hankow Bund. Beyond that somewhere is the house where it all happened just over a year ago. The place where Tom slipped away. A white-pointed sun on a blue flag is flapping from the harbour master's office.

She hears the faintest of sounds over the gush of the *Haitun*'s wake and looks right to scc Tom again, standing by the railing, gazing at the river behind. Not another soul to be seen, though she can hear the sound of the cook chopping away in the galley just below.

Her brother turns and points into the churn of the wake. A white sampan is gliding up to them, closing rapidly, as if hovering on the water. No one to be seen under its white bamboo canopy, just a shadowy figure sculling it towards them. Every square inch of Ruby's skin is sparking now with the pins and needles feeling, the last of her tears cool on her cheek in the morning breeze.

'Goodbye,' Tom says. '*Zai jian,*' and he climbs easily over the rail and steps down onto the ghostly sampan that's now nose to tail with the *Haitun*.

'*Zai jian,*' Ruby whispers.

And then, soundlessly, powerfully, the white boat veers to port, turns across the greeny-brown wake and slips away into the mist. Tom's figure is still just visible, upright, face lifted to the sky, then a shimmer, a faint silhouette.

And then gone.

第二十二章

BEYOND DEAD MAN'S CURVE

Something inside her lifts.

A weight that's been kept bottled tight for more than a year, kept locked down on the dreary British gunboat as the teacups rattled and no one talked about what had just happened, held tight by Mother and Dad during the return to school and the move to the antiseptic Mansions.

Even last week with Charlie, crouched in the sparrow-haunted bushes outside the Mansions, only a bit of the pain and guilt had come.

Now sobbed out, despite the sense of renewed loss, despite the shock of the encounter, it has lifted more. She keeps watching the spot on the river where the white boat disappeared, hoping for a last glimpse of Tom standing there – but knowing that she won't see it.

He's gone for good, like he should have done

215

months and months ago. Somewhere else, maybe to be reincarnated into *something* else, she thinks. Something or someone wonderful.

She hears voices behind and turns, not yet ready to talk to anyone else, keeping her head down so the brim of Jin's Fedora shields her face with its tear tracks and snotty nose.

The voices on the foredeck are louder, the *Haitun*'s engines pushing harder upstream. For this moment she doesn't care what's happening, or why. Just wants to hold the image of Tom.

She goes back into the corridor, pushes open the door to cabin nine and hovers in the doorway. There's a stillness there, so thick you could cut it, like the darkness in the well at White Cloud. She looks at the spot on the bunk where her brother sat, where they held each other just a few minutes ago, but already it feels like ages and ages. How on earth did the night pass so fast?

'Ruby?'

She jumps. It's Charlie calling her name, coming closer. 'Where are you?'

'Here!'

Crossing the cabin on her bare feet she rips open the curtain, keen for light and warmth. Lemon sun spills through the window and falls on the far end of the bunk, on to Tom's discarded monkey. She picks it up, fingertips still shaky from the emotion and the cold of the deck, and winds the key a few quick turns.

Nothing happens. The monkey's lifeless painted eyes look at her mournfully and she bites her lip as she feels the emotion again. But this time it just wells for a few seconds and then dies away . . .

'There you are!'

Charlie's in the doorway, face creased with worry. 'Where did you get to?'

'I was in here,' she says, gathering herself quickly. 'I was in here half the night talking to – the other passenger.'

A look of bafflement crosses Charlie's face – but also something else, something that spikes his words back. 'You weren't. I looked in the middle of the night and there was no one in here, Ruby. No one. And who was it anyway? Who were you with?'

'I told you, the mystery passenger.'

'That sword of yours was shining like anything,' Charlie says, struggling to keep hold of his voice. 'It was really bright.'

The tingles dance the length of her spine again. She holds up the monkey as if that will answer everything, and looks into Charlie's deep eyes. 'I was here! It was – amazing. I was with Tom, Charlie! And I talked to him for hours somehow. And then he got up and went to the back of the boat and he climbed into a white sampan. He's gone for good, I think . . .'

Charlie looks as though he's about to argue, then takes a hesitant step forward.

'What did he want? I mean, did he tell you anything . . .' His voice falls away uncertainly.

'So you do believe me?'

'I saw him myself back in Shanghai, didn't I?' Charlie sighs. 'And after what I saw at Peach Blossom Village I'm ready to believe anything. I'm even starting to wonder if Straw really was the dog my dad told me about from his childhood all those years ago. The way he ran straight to that old man like he knew every path . . .'

'I'm glad you don't think I'm crazy.'

'I didn't say that,' Charlie says with a stifled laugh. 'But at least now we're as crazy as each other.'

He moves away to the porthole and looks back at Hankow. 'Did you see? The Nationalists have taken the city. I need to tell Tian Lan and see if she's got some ideas about what we can do next.'

Her mood falters. 'But we're keeping together right?'

'Of course. As long as possible,' Charlie says, looking at the Yangtze streaming past. A nagging worry slips through Ruby's head – the sting of jealousy again – but she shoves it away. With that weight of grief lifted it feels just now that she can face what lies ahead with more courage.

'Good. And I need to ask the Captain some questions.'

'So what did you think of our mystery guest?' Marlais asks again.

He's sitting opposite Ruby in the *Haitun*'s stateroom, thick fingers knotted on the table in front of him.

She gazes back at him. It's felt like he's been holding something back ever since the first moment they met in Nanking. Perhaps it's better to find out what Marlais knows first, before blurting everything out.

'He's gone now,' she says. 'It was – did you know who it was?'

The Captain shakes his head slowly. 'No. Just that I was told you might know the gentleman.'

'Who by? Please tell me what you know. It's just not fair if you won't—'

He holds up his hands, as if surrendering. 'OK, cards on the table. We're about to sail from Shanghai and make a run for Wanhsien before the river is closed. It's the day before that scuffle between the Communists and the Green Hand. Well, we're just about to cast off and this strange Chinaman comes up to me on the dockside and gives me a hundred dollars. Counts them straight out of his hat and squashes them in my hand and says he has a special passenger for me – a very special passenger who needs to get to Hankow in a hurry. But *very* secret. He would be smuggled on when I wasn't looking – and I should keep a cabin ready and no one was to look in there. He was wearing a . . .'

Marlais is squinting at the Fedora pushed back on her head. A strange sensation starts to crawl over Ruby's scalp.

'A hat much like yours, Miss Harkner. He was quite impressive,' he grins, 'and I found I was nodding and agreeing before I'd even counted the money. Not much to him – but a way of talking, even though he looked like some old bum down on his luck.'

It sounds like Jin, she thinks. Not the hat of course, there are hundreds, thousands of those on the heads of men in Shanghai, but she can feel Jin's presence now, his charisma reflected in the Captain's admiring tilt of the head, the spark in his eyes.

'Go on.'

'I'd have done it for nothing to tell you the truth, he was that persuasive. But I needed to pay off the crew, so I took it and looked the other way and told no one to go near nine. Thought maybe it was a general on the run. Or a Red.'

Ruby taps her finger away busily at her teeth. 'And you didn't know when the passenger came aboard?'

'Nope. But Old Mister Lee knew it well enough as soon as he started passing those messages back and forth under the door. He wasn't happy about it. Said we had a lost soul on board. Now I thought he meant that by way of a figure of speech. But I pretty soon figured out that wasn't the case. He meant it more literally, didn't he?'

Ruby nods. 'It was my brother, Mister Marlais. The ghost of my brother.' She glances up, wondering if she'll see a mocking smile come back at her, but Marlais just shakes his head.

'Well, whaddya know? I think I felt it. Woah.' He blows out a long deep breath.

Two shadows flit past the windows, blocking the rolling green land beyond: Charlie and Tian Lan, chatting away again. That invisible hand tightens Ruby's guts again, but she tries to ignore it.

'I wanted him to stay. But he had to go.'

'Everything is a matter of timing, Miss Harkner. That's what I've found in life.' He points at her hat again. 'Sometimes we have to get it just right. That's what that Chinaman said to me on the docks. He shoved me another hundred bucks and told me to keep my eye out for anyone in trouble. That I'd be bound to find people on this trip who needed my help. He told me to keep my eyes peeled as I went upriver and look out for a slim Chinese boy and a pale English girl and help them if I found them. Now – what do you make of *that*?'

Ruby's scalp is buzzing, the hairs riffling up. It was Jin at the docks, no doubt about it. Not long before everything went so horribly wrong. He must have known somehow all this was going to happen. Maybe he even knew he was going to die? She steadies herself and looks back at Marlais.

'It was a friend of ours. He was a Taoist priest or something. He was killed the next day . . .'

Her voice flounders.

Marlais gets to his feet and looks out at the hills rising and falling outside the porthole. Sunlight battling dark cloud.

'Then I'm very sorry. He seemed like a good man.' He clears his throat and then steps over to the barometer on the wall and raps it hard with his knuckles. 'To be practical for a moment, this thing can't tell us one way or another. Either things are calming down in the heavens, or there's a lot of stormy weather yet to come. I'd better see to the ship, Missee Harkner. Next stop Shasi and then, day after tomorrow it will be the Gorges, the rapids, the whirlpools, and then

I'll show you what this old tub can do! We'll find your bandit for you. And I'll sail on to Wanhsien and rescue my girl.'

Half the day burns like late summer, the other half chills like autumn as she turns the puzzle over and over in her mind. How did Jin know what was going to happen? And why – if he did – couldn't he stop it all happening? Why not divert Fei or interrupt Dad or hide the gun so Andrei couldn't kill him? As a shower cloud drifts away a rainbow hoops the river for a fragile minute or two – and then is gone again.

They pause to drop the monk on a small village jetty on the south bank. As he steps gingerly into the ship's rowing boat he turns to Ruby and throws her a smile.

'I'm nearly home,' he calls. 'We all go home in the end. Remember that! A bit older – and hopefully a bit wiser!'

Some chance, she thinks. I just feel more confused the further I go . . . Nothing really makes sense. But she can't imagine *not* being here, *not* chasing upriver, *not* seeing Tom. All this had to happen . . .

Shadows thicken the folds of the hills as the engines thrash against the Yangtze's growing current. She heads back to the cabin and glances down at the increasingly alarming sound coming from below – and sees green light seeping from the open mouth of Jin's pack.

Her hands fumble the bag open to reveal the sword shining steadily, the green stars and characters staining her fingers with colour. Marvelling, she takes it in both hands, steadying herself, and stares at the blade, trying to relax, to breathe, to remember what Jin said . . .

. . . and slowly she feels the sword move, cutting a shape in the air. At least that's what it feels like. She sinks her weight down towards the *tandien*, trying to feel where it wants to go, carving arcs to the left, over to the right, pulling her shoulders around with it and loosening the tension there.

It feels good, like it's loosening that knot that's been cramping up her stomach. Cutting through it! Better than muddling all those thoughts and getting tangled up in them, she's moving, like someone is taking her hand and saying you just go this way, Ruby, then this. Now here, now there. *That's it, you've got it.*

Almost like Jin's with her again, whispering instruction. If he knew she would be here then it's almost as if he is too.

She closes her eyes and the sword moves faster, her bare feet whispering on the boards of the cabin and the *Haitun* steaming full speed, engines pumping them all deeper up the Yangtze. Into the lengthening shadows.

第二十三章

STINKING APE

A night and day pass.

The river level falls and the mood of the *Haitun*'s crew eases. Marlais prowls the ship from dawn to dusk, beckoning Ruby and Charlie to witness as he urges his stokers to shovel hard, or stands beside Lee and studies the unfolding reaches of river. He makes sure they know what's happening, makes them eat and rest – and finds Ruby a pair of soft Chinese shoes to wear, and a dark blue padded Chinese jacket.

'Colder weather coming,' he smiles, looking down at her bare feet. 'I'm sure your parents would want us to take good care of you. Not let you catch cold!'

'Thank you,' Ruby says, pulling on the snug shoes and tying them tight. It's better, more like Shanghai Ruby should wear, better fitting. And the jacket's warmth is welcome too.

225

But the comfort of the borrowed clothes is undermined by the way Charlie's behaving. After that moment of closeness and understanding in the cabin he's pulled away again, wrapped in his own guarded thoughts. When he does answer her questions he does so with half sentences, and then just throws a smile on top of that to reassure when she presses. And every now and then he slips away on some excuse or other to chat to the Lanterns and Tian Lan.

Just past Changsha they put ashore looking for coal and supplies, but there's not much to be had. The docks are nervous, coolies glancing over their shoulders as they bring provisions to the boat. The coal to be had only just covers the floor of the *Haitun*'s bunkers and is mostly dust. Everything seems dark, from the faces of the dockside workers, to the skies overhead, to the water running harder in the channel.

And when she goes to sneak a look at the sword she finds it's still shining steadily.

Junks fall past on the downriver channel. Each is hailed by the *Haitun* for news and, towards sundown, a brace of Chinese boats lashed together as if for comfort comes close enough to have a clear, short conversation. Two pieces of information: yes, the water in the Gorges is higher than normal, but not too bad. And yes, a foreign motor launch has gone past.

The *Sea Witch*. Not three hours ago.

The news electrifies Charlie. In seconds he's on the bridge, fronting up to Marlais, eyes burning. He's been so quiet since the disastrous journey to Peach Blossom Village, but now the words tumble out.

'We need go faster. Moonface there.' He jabs his fingertip beyond the prow of the *Haitun* to where the river slides around the shoulder of a scrubby brown hill. 'Fast. We go now!'

Marlais ignores him, turns to grumble an order to the new helmsman.

'Tell him, Ruby,' Charlie says. 'Tell him we've got to go faster.' He turns to the Captain again, spinning his hands as if winding engines faster.

Marlais shakes his head. 'Not this evening. Bad water ahead. Sandbanks and the current's switching like a snake in a sack. Besides we could miss your old gangster in the night if he was moored tight and had his lights out. No. We'll do thirty more minutes and then we'll have to find a mooring ourselves. And we're going to need more coal damn soon.'

'What's he saying?' Charlie snaps.

'He's saying it's too dangerous—'

'Then we'll take the ship over,' he shouts.

'You're being silly, Charlie! You're not thinking straight.'

227

'Then we'll go on foot. Tian Lan knows these hills like the back of her hand, and she knows a short cut. We can get another boat maybe at the next town. A faster one.'

'She's a good fighter, but she doesn't know everything,' Ruby says, frustration giving the words an extra shove. 'You've seen the Shadows, you saw the ghost in your parents' old village. She's got your head all in a spin.'

'Now *you're* being silly!'

Charlie colours as he says these last words, really colours, something she's never seen before. And Ruby feels herself colouring back, the beetroot seeping up her face to her hairline.

Marlais snorts. 'Could you two take your argument somewhere else, I've got to find a safe place to moor.'

'Then I'm going on foot,' Charlie says, ignoring the captain. 'We can't let him get to that stronghold. He's probably got half an army and Heaven knows what else on his side. Tian Lan says we could commandeer a lorry or something. She knows this part of China, Ruby, and you don't.'

'But we said we'd keep together—'

'As long as possible. I want to be with you, but I've got to do the right thing for Fei, no matter how much I—'

He shuts his mouth tight and looks at her in a weird way, like someone who just managed to stop in time before falling over a cliff.

'No matter how much you what?'

'Forget it. I'm sorry.'

Charlie dodges her gaze and dashes past her from the wheelhouse.

Marlais gives Ruby a nudge in the ribs. 'Well, go on. Go after him . . . or you can let that stroppy girl calm him down. Your choice.'

She hurries down to the foredeck and sees Charlie walking briskly towards Tian Lan and the Red Lanterns. The girl looks up, calls out his Chinese name and beckons him over, her face brightening.

Damn and blast her, Ruby thinks. We should be sticking together right now and she's messing it all up. Can't let it happen.

'Charlie!' she calls. 'Charlie, I need to talk to you. We agreed we need each other.'

He hesitates and glances back, face taut, frustrated – but determination burning in his dark eyes.

Tian Lan calls again. 'Jia Li. Come to your friends. Or would you rather be kissing your pale ghost of a girlfriend.'

The others laugh softly in the dusk.

She hears Charlie's mumbled reply over the lap of the water. 'She's not my girlfriend.'

For a moment his comment knocks the wind from her sails, but then Ruby gathers herself again and marches forward, chin lifted, defiant. The others get to their feet and form a half circle behind Tian Lan, watching her with a mixture of curiosity and contempt.

'Go on,' Tian Lan hisses, waving Ruby away with the back of her hand. 'Run home little girl. Leave China to us. Jia Li says he's joining us – that he's coming with me. We're going over to the Communists. They'll help us rescue his sister from that stinking toad of a gangster.'

Ruby's gaze slips to Charlie, waiting for him to deny it.

'Is it true? Are you a Communist too now?'

He throws his hands into the air. 'I don't know. But we can cut over the hills past the next bend. If we act now we might catch him before the Gorges—'

'But what about spirits and Shadow Warriors?' Ruby shouts. 'What about what the ghost or whatever it was said to you in the village? This lot might be OK against flesh and blood but we're facing the Otherworld. I'm your best help for that. The spirit sword is coming back to life. It's guiding me! Cross my heart!'

'There are no ghosts or monsters any more,' Tian Lan snorts. 'That's all fairy stories of the past. There's just good people and bad people and we're going to do away with the bad—'

'You saw Tom, Charlie. And that old man in the village, tell them!'

Charlie twists his mouth up and looks away as the girl snorts again.

'The bad people will be swept from China,' she says firmly.

'You mean foreigners like me?' Ruby steps forward to within a yard of Tian Lan, meeting her gaze.

'Stop it,' Charlie whispers.

Ruby doesn't move her eyes from the girl's stare.

'Jia Li told us all about your stinking ape of a father and what he did. That's what we're dealing with. What's the life of an innocent Chinese girl when there's money to be made or some deal to be done to bleed this country dry.'

The fuse is lit. Ruby feels the anger burn through her and shoves Tian Lan hard. But her timing's wrong, or the emotion has knotted the *ch'i*, because the Chinese girl hardly rocks back at all. Like trying to shove something rooted in the ground.

'How dare you,' Ruby hisses, pushing her face towards Tian Lan's.

'Stop it,' Charlie says again, his voice firmer. 'Stop it, will you?'

Ruby turns to him. 'And is it true? Are you going with them?'

Charlie groans.

'Just to try and cut Moonface off. Or see where he is. I'll come back. Soon.'

'But—'

'But nothing. You stay on the boat. Meet us at the next town. Full Moon Bridge. And if I don't – if I'm not there, I'll see you back in Shanghai. At the temple as soon as I can.'

He turns to Tian Lan and nods.

It can't be happening, but it is. He's going to leave me again, Ruby thinks, abandon me half way up the river. And go off with the Red Lanterns and everything else is going to be forgotten.

'Charlie, you and I need to stay together.'

'I won't go far. Just to see if we can find the *Sea Witch*. Or get some more help. My mind's made up. I'm sorry.' He stalks away down the deck, towards the dinghy, and when she tries to follow, one of the Lantern boys blocks her way with a strong hand and shakes his head once.

'You heard him.'

Feeling eyes burning on her back, Ruby turns and

232

runs to the cabin, the anger and frustration bringing a fresh sting to her eyes, and beyond that, the dizzying sense that for the moment she is alone.

Completely alone.

She lies on her bunk, gripping the spirit sword tight.

I should have told him earlier, she thinks.

I should have told Charlie how I felt ages ago and then none of this would have happened. Maybe we'd have run away somewhere – or he'd have told me more about what was going on in Shanghai and I could have stopped Dad telling the Green Hand where Fei was and none of this would have happened.

He's being an idiot, but it's my own stupid fault.

And now it's too late.

She pulls the blanket over her, a bitter taste rising in her mouth.

The Chinese girl's impressive, she thinks, there's no doubt about it. Tall and slim, graceful, not like me and my clumsy ways of doing things. She's beautiful too, long black hair, cheeks like polished wood. Not my fault if I was born this way. I wish I'd been born Chinese and then . . .

But how dare she call Dad a *stinking ape*? He's a good man, underneath it all, no matter what trouble he's fallen into. Charlie himself said we don't really know what hooks the Green Hand have got in him. He looked so miserable that night in the Chinese City, like a prisoner about to be executed for something he didn't fully understand. And yet, as the bullets flew, he came alive again. A hint of the Dad I used to know. The spark, the silly jokes that even Mother used to laugh at on a good day. Maybe I should head home, try and help him. Forget all this, forget Charlie—

There's a knock at the door, a soft three beats, and Charlie is standing there, hands clasped. For a long moment she can't say anything, not what she really wants to say, and when she does speak the tone comes out wrong again.

'What do you want then?'

'To say sorry—'

'Are you really going with them?'

He nods slightly. 'We're close to Moonface now. Tian Lan says there's a Communist cell near here, near Full Moon Bridge. I didn't want the others to hear. We can reach them and they can take us by lorry upriver and maybe we can cut him off before—'

'And what about me? Take me with you—'

'You can't come, Ruby. They won't have you.'

'But – what about you? Don't *you* want me?'

'It's not that *simple*.'

The *Haitun*'s engines die abruptly and a few seconds

234

later there's the sound of reeds shushing a long drawn-out sigh down the starboard side of the hull.

Ruby scrunches her eyes tight. 'It shouldn't matter what colour my skin is,' she moans. 'Should it?'

Charlie shuffles uncomfortably.

'Should it?'

'I like your skin colour, Ruby,' he says. 'And I like you. I had a dream last night, when I couldn't find you . . .'

There are voices outside and his voice loses its way.

'What kind of dream?'

'It was – scary. But kind of nice. I saw something. I saw you.'

'And?' she says, straining to keep the conversation going, trying to hold him.

'I'll tell you when I come back. When I see you again. Maybe tomorrow.'

For a moment she had thought he was changing his mind, but that sentence is crisp, decisive. She keeps her eyes shut. 'And what if we can't find each other then?'

'Then as soon as I can. I'll find you in Shanghai. At the temple. On that cross you drew on the ground . . .'

She feels his hand rest briefly on her shoulder, the weight of a sparrow on a branch and no more, and then it lifts away . . .

. . . and when she opens her eyes Charlie's gone.

第二十四章

MOTHS AND MUD

She tries not to listen to the sounds on deck, even stuffs her hands over her ears as she lies on the bunk to block it all out. But a part of her mind keeps listening. Above the river chatter she can hear Charlie's soft voice, Tian Lan's bright syllables clipped over the top of it. She hears Marlais ordering the boat to be made fast, the run of bare feet on deck, the creaking of rope and wood as the *Haitun* heaves to the bank.

Then silence.

An enormous silence, unbroken for five long minutes, maybe just the plash of an oar, a voice lost as soon as heard, then nothing.

This isn't what was meant to happen, she thinks, her heart aching.

I'm sure of it. All the rest of it has felt like it was destined to happen. But not this. Not Charlie going off and me lying here like this. It's time to act, I'm sure of it, not wait around like Mother's waited all her life for something to happen that's never going to come.

Shanghai Ruby never used to wait for anything, she thinks. I made things happen. And look at me now, look what I've done these last few days. I've trapped a fox, fought shadowy ghosts, hopped a train and a steamship across a war-torn country. Been shot at by bandits. So I'm not going to just jolly well lie here and wait, she thinks, swinging off the bunk. That would be the stupid thing to do. That wouldn't be me.

Maybe I can go with them, just keep my distance. Be with Charlie, even if I'm a hundred paces behind him, hiding in the shadows. Half tiger, half mouse at the same time. But not doing nothing.

She pulls the hat down on her head, then, cautiously, reaches for the spirit sword. The characters on the copper are still shining, the pattern of stars particularly bright now. Seven fiery green dots dancing in front of her eyes.

It must mean Charlie's going to need *me*.

She's glad of the soft-soled shoes as she slips down the corridor, dodging into an empty cabin at the sound of footsteps, then making a rush for the rear deck. The *Haitun* is pulled tight to the reedy bank, water level still high, a long wooden pole spliced to the mast overhead and stretching out to bind them to shore. The ship's rowboat will make too much noise and anyway the bank is so close. The mooring pole is the best bet.

From overhead there's a cough and she glances up to see a sentry silhouetted there, standing on the roof, rifle slung over his shoulder, pale smoke curling from his nostrils. Above him the clouds have parted, pinpricks of a thousand thousand stars in the fabulously black sky beyond.

From the far side of the *Haitun*, far away across on the other bank, there's a strange kind of bark then, a jagged shriek in the silence. The sentry turns away to look, and quickly, silently, she scurries across the deck and clambers over the rail.

Reaching as far as she can along the pole, she gets a firm grip overhead with both hands and then pushes off hard, feet swinging out across the dark water. Her weight sags, threatening to rip her hands loose, like they always came loose on the monkey bars in the gym at school. She grips harder, ignoring the ache in her shoulders, frees her right hand and reaches further out, not daring to look down, then transfers her weight and swings. Her fingers grip and quickly she does it again with the left. That's it, *mei wenti, mei wenti*, she thinks, chanting the words like a coolie. Her bare legs brush the first of the reeds, but now her right hand is losing grip, threatening to drop her . . .

The unearthly shriek sounds again across the water. Longer.

She manages two more clumsy swings and then she's slipped, falling, the reeds whispering as she thumps into the mud, sinking to her ankles, toppling to one side and plunging her arm up to the elbow in slime.

'Who's there?' The sentry's voice barks into the darkness.

She crouches low, keeping her face down. The mud feels so watery she's worried she's just going to sink into it and never stop, and she starts to fight against the downward suck. Her arm gloops free, black as pitch, stinking. It makes a hell of a sound as it comes and she hears the sentry's voice again, shouting. A moment later a searchlight burns the reeds, moths dancing bright in its beam as it sweeps the bank. She pushes herself flatter to the mud – and then smears some of it on to her face for camouflage, the rich, bitter smell filling her nostrils. The floodlight cuts over her head as she wrenches her legs loose with two long squelches and desperately claws forward through the brittle reeds. The mud grabs at her legs, but then the ground becomes firmer, and she crawls up the bank and throws herself over the top just as the searchlight scorches past again.

Breathing fast, she turns.

A wide flat landscape lies before her: patchwork fields stretching to distant hills holding up the night sky. Away to the east a chunk of waning moon sticks out of the edge of cloud, shedding light fitfully across the overgrown bank, illuminating a faint path that leads away from the river. Following it she can just make out figures heading inland, Charlie's slim form recognisable even at a few hundred yards. Not out of sight yet.

She hurries along the bank, keeping crouched, then drops down the landward side, on steps hacked roughly in the steep slope.

I'll keep good distance for now, she thinks. No use barging up to them, I'd just be sent back. Maybe Tian Lan might even lop my head off, she thinks grimly. She tugs her own sword free of the pack, the emerald light still bright, and holds it in front of her two-handed, like she's seen the swordsmen do who busk their skills on Bubbling Well Road.

Then she jogs forward into the darkness, feet slurping mud in the cloth shoes, one eye on the group ahead and one on the copper blade, watching as it slowly but surely burns more and more fiercely.

* * *

For a good half hour she trots along a raised bank that jinks between flooded paddies, past mulberry trees that sigh on the stiffening breeze shedding the first of their autumn leaves, the trickle of unseen streams and gurgle of drainage channels at her feet. Charlie and the Lanterns are visible now and then, small dark forms scurrying under the star-speckled sky. She checks back over her shoulder, remembering the route, determined to fix it in her mind so that, if the worst comes to the worst, she can turn and get back to the *Haitun* before dawn.

The stars and characters on the copper blade are so bright now that they're lighting the ground in front of her like a torch. It helps to see the uneven pathway, but it makes everything else that much darker, like she's wading into nothingness. She grips the handle tighter. Again she remembers the day at the beach when the waves nearly took her down. A huge force threatening to engulf her after *venturing too far out, as usual*. When Dad at last came to the rescue he looked furious, then relieved, then – after ten long minutes – a smile twitched the corner of his lips, blue with cold. *You always go too far*, he had said, watching as Mother towelled her ridiculously hard to get her circulation going again. *One day you'll go too far for me to help. God help you then!*

And then he said something else—

A splash to her right, close by, startles her, shutting the memory out. A violent thrashing in the near silence – and then a quack as a wild duck beats the water and takes to the night.

She steadies herself and moves on. In the distance a dog starts to bark and she peers into the gloom, tucking the sword behind so its light doesn't distract. Charlie and the rest have stopped on a path that rises from the flooded fields, its flagstones shining in the moonlight and climbing towards some thatched huts huddling under a huge pine. No lights to be seen, just the steady snarl and bark of what sounds now like a really fierce watchdog. The group seem to be having some kind of debate – and then suddenly all their heads lift and they dash across the open ground, heading left, parallel with the river and obviously intent on skirting the hamlet at speed.

Ruby runs, faster now, trying to keep pace. The mud on her legs and arm is tightening the skin and that's mixing with the fizzing of the pins and needles coming again all over.

The dog at the huts is barking even more ferociously. Sounds like a real beast, she thinks, glancing nervously in its direction. Often they're allowed to roam at night and take a bite out of anyone on the road.

Blast it, she's lost sight of Charlie now.

Her eyes whip across the landscape. To the left there's a low hill, a weathered mound a couple of hundred feet high that the river bends around – and yes, there's the Lantern group, making their way up it. The moon glints off Tian Lan's swords, Charlie just behind her, half way to the top already. Hurrying, Ruby picks her own path to close some ground, rushing forward through the brittle thistles and grass.

As the others make the crest she reaches the steeply sloping side of the hill. There's a real maze of tracks ahead of her, criss-crossing around strange, warty bulges. She takes a breath and climbs fast, the sword flaring with colour, staining the dying nettles, the dusty ground as she gains height.

Something just doesn't feel right about this hill though, something that makes her legs heavy – like they do when you're trying to run in a dream. She grits her teeth and pushes on up, gaining yards as her breath labours, and then a smooth-soled shoe slips beneath her and she stumbles . . .

. . . and she sees the first bone.

A milk-white thigh bone is sticking up out of the hillside, a moonlit, bright exclamation mark that makes her pause where she's fallen.

Ruby looks around wildly as the spirit sword flares even harder – and in its light she sees the empty eye sockets of a skull staring at her, another lying just beyond that. A bleached ribcage nearby is tangled by the weeds. She looks further up the hill, heart punching her chest, and sees now that some of the weird bumps on the hillside have holes in them like small doorways.

Mei wenti, she mutters, her lips dry.

Just a few paces away a long box sticks out of a collapsed doorway and from it trails the broken arm of a skeleton, its remaining three fingers splayed as if about to push itself upright. As if the coffin has drifted straight out of the hillside . . .

She looks from side to side, fighting the panic, and realises she's in the middle of some kind of huge, derelict cemetery. The lintels over some graves have fallen, others broken open by thieves or animals or Heaven only knows what, and as she picks herself up and climbs higher, she spots bone after bone on the dark ground.

Another skull. A jaw.

Another thigh bone, half chewed.

The shakes reach up through her mud-locked feet and she grips Jin's sword tighter, picking her way round the bones, wishing she still had Amah's Buddha cap or a fresh talisman to burn and drink. And where's Charlie now?

She looks up to see the group's already dropping out of sight over the crest of the hill.

The thought of being alone on this hillside of the dead is too much. She opens her mouth, about to scream his name – whatever the consequences – when she sees a curious procession of other figures coming up from the left, from the direction of the river. One is holding a banner of some kind that blows in the breeze, the others marching jerkily behind.

Crew from the ship? Bandits? Communists?

Something really weird about the way they're moving. Cold dread seeps through her as she watches them move into the moonlight, and creeping realisation dawns. Five, six, seven ragged figures, striding up the ridge towards Charlie and the others, their legs and arms held straight and locked, moving swiftly. The wind tugs at their Chinese gowns, the ribbons on their headgear.

Her own arms and legs lock up tight, her blood running cold.

It can't be. Surely not . . .

Jiang shi. Hopping vampires.

She knows it's true as soon as the thought has formed. One gloomy evening Fei invented a game where each member of the gang took turns at being a *jiang shi*, tightening up their limbs and shrieking as they chased each other, corpses reanimated from the grave and desperate to feed off the *ch'i* of anything living they can find.

Even that had scared her witless. But that was just a game.

These are real. Real hopping vampires – and they're after Charlie.

第二十五章

TERROR ON BONE HILL

In that moment of shock the Lantern group has slipped out of sight over the hill's dark lip. The *jiang shi* are only fifty paces or so behind, twitching along in the moonlight like badly operated puppets, moving at a horrible speed.

Her hands grip the sword, knuckles white.

Got to do something. Got to think of *something* . . .

But the terror of what she's seeing has dulled her mind. Fragments of half remembered folklore and stories trip over each other. Do you need a mirror – or is that for European vampires? Or is it both? Or are you meant to push seeds into acupuncture points on their back or something? And wasn't there something in the Almanac about the blood of a black dog – or a black donkey?

It's all a stupid muddle. Maybe the spirit sword will

slice them like it sliced the Shadow Warriors.

And maybe it won't. Only one way to find out . . .

She takes an enormous breath into her belly, then scurries up the boneyard as fast as she can, dodging through a hundred, a thousand, shattered pieces of people scattered and forgotten on the desolate hill. Broken coffins jut like bad teeth from the rutted ground, rats scurrying away in the livid green light of her sword.

The panic keeps threatening to overwhelm her, but the blade gives a little tug now, like it's encouraging her, urging her on, and it calms the fear just a tiny bit, enough to let her run.

Behind her the guard dog is still barking, but something else too. A sharp yelp that chops the night twice. Glancing back she sees the river unfolding its silver path between low hills. You can even just make out the *Haitun*, a few lights burning—

There's a screech ahead of her, an unearthly sound, and she rushes on. Didn't Fei once say that martial arts experts can fight hopping vampires? Maybe some kind of *ba gua* move.

Another scream cuts the thought in half. That was human this time . . .

She clambers the last steep yards of the hill and below her sees a stone stairway dropping away to a collapsed gateway. About a hundred yards lower there's a cluster of buildings, a small temple complex of some kind around a courtyard. And there's Charlie and the others, surrounded by the *jiang shi*. More of them now, maybe a dozen, encircling the shore party and moving towards them.

'Charlieeeee!'

With every bit of air in her lungs she screams his name and rushes down the hillside, taking the steps two at a time, lifting the sword high.

Some of the weird, stiff figures are already turning to face her. The fear threatens to buckle her knees again, but the sword is *really* moving in her hands now, guiding her. To her right something large and dark hurtles through the corner of her vision, a fleeting shadow, but it's all she can do to concentrate on her feet, make sure she doesn't tumble on the broken stairway before she even joins battle.

'No! Ruby!!' Charlie's voice is tight in his throat, desperate. 'Keep back!'

Tian Lan has drawn her swords, circling them uncertainly in the air. She leaps forward and hacks at one of the closest *jiang shi*, but the blade just rebounds with a thud that jars her to the shoulders, and she stumbles back, off balance, her face white. The girl with the plum scarf raises her pistol two-handed and aims at the same vampire, and fires once, twice. Puffs of dust show where the bullets hit the temple wall behind, but the *jiang shi* keeps coming. The girl fires three more frantic blasts then drops to her knees, fumbling more bullets into the chamber, unable to tear her eyes from the thing coming at her, whimpering. Charlie is rooted to the spot, mouth wide open, eyes reaching out to Ruby . . .

The copper blade twitches hard then, it's seven-starred pattern blinking furiously, and before she's really sure what she's doing, she charges down the last of the steps. Oh God, she murmurs, bracing for the fight, but at the last the sword pulls her sharply to one side, as if to circle the *jiang shi* rather than dash straight into their midst.

Two of the things give off that horrible squeal, and come staggering towards her, advancing fast. Their faces are awful to look at, half the features there, half not, blunted by decay, a musty stink of earth coming off them as they rush forward.

The first of them reaches out, its long thin hand jabbing for her. She chops down with the spirit sword – or it brings itself down, it's hard to tell – the timing just right. But instead of slicing effortlessly as it did with the Shadow Warriors, the blade just chunks in half an inch – and sticks there. The *jiang shi* screams, foul breath billowing as it clutches at the sword, its awful strength twisting Ruby around as she struggles to free her weapon. The vampire's dead eyes look right into hers for a second and then it flings the blade free, sending her tumbling, falling, sprawling in the dirt behind the largest of the temple buildings.

'Rubyyyy!' Charlie's voice wails her name.

Two more gunshots detonate. Dazed, she looks up to see Plum Scarf wrestling with a *jiang shi*. It grabs her throat, lifts her off her feet and then hurls her through the air to where she slams against a wall and slumps to the ground.

We're done for, Ruby thinks, stumbling to her feet, spitting soil from her mouth. But she still has Jin's sword and writhing snake-like it moves in her hands again. She takes a few steps sideways just as a *jiang shi* bursts through the rotten plaster and timber of the back of the main building. It misses her by a fraction, and this time, when she swings with *all* her strength, all her desperation, the blade digs deeper, chunking into the dead centre of the vampire's back and knocking it to the ground.

It shrieks, rolls . . .

. . . then gets slowly, steadily back to its feet.

No hope. That was my best shot, Ruby thinks. Can't hit it any stronger than that. Can't do better.

Got to get away.

She backs through the hole in the wall, up onto the raised floor of the old temple building. Pale moonlight chases the shadows inside – nothing much left in the building, just a smashed-up altar, fragments of wall hangings, some candlesticks scattered on the rotting boards. The hopping vampire is coming after her now, clambering stiffly through the hole it made, backing her away around the remains of the altar.

The stars on the blade are glowing harder than anything else now, the seven points of green light twinkling in front of her in the gloom, pulling her eyes away from the horrible thing. Suddenly they all wink out, then – one by one – start to light up in sequence, blinking on and off in a pattern: lower left, upper left, lower right, top. Then repeating again. The creature is closing again, as if it has regained strength. It hisses through the gaping hole of its mouth. Still she has half an eye on the stars on the sword. They keep blinking that same pattern, as if firing out an urgent message, and slowly, carefully, she starts to copy it, moving the tip of the blade to lower left, upper left, lower right, top. It feels like the blade wants to move that way, and she repeats it now harder, faster – and then again. On that third repetition the vampire loses momentum, and comes to a halt in front of her, gently swaying on the spot, its eyes fixed on the blade and the pattern it's making as if hypnotised.

'Get back!' she snaps. 'Let me past.'

She takes a step forward and, after a sickening pause, the vampire staggers back a pace, its gaze still trained on the sword. Each movement of the sword tip now seems to move the *jiang shi*, a bit like the feel of having a really strong fish hooked on the end of your line, but in reverse. And it feels like one wrong move and she'll lose her grip on it. Carefully she takes another pace, and again the thing retreats the same distance towards the shattered remains of the main door. There's confused shouting outside now, and then another sound: a roar, like a huge wind has suddenly risen, and then a horrible shriek.

Tian Lan's voice shouts over the roaring: 'Run, run for it!'

The sword is shaking in Ruby's hand. No time to think, or even to breathe, just to focus on driving the vampire backwards, towards the main entrance and back down into the courtyard, and see what's happening.

The sound is horrific outside now. Charlie's voice is calling her name wildly, but is suddenly cut short amidst the roaring wind and the unearthly squealing of the *jiang shi*. Ruby pushes forward, shoving the vampire with whatever invisible force the sword is generating. It's fighting back now, she can feel it through the blade, and, as she staggers from the building, she sees something so shocking that her focus is lost for a moment, and the sword wavers, falling in her hands . . .

In front of her is a vision from a nightmare: a huge four-legged creature is ripping at the throat of a felled vampire, its feet pinning it to the ground as it snaps away. The *jiang shi* twitches, shakes – and then stops moving, and the figure straddling it straightens, rearing up on its hind legs, its huge red brush of a tail suddenly visible, sweeping the ground red.

A fox spirit, a huge fox spirit. Just like the *huli jing* from White Cloud but this one looks *far* fiercer, *far* bigger, *far* more powerful than the one they trapped and dropped bottled down the well.

The fox lifts its head and then shrieks into the night air. She takes half a step backwards, eyes roaming the scene trying to take it all in, and then sees Charlie lying on his back to one side, staring up at the night sky, his arms and legs still.

The last of her concentration is well and truly shattered and the *jiang shi* in front of Ruby wrenches free of the sword's grasp – but her eyes are fixed on the shrieking fox.

If you can call it a fox. Just as in White Cloud it

looks like something trapped halfway between animal and man as it rears up, the tail beating the air so fast it seems there's more than one. Tian Lan is at the edge of the courtyard, eyes popping from her head, the remaining Lanterns gathered behind her. Some of the vampires are backing away from the fox, but two of them are stiffly advancing on Charlie's immobile body.

The *huli jing* turns towards her, tongue lolling and pale grey eyes picked out by the moon. It's completely impossible to read his wild look – it could be anger or contempt or hunger. Or something else entirely. His eyes bore into hers and for a second she feels she has looked into those eyes before.

'Help!' she chokes. 'Please help him, Mister Fox!'

The creature blinks, lifts his head and seems to grow even taller, his brush beating the ground faster and faster, blurring. As the tail thrums, a noise gathers, seeming to come from all sides at once, something like distant thunder vibrating in the walls, coming up out of the ground. Yes, the ground is actually shaking, she's sure of it.

The *jiang shi* are all turning towards the fox now, the shrieks and cries dying on their crumbling lips. Bright sparks start to fly from where his tail strikes the stone slabs, shooting into the air like fireworks – and then he jumps, leaping high into the air, higher than the buildings, lifting into the dark. He hangs for a heartbeat, silhouetted – and then drops.

As the fox's paws strike the ground there's a thunderbolt of an explosion. A blast wave hits Ruby, lifting her off her feet, sending her stumbling back, blinded, clunking against the stone steps behind. Her head bangs hard, her vision whiting out. Desperately she rubs her eyes as she struggles back to her feet, one hand still gripping the sword in case any of the *jiang shi* are coming back for her.

But as her vision clears, she sees the hopping vampires – all of them – lie motionless, toppled like ninepins where they stood. Not a movement, not a sound coming from them, no more now than bone and flapping cloth and night air.

Of the mighty fox spirit there's not a trace. Just a distant sound like retreating thunder back over the cemetery hill. And Tian Lan and the remaining Lanterns are gone too – fled it seems down the path and somewhere into the tangle of night-locked fields and hills beyond, the girl with the scarf disappeared with them, either recovered or carried away.

For a heartbeat she thinks Charlie's gone too, but then she sees him, lying face down in deep shadow at the edge of the courtyard, and she rushes to him, skirting the fallen vampires, calling his name over and over. He's not moving at all. Quickly she crouches down and rolls him onto his back, the pale moon falling on his tightly shut eyes.

She shakes him by the shoulder. 'Charlie!'

His eyelids flicker and then – suddenly – open wide, fear filled, confused.

'It's OK, Charlie. We're OK,' she says, the relief flooding through her.

A single syllable bubbles in his mouth. 'I – I – I . . .'

From the river comes the long wail of the *Haitun*'s hooter. It mingles with the ringing in her ears from the thunder blast or whatever it was.

She grips him by the shoulders, takes his weight and hauls him to his feet, babbling words out. 'Did you see? Did you see him, Charlie? It was a fox spirit. I think it might be the one from the temple.'

'Where, where,' Charlie mumbles. 'Where's Tian Lan?'

'They've gone. And the *jiang shi* too. The fox got them.'

Charlie shakes his head, but he's not arguing. Just fighting for breath, for his head to clear, for things to make more sense.

The *Haitun*'s hooter blasts again.

Any twinge of jealousy she feels at the mention of

Tian Lan's name is washed away by the joy of seeing Charlie alive. She throws her arms around him and hugs him so hard the air sighs out of his slim chest.

'I thought you were dead,' she gasps. 'I thought it was all over. I can't believe it.'

But Charlie's not listening. 'Where are we?'

'On the other side of the hill. Above the river. I was so scared when I saw those things . . .'

Charlie shakes his head, pushing himself up on one hand. 'I can't think straight. I remember leaving the boat and climbing the hill. Listen,' he says, gazing right into her eyes, urgently, 'I need to tell you something important.'

He groans and closes his eyes again. Ruby glances at one of the piles of bone and rag and shakes her head. 'Not here. Let's just get back to the boat. In case.'

A few hundred yards from the *Haitun* the fox glides soundlessly through the reeds, his silver eyes wide. He shakes his head, the cold, earthy taste of the *jiang shi* still in his mouth, limbs heavy from the effort of the fight. The boat's engines are already spewing white water from the stern, the girl and boy being helped onto the dinghy and then lifted back up onto deck.

Not now. Not yet.

Time to go back to ground, to go home.

He stops and dips his head towards the wavelets lapping the river bank and drinks deeply, and feels nothing, his silver-grey eyes reflected in the black water.

第二十六章

FULL MOON BRIDGE

In the first light of dawn Marlais looks tired, the lines around his eyes scored like a ploughed field. But the blue of his irises is undimmed, bright and intense as they gaze at Ruby.

'So. What *did* you see, my girl? It looked like there was a hell of a fight up there,' Marlais scowls. 'Or a whole keg of gunpowder gone off.'

'We were attacked,' Ruby says. 'And someone saved us.'

'Don't hold back from old Marlais now,' the captain says. 'You were both as white as winding sheets when you scuttled back on board. Your young man looked dead to the world. He'll be a long time asleep I reckon. Must have taken a blow to the head or something.'

Your young man. The phrase pulses a bit of warmth

to her cheeks, but she doesn't bother trying to hide it now.

Marlais grinds the walnuts in his hand. 'So come on – tell me what you saw.'

On the bank the reeds are tumbling with the stiffening breeze. There's that peculiar sensation again, like she had in Shanghai when Straw was padding along behind her the night she fled the Mansions. The distinct sense of being watched, that there's more out there than the reeds and the grey-blue hills. Marlais seems to have an open mind, she thinks, fingernail tapping away at her teeth. He believes all that stuff about Joe Munro. About Tom.

She shakes her head. 'There were horrible, horrible things. In a graveyard.'

The Captain folds his arms and tilts his head to one side.

'Horrible things?'

'I think they were *jiang shi*.'

Marlais raises his eyebrows – but he's not laughing at her.

'Ghosts I can buy, Miss Harkner, but *jiang shi* . . . ?'

'It was real.'

'Maybe we each see what we need to see. I don't doubt your brother was here because you needed to see him. Maybe last night you saw those things

261

because you needed to . . .' He sighs.

'But what's *happening*? Do you think – do you think I'm going mad?' Ruby says, voice hesitant.

'No. Not at all, no more than yours truly.' Marlais puts a hand on her shoulder. 'You're just going a bit . . . deeper . . . than normal, that's all. Things happen because they have to, that's been my experience. And just because something's real today, won't mean it's real tomorrow.'

'I don't understand.'

Marlais drags a hand across his face, then forces a smile. But this one is tired, resigned. 'You will, my dear. You will. Now if you'll excuse me I have to check on the coal. We need stocks before the day is out and we may have a job to reach Shasi on what we've got. You get some rest, like your friend.'

Back in the cabin she stands for a long while looking at Charlie.

Once they'd bundled back on board last night, his eyes had closed again at the first opportunity – and he's hardly moved a muscle since. At one point, dead middle of night, he whispered her name. But he was fast asleep – or deeper than that. Curled on the bunk with his spectacles off he looks exposed, vulnerable, and with sleep he looked vulnerable too.

Your young man, Marlais said.

She curls up on the lower bunk and pulls the blanket over her head.

As ever with Charlie it's hard to read whether that important thing he wanted to tell her was something really good – or something really, really bad.

She wakes to a rough shake of the shoulder, mouth so dry it feels like cardboard, a confused nightmare interrupted midstream. The blanket over her head is tugged away and orange light floods her vision, dazzling.

'Ruby! Wake up!'

Charlie is bending over her, hand still on her shoulder.

'What's going on? Are you OK?'

'We've been asleep for ages. Ages! I think it's nearly evening. And we're not moving, the engines have stopped.'

'Where are we?'

'Past Changsha I guess . . .'

She rolls over, feels the stab of pain from one of the bruises on her arms. It's reassuring in a way. If you can feel pain then you're still alive. Still breathing.

'How are you?'

'I – I still feel *really* tired,' he says. And as her eyes focus she sees with a shock how pale his features are. Almost as pale as hers. 'I had this terrible dream about being on the hill with Tian Lan and this thing attacked me.'

'It was real, Charlie,' she says quietly. 'But we survived. You're OK now.'

He looks at her, as if he's still struggling out of that deep sleep. 'I don't want to leave you again, Ruby.'

That knot of tension in her belly eases. For the first time in days she can sense the breath move there, feels Charlie is close to her again.

'I'm glad.'

'I'm sorry if I was snappy, I—'

'I know you just want to get Fei.' She pauses. 'What – what were you going to tell me? Last night.'

Charlie glances away, massaging the back of his neck. 'I don't know. Did I say that?'

'Yes. Just before we came back.'

'I'm sorry. I just don't know. Come on, we need to get this thing moving again.'

From the deck they see puffed-up clouds sagging overhead, but not a hint of smoke from the funnel. The sky is smudged on the rippling river and around them the hills are steeper now, taller, crumbled cones of pale grass and yellow earth rising up from boulder-strewn banks.

Charlie screws up his face. 'Why aren't we moving?

We've still got daylight.'

There's no sign of Marlais on the bridge, but Old Lee stands at his post, eyes fixed on the next bend in the river, watching a junk coming downstream.

'No coal,' Old Lee says quietly. 'The Captain has gone to look for some at Full Moon Bridge. Safer than Ichang.'

'But what about Shasi?' Charlie says, looking at the chart open on the wheelhouse table.'

'We're past Shasi,' Old Lee smiles. 'We were doing fifteen knots 'til the fires went out.'

Charlie groans. 'But we'll never catch Moonface now. Not before he gets to his stronghold.'

Ruby squints at the characters and stabs her finger on the chart. 'Is that Full Moon Bridge?'

Old Lee nods.

'And where are we now?'

The pilot reaches out with his long fingernail.

'You see, not far. He will be back soon.'

Ruby looks at Charlie. 'It can't be more than a few miles. How about going to have a look, rather than just sitting and waiting? We could ask around if anyone's seen Moonface's boat.'

Charlie nods, but when he looks away at the bare hillsides to their right there's fear dragging at his eyes. The slanting afternoon sun is picking out the telltale bumps and lumps of more graves. Ruby gulps back the plum stone rising in her throat again at the thought of *jiang shi*. So many graves – and yet they've seen so few people on the roads, in the villages they've passed. It's like there's more dead than living in the Interior.

She looks back at the chart, trying to sound decisive, brave.

'There's a path along the river. Let's stick to that. I mean it's daylight after all so . . .'

Old Lee pulls his eyes from the river and looks at her. 'Don't worry. You'll be safe enough. Just get to Full Moon before nightfall.'

It feels good to be doing something as half an hour later they jog the well-trodden track alongside the Yangtze. The hills are closing in now, confining the river, and the path lifts over spurs of hill that dive down to the water. The reeds and mud banks of the lower river have given way to a rocky shore, and the flow of the Yangtze is quickening: when a solitary junk passes below it sweeps downstream at an almighty clip.

Ruby stops and looks over her shoulder. She has to keep waiting for Charlie who seems unusually slow. His stamina hardly ever gives out, but now he's panting hard each time as he catches up. 'Wait up. My legs feel like lead.'

'We can go slower if you want,' she says, 'but you look fine.'

It's a lie. In the autumn afternoon light he looks washed out, ill in fact. Maybe he's sickening like Tom did?

'We can rest, Charlie.'

'No. I want to get there. Maybe someone's seen the *Sea Witch*. Or maybe we'll find Tian Lan again.'

Ruby stops dead. 'If we do, you can't disappear with her—'

'No.' He shakes his head. 'I need to stick close to you. I know that now, after . . .'

'After what?'

'After what we saw on the hill.'

'So you do remember?' Ruby asks excitedly.

Charlie nods. 'I think I do. But I don't want to talk about it.' He glances up the hillside. 'Let's keep moving.'

They jog on in silence. The path twists past shrubby pines, worn to a deep, sandy groove between the rocks. Above them now broken old graves are caught by the light of the lowering sun, casting long shadows down towards them, and Charlie's pace increases.

As the afternoon fades, a last breathless climb of worn stone steps takes them over a ridge, and then before them lies Full Moon Bridge, a tight cluster of tiled and thatched rooftops huddled around a narrow valley floor. Smoke feathers up from the houses and you can see figures moving in the fields around. Real people, living real lives. Not ghosts or *jiang shi* or foxes, just a small Chinese town on an autumn afternoon going about its business.

A smaller river cuts down through the hills from the north, carving out the valley where the settlement sits, tumbling down through the town and under the arc of a roofed bridge. A hundred yards or so beyond it merges into the colossally bigger Yangtze.

A man's coming up the track now, studying her with interest. Two wicker baskets are dangling from the pole across his shoulders, one full of quacking ducks, the other bubbling with bright red peppers. The kind of China she's always longed to see, hard to tell which century it is even.

Charlie's already hurrying down the stone steps and she runs after him, fresh power in her legs, taking off the Fedora for fear it will blow away, her blonde hair tumbling in the wind as she hurtles past the startled local.

The track drops between ramshackle buildings, the smell of open drain and cooking mingling in her nostrils as they turn onto the sloping main street and towards the Yangtze, past market stalls selling peanuts, small oranges, the little river below them hurrying over a last rapid and then flowing under the perfect half circle of the bridge.

It's not hard to find Marlais. A gaggle of hopeful merchants and farmers are scrummaging around him near the jetties, all holding out their wares and shouting bargains. The Captain, a half head taller than anyone else, is dutifully inspecting everything shoved under his eyes: corn cobs, ripe peaches, boxes of singing crickets – but shaking his head at each with a sorrowful smile.

'Just need plenty coal,' he says. 'Chicken. You savvy? No wantee peach. Or blasted crickets.'

His gaze sweeps over the heads of the traders and locks onto Ruby – and a resigned smile lifts his face.

'I wish you two would keep to the old *Haitun*,' he bellows. 'Much safer by far. There's brigands in the hills shooting at anything that moves apparently. And Communists not far off. They'd all like us for a big fat ransom. But we've got the coal, I think! And that boat you're after cleared the jetty here this lunchtime. We may get them yet.'

Charlie shakes his head, not sure he's understood right.

'Moonface?'

The Captain nods.

'So when we go?'

'An hour. I've got them loading a boat for us and we'll have to transfer that to the *Haitun*. Maybe an hour for that. And then it'll be nightfall—'

Ruby's eyes scour the dockside, the small junks tied up. Beyond the longest of the wooden landing stages there's the rusted hulk of a shipwrecked boat parting the swift water. 'Can't we take another boat or something?'

Marlais shakes his head, and nods back at the river below. 'Nothing else as fast as us around here.' He nods at the wreck. 'See that? That's one of the Yangtze Rapid's old boats. Shows we can't mess around. But we'll be on the way soon and then . . .' his eyes shine brighter than ever, '. . . and then it's the Gorges and life becomes very interesting. Take a moment, my young friends – take a look at the bridge.'

Charlie goes to argue, but Ruby grabs him by the sleeve, pulling him away.

'Nothing we can do about it. Let's look at the bridge. Please?'

She looks into his eyes, senses him pulling back inside his shell and decides to press. 'If you remember what happened on the hillside, you must remember now what you were going to tell me. It sounded important.'

'I'll tell you,' he mumbles, 'but let's go to the bridge.'

Marlais' voice rolls down the street after them. 'If you hear my whistle you get down to the dock quick sharp, y'hear?'

Charlie walks ahead, and as Ruby follows she feels her pulse picking up. A sense of anticipation taking hold now, as if something important is coming.

'Wait for me.'

'Let's take a look from the other side,' he says, trying to sound matter of fact, but there's something snagging his face too, a look she hasn't seen before.

'What about this dream?'

Charlie goes to say something, then carries on down the street to where a wooden platform has been built out over the little river. Stairs climb the steep curve of the bridge in front of it, up through vermilion gates and under the tiled roof of the building that sits on top.

'Let's look from there,' he calls over his shoulder.

That feeling of anticipation won't let go. As she joins him she tugs the sleeve of his jacket again.

'Charlie, you said something about a dream? Was it about Moonface? Or were you dreaming about Fei? Or about Tian Lan—'

'No,' he says quietly. 'It was about you. You and me.'

Ruby's heart misses a beat.

Mother's always saying her *heart missed a beat* – usually over something trivial – but this is the actual thing. One moment it's whumping away, and then suddenly there's silence, a gap in the beats – maybe two or even three – and then the pulse is back again.

'You and me,' she echoes, waiting for more, but Charlie looks away, pointing.

'You can see why it's called Full Moon.'

The late sun is behind the bridge now, the near side in shade, but the water through it still brightly lit. The dark half circle of the arch meets its own reflection in the water, and joined up it becomes a perfect whole, cupping a shimmering disc inside it like the moon. On top, the red gates and the terracotta building glow in the last of the sun. It's beautiful, the kind of thing she's longed to see, but the question keeps nagging.

'Charlie, what do you mean, *you and me*? What was this dream?'

He screws his face up, picking words carefully. 'I – we were miles and miles apart. I don't know, I'd gone off with the Lanterns or something. And I knew *you* were hundreds of miles away . . . And, well, I was worried about you. Really worried – that I wouldn't find you again.'

In the gap the river gurgles past them, rushing the last few hundred paces to the Yangtze.

'And – come on, there's something more. *Tell* me.'

'And I suddenly realised, everything was OK, because I had a link to you. I remembered about the red thread and looked down and saw it tied to my little finger and I knew it went all the way across the country—'

'A red thread?'

'Yes – you know – the one in the old stories. The thing that binds two souls together.' He pauses. 'Who are destined to be together.'

The tingles shoot from the roots of her hair to the soles of her feet. Of course! She had forgotten that piece of folklore, even when she saw the fine red line twisted around her finger at the fortune teller, but now it comes back in a flash. Remembers Fei going on about it and wondering who her thread linked to and hoping it might be a film star like Rudolph Valentino.

All of Charlie's pallor is gone, his eyes shining. 'I saw it, Ruby – I saw it when I was dead beat in Nanking, just before Marlais found me. At least I think I did.'

'I've seen it too,' she gasps. 'I saw it. Just after I was bumped by the van I saw the thread, but when I tried to follow it disappeared.'

Automatically they both glance down at their hands. Then at each other's, but there's nothing to be seen. An uncomfortable thought darkens Ruby's head. 'But maybe your thread linked to someone else. Maybe Tian Lan—'

Charlie shakes his head. 'No. I knew at once it linked to you. I didn't know how to tell you and then there was no time to ourselves . . .'

'But you should be with someone like Tian Lan. She's clever and a real fighter, not messing around like me. And she's beautiful—'

'Don't be daft. She'd never look twice at me,' Charlie says, snatching the spectacles from the bridge of his nose. 'I'm thin and weedy and I can't see straight. I'm only good for bookwork, not sorting the country out, not fighting.'

Ruby shakes her head.

'But you're so brave,' she says. 'And you're so much stronger than you think you are . . .'

Her heart's hammering now, matching the pulse she can see fluttering away at Charlie's throat.

'I saw it,' he says quietly, and then, with a quick, awkward motion, he leans towards her, holds her shoulders and puts a kiss on her cheek. It's over in a second and she stands there open-mouthed again watching him pull away.

'Sorry,' Charlie mutters.

Ruby looks back at her little finger. Not a trace of the thread to be seen, but it's like she can feel it, tight around the base, throbbing.

She looks back at Charlie, the sensation of the kiss still on her cheek. 'I thought you didn't really like me. That way, I mean.'

'I wasn't sure,' Charlie says. 'But when I set off with the Lanterns, I felt terrible every single step I took . . . there's something special about you.'

Vaguely she's aware of a repeated whistling from the riverfront.

'Special?'

'You don't care about all that other rubbish of what people think. It's great the way you do things just because you think they're right.'

She can hear Marlais calling her name.

'We're here!' she shouts, then looks back at Charlie.

'We'll rescue Fei,' she says. 'And then we'll run away together somewhere. Somewhere quiet.'

Half a smile steals across Charlie's face. 'Don't think quiet suits you, Ruby.'

Captain Marlais comes jogging up the main street, trailing the two crew from the *Haitun* in his wake, a throng of disappointed merchants behind them. His face is scrunched up with concern.

'Fun's over, shipmates! Just heard there's a nasty bunch of bandits coming into town. Maybe a hundred or more. We're getting out with whatever coal's on the junk or our journey might be about to end here.'

He drags a finger across his unshaven throat.

From somewhere on the hill above a rifle shot shatters the evening stillness, ricocheting off the cliffs. Then another. Marlais grimaces, watching the townsfolk scattering for their houses, ducks quacking frantically, dogs barking.

'A grim lot. They still do the death by a thousand cuts business, apparently, and I'm not about to find out what that feels like. Let's be quick about it, friends, and run for Ichang.'

第二十七章

RADIO SIGNAL FROM FAR AWAY

The hurried retreat to the river, the clanking of the gangway underfoot, Marlais' unusual panic: all this is dulled by the thought of what Charlie has said, and by that brief kiss below the bridge.

There's hardly any fear now as she hides from sight on the little junk. She just keeps hearing Charlie's words, and her own that answered him back, like she's playing it over and over again, every little syllable and hesitation recorded perfectly – just like when Dad made her and Tom talk into the Vitagraph machine on Nanking Road.

It's you. I want to be with you.

And the kiss? It was real. Brief but real.

She looks at Charlie. He's standing on the flying rear deck of the little junk peering back at Full Moon Bridge. He glances round, darts her a reassuring smile and then motions her to get down. Marlais and his two men are crouched under the junk's arched roof, rifles trained back on the town. The hull creaks as the current grips them, and then they're moving away from the jetty, past the old rusting hull.

There's another gunshot and some distant shouting but it's as if all that is happening far, far away. Maybe I should have said more when I had the chance just now, she thinks. Maybe I should have kissed him back. Bother it, maybe the moment's gone for good . . .

One of the junk crew is squatting on the low roof over her head, elbows on knees, looking down at her like you might look at something exotic in the zoo. He puts a long pipe to his mouth and blows out smoke, his nose wrinkling.

'Good evening,' she says. 'Thanks for your help.'

The man takes another suck at his pipe. 'You heading upriver?'

'Yes. As soon as we have coal on board.'

'Then you're either very brave, or very *stupid*.'

He spits out the last word.

'Why?'

But he just shakes his head and turns away.

Charlie comes towards her on the swaying junk deck. He's trying to look nonchalant as he slumps down beside her, but she can feel the tension. And he looks exhausted again.

'Charlie. *Ni hao ma?*'

He nods. '*Hao*. Fine. How about you?'

'I'm fine,' she says. 'Just fine.' And her eyes drift down to her little finger. She wiggles it around and around, wondering if she can still sense that thread tightly bound at its base.

'That's good,' he says and she feels, reassuringly, his shoulder lean against hers. 'That's really good.'

As the coal is loaded sack by sack, painfully slowly, into the *Haitun*'s bunkers, Ruby watches night fall piece by piece on the Yangtze. Charlie is tapping his foot impatiently beside her and suddenly shivers hard.

'Are you all right? You don't look well, Charlie.'

He bites his lip. 'Don't I? I don't feel great. I wonder – I wonder if one of those things on the hill got hold of me. I keep feeling cold and tired ever since then.'

'I'm sure you'll be fine,' Ruby says briskly, not wanting to take that thought any further. 'Maybe you just banged your head. Or you've got a cold coming on.'

Marlais passes, face dusted with coal, the whites of his eyes shining bright. 'We'll move as soon as we can. Promise. It's pretty poor stuff that coal they fleeced us for, but it'll get us to the Gorges at least. Join me on the bridge? It'll be safer.'

Smoke starts at last to billow from the stocky funnel, the *Haitun*'s searchlight flickering into life on the shadowy water ahead. One by one the armoured shields clank down into place on the starboard side, the reverberation echoing across the water.

And one by one the junk crew silently retreat to their boat, their thin figures no more than shadows now in the dusk. The last one to leave is the sour-faced man with the pipe. He taps Ruby on the shoulder, the sour smell of sweat mingling with the tang of the smoke.

'Go home,' he whispers. 'While you can. You seem like a good devil to me.' He sweeps the black river with his hand and then spits a gob of white phlegm into the gloom. 'But there are plenty of bad ones out there.'

Huddled in the wheelhouse a half-hour later, Ruby watches as the *Haitun* fights the current round the bend and steams full speed towards the little port town. Lights are burning in the houses, but all seems very quiet there, just a few dogs barking. The *Haitun*'s Lewis gun is stripped and ready for action, all hands waiting for firing from the bank, or an attempt at boarding by the bandits.

But there's nothing.

Marlais braces his elbows on the shuddering hull and squints through the binoculars at the town. Above him the radio on the wall is hissing quiet static.

'Maybe the bandits have already gone,' he says. 'But it's weird. Someone must have tipped them off about us, some nice juicy Westerners to hold hostage, or sell on to the highest bidder. So why haven't they tried anything? It feels like we're being let past.'

He turns to scour the river ahead. 'I want all hands posted to watch for other river traffic. Nothing on the radio, but we can't let anything ram us in the night – or miss our quarry. All lights up now, let's light her like a bloody Christmas tree so nothing can miss us.'

'What about Charlie and me?' Ruby says, 'We want to do something to help.'

'Then get on deck. Keep your eyes open for anything. The river's still high and there could be all kinds of flotsam and jetsam coming at us. Ghost boats even.'

Together they lean into the night breeze on the foredeck, the frothing water chattering away at the *Haitun*'s prow beneath them. Beside them the young depth sounder stands poised, his bamboo staff ready to check the fathoms. When she glances up at its tip,

Ruby sees a fabulous blaze of stars splashed across the heavens.

'The Silver River,' Charlie says, gazing up at it. 'You can't see it like this in Shanghai any more. Not with all the lights.'

'It's a better name than what we call it in English. That just makes me think of cows. It's a shame we can't see it any more.'

'Progress isn't a shame,' Charlie says, matter-of-factly. 'Lots of people are desperate for electricity. The new China will be so bright—'

He pulls himself up short, eyes still fixed on the Milky Way gleaming overhead. 'But it is beautiful . . .'

A long, cold hour passes, and then another, as the hills roll even closer, and apart from the occasional tiny light on the banks there's nothing but shades of black, blue-black, dark grey.

Tiredness creeps with the chill. Now and then the *Haitun*'s engines come down to half speed, or even slow ahead as Marlais calls out orders, and you can feel the anxiety run through the crew. In the sweep of the searchlight Ruby sees telltale ripples shimmering over submerged sandbanks, a half tree careering along on the current, an unlit sampan night fishing.

Charlie clears his throat, eyes up at the narrowing band of stars overhead.

'There's something else I wanted to tell you.'

'Me too,' she says. 'Back at the bridge—'

'No, before that. When I was in Peach Blossom Village talking to that old man.'

'What about him?' she asks, slightly disappointed, but then that's brushed away by what Charlie says next.

'He looked – well, he looked rather like Lao Jin. I mean, much – much – older. But he definitely reminded me of Jin. Maybe he was a relative or something, an uncle – maybe that's where Jin comes from too?'

'Why didn't you say before?'

'I don't know. Do you think it's important?'

'How like him?'

'Very,' Charlie says. 'But I only realised it after it had all happened if you know what I mean.'

The ship suddenly lurches to port, a long growl coming from below deck, then stabilising again as the *Haitun* steadies herself, and she hears Marlais bark out an ugly swear word.

'I'm going to see how we're doing,' she says. 'But no more secrets from each other, OK?

Charlie nods and turns his face back to sweep the river ahead.

In the wheelhouse Marlais has taken off his cap, white hair glowing in the flickering lamps, sweat shining on his forehead. Even Old Lee is tense, leaning forward, that long shard of a fingernail tipping back and forwards as he guides the helmsman.

Ruby hesitates, afraid to break the concentration. 'Is everything OK?'

Marlais tilts his head to one side. 'Channel's completely different to normal. Must have been that last big push of floodwater.' He turns to her and wipes the sweat away. 'Know what turned my hair white, Miss?'

She shakes her head.

'It wasn't being shot at a hundred times, it wasn't the near misses in the fog, it wasn't even old Joe Munro and his ghost. It was one bad night in the Gorges when I thought we were going to be chewed up in the Grinder.'

'The Grinder?'

'My name for a set of rapids. Bad ones. You'll see them soon enough.'

'What happened?'

'We lost power, went sideways, tracking ropes broke and we went slamming towards the rocks. Would have all been splintered.' He whisks his hand sideways towards the other one, balled in a tight fist. 'And then something, some big freak of a wave, just lifted us up clean over the thing. And when I woke up in the morning my hair was white as the snow. You never know what this thing's going to throw—'

A crackle from the radio cuts him short then, a furious burst of static like you get when the typhoons are chasing in to Shanghai and messing up the wireless.

'That's trouble,' Marlais frowns. 'Yangtze Patrol maybe, or even your lot—'

Another three loud fizzes of interference hiss from the grille and then a voice fills the wheelhouse – a slow, deliberate voice, speaking in Chinese-accented English. The reception is broken, static swirling round it, but the first words Ruby hears turn her blood cold.

'This is Moonface calling. This is the *Sea Witch*. Do you read me? Come in, *Haitun*. Over.'

She looks at Marlais. The grooves on his forehead have deepened as he stares at the speaker grille. The radio squawks again and the voice is back. 'Go back. Save yourselves. You cannot catch me where I am going. You cannot follow me to Hell's Throat. No one can follow me there.'

Marlais snatches the handset. '*Haitun* calling, *Haitun* calling, over.'

There's a long pause and then the guttural voice comes again. 'Go ahead. Over.'

'Give up the girl to us. What can you possibly want with her? Give her up and tell us your ransom demand

and I will see to it that it's paid by—'

'I need the girl,' Moonface's voice cracks back. 'I need her. And she will lure my enemy to Hell's Throat. Turn around at once, or face the consequences. You are on a river you do not understand. Turn around. Or drown. Over and out.'

Marlais cranks fresh charge into the radio. 'Come in, *Sea Witch*. Come in, this is the *Haitun*. There are British gunships upriver and we have radioed them for assistance. You cannot escape. Over.'

Ruby looks urgently at Marlais. 'Have you? Have you really?'

The captain shakes his head and cranks the radio one more time. 'Come in, *Sea Witch*.'

The static grinds from the speaker, dies. And then, suddenly, very clearly, as if the words are being spoken right into the shell of her ear, Ruby hears Moonface again.

'And you, Missee Harkner. Go back to Shanghai and try and save your miserable double-crossing father while you have the chance.'

Charlie is in the cabin now, his eyes wide in the gloom, staring at Ruby, the speaker, at Marlais.

'You do not understand what is happening,' Moonface shouts, every word punching from the speaker. 'GO HOME!' And in the half second of live

286

radio air between those last thundered words and the abrupt silence that follows, they all hear an unmistakeable girl's voice shouting.

'Help me! Charlie! Rub—!'

The contact is broken as Fei's words are chopped clean in half.

Charlie grabs the handset from Marlais. 'Fei? Fei? Are you there? Hello?'

And then a fresh burst of interference snarls back and through it, very, very distantly, as if signalling from a thousand miles away, from another planet, they hear a clipped, precise English voice. 'This is HMS *Cockchafer*. Identify yourself. Identify yourself at once. All foreign vessels are to head for port. The river is closed above Hankow to all—'

Marlais growls, from deep in his stomach, and grabs hold of the radio, tearing grille and cab apart and sending them clattering to the wheelhouse floor.

Charlie swings around, eyes furious. 'What you do that for? Now we get no help.'

'We don't want their help,' Marlais snaps.

'Don't talk rubbish,' Ruby says. 'Our gunships could stop Moonface before he gets to the Gorges. Or we could get some of them to come ashore with us if he's reached this stronghold place of his.'

Marlais shakes his head and stalks out of the cabin,

face black as Charlie looks at the broken radio on the floor.

'We're going to be too late. And now we can't call for help, damn it.'

Old Lee looks at him, weighing whether to say something or not.

'Let Marlais be,' he says, whispering. 'He has had some bad news. Someone he loved has died. Let him be and let the rest of us concentrate now. The river isn't right. It isn't right at all. Don't tell anyone,' he adds under his breath, 'but we are a bit lost. Not sure if we're still this side of Ichang or already past it. Should have seen the lights about an hour ago but there was nothing.'

Ruby puts a hand on Charlie's hunched shoulders. 'It's going to be alright. We should get some rest.'

Charlie shakes his head. 'I'm too worried.'

'But you're dead beat, Charlie. You look awful.'

A long, drawn-out yowling comes from away on the port bank, its voice curdling across the river, making them all turn their heads as one.

Old Lee grimaces.

'Fox,' he says. 'An angry one. Really angry.'

'I need to get something,' Ruby whispers to Charlie. 'Wait here.'

* * *

She's surprised to find Marlais sitting in the cabin, head hanging between his shoulders, the walnuts cracking away in his hand. He glances up as she comes in and she sees a whisky bottle clutched in his other fist. The Captain waves it at Jin's pack sagged at his feet. Green light is spilling from it, pulsing, lighting the floor.

'So what have you got in there then, young lady?'

'A present,' she says, shocked now to see how brightly it must be glowing. 'The sword I got from the man who paid you in Shanghai.'

'Let me see.'

She parts the drawstring with trembling hands and gingerly lifts the sword free, the green on its blade now burning steadily, characters and stars aglow.

Marlais whistles through his teeth. 'Now isn't that just *something*!'

'It feels like it's alive sometimes,' she whispers. 'And I think it gets brighter when there are things close by. Ghosts, spirits, things like that – but it doesn't always seem to work like that.'

Marlais takes a long slug from his whisky. 'Maybe it's more about *where* you are rather than what's near you.'

She feels the blade lift slowly, lets her hand follow it and sweeps a long trail of lime in the air.

'It's the dandiest thing I ever saw,' Marlais says, following the curves she's cutting, hypnotised. 'And I've seen a dandy thing or two.'

There's a hushed silence between them. The Captain takes a pull at the neck of his bottle. 'Have you noticed something, Miss Ruby?'

'What?'

'Haven't you noticed how empty the landscape seems now? I thought it was just because of how bad things are upriver, that everyone was hiding, but it's not that. There are villages I've passed a hundred times, that teem with life normally and now are empty. And even the hills don't look right. Like they've moved, or grown. Either my memory's playing tricks or something's really wrong . . .'

His voice dies.

'I don't understand.'

'Maybe we're not on the normal Yangtze any more,' Marlais whispers. 'Maybe we're on another version of it. A kind of shadow . . .' He hangs his head again. 'Maybe that thing of yours is trying to give us the dope about where we are. *Way* off course!'

The goosebumps ripple over Ruby's skin. It feels instantly right somehow, what Marlais is saying.

'I had a book – an old Taoist book,' she says excitedly, 'that talked about the Green Frontier. And we were in a tunnel under the city and it was full of green moss and then all the really weird stuff started to happen to us, and some gates we went through in the city . . . but we haven't been through anything else green. Not even before we saw the hopping vampires on the hill.'

Marlais takes a big swig from his bottle and snorts. 'Never noticed the name of my old boat? The *Lu* Haitun?'

The *Green* Dolphin.

'But a boat couldn't be a frontier, could it?'

'Couldn't it?' Marlais says, his voice thick and heavy. 'It moves you from one place to another, from one time to another. Why not?'

Ruby feels the blade shift her hands again and she goes with it, lifting up and rolling her shoulders, stretching muscles and *ch'i* channels, that feeling of electricity on her skin, flowing through her body. But now it's as if that tingling is something else other than fear: it's strength – opening her joints, the *ch'i* reaching through every blood vessel, every pore, every sinew.

Marlais watches entranced, his cool blue gaze on the girl and her sword, the bottle in his hands forgotten for a moment.

One more big circle and slowly the blade calms in

her hands, coming to rest. She takes a long, deep breath and turns back to him.

'Captain Marlais?'

He doesn't answer, his gaze dropped back to the floor.

'Mister Lee said that you had had some bad news.'

'Very bad,' he says, voice thick.

'What was it?'

'A friend of mine died.'

'Who was it?'

The walnuts are click-clacking away in his fist. 'The woman I told you about. My wife. The woman I loved . . . She died, it seems, at Wanhsien. I got the message earlier. From one of those idiot Brits . . .'

His voice stumbles.

'I was too late . . .'

Marlais puffs out his cheeks, stares down again at the bottle. It's strange to see this energetic, forceful man so broken, so hunched over. She takes a step towards him.

'I'm sorry.'

'It's not your fault.'

'No, I mean I know what that feels like.'

'How could you, at your age?'

'I meant Tom. I know what it's like to feel guilty someone died.'

'Your little brother?'

Ruby nods. Sees Marlais struggling to hold his own emotion in.

'Captain Marlais, what will you do now?'

He sniffs. 'What do you mean?'

'If you don't need to go up to Wanhsien any more? Are you going to turn round?'

'Hell's bells, Ruby,' he growls. 'We're going to finish our damned mission,' he says, looking up, eyes fierce. 'Help you and your young man. I'm going to try and be as strong as you are. Just because one injustice has happened doesn't mean we need to let another, God help me.'

'What if it's true?' Ruby says. 'What if we are really on the frontier, nearly in the Otherworld?'

Marlais gets to his feet, setting his shoulders.

'Then you better practise like crazy with that sword of yours. Heaven only knows what we'll face above the Grinder . . .'

第二十八章

INTO THE GRINDER

Silently, intently she works the sword in her hands again for long minutes after Marlais has gone. As the copper burns its steady flame and swirls in the darkened cabin the journey plays in her head.

She thinks of Tom slipping away on the ghostly sampan. She thinks of Charlie and that half-kiss he planted on her cheek. She thinks of the long way they've come and how she really has had *far to go*. And so much more yet before she's home.

Home.

I'll need every bit of energy, she thinks, all the *ch'i* I can gather if I'm ever going to get back there again. Maybe I should just *rest my eyes*. That's what Dad always says when he comes back from the Customs House exhausted and slumps in the armchair and then is snoring within five minutes with the newspaper crumpled on him. Always the same, she thinks, whether it was the old house on Bubbling Well, the Customs place in Hankow, the new flat, before Tom, after Tom. A ritual that didn't change. Mother would come in and sigh and raise her eyes. And she might adjust Dad's leg to make it more comfortable.

That image is strangely comforting, and for a moment she wishes he was there, sitting beside her – even giving her one of his 'lectures'. He always knew what to do – at least he always used to know.

I've hardly ever seen that false leg – not really, she thinks. He always kept it under trouser legs even on the hottest, steamiest Shanghai days. Just a glimpse now and then of the prosthetic foot and lower part of the calf. It held a grizzly fascination for both Tom and her and when they talked about it they always did so in whispers.

What do you think did it?

A shell? More than a bullet.

He takes it off at night. I heard him looking for it once. He was saying, where's my bloody leg?

We both laughed at that, she thinks, embarrassed now. And then she remembers something more: the day at the beach, the day she pulled herself into the dark blue water and went under. When Dad had pulled her back and lay exhausted on the beach, she saw the stump. As clearly as she'd ever seen it, wet from the sea, milky white and glistening and smooth. It made him look so – vulnerable, despite all the stiff upper lip, despite the bluster. Maybe Jin was right, maybe Dad was just doing his best. *That's all we can do, Ruby, make the best choices we can and hope we make enough good ones in a lifetime.*

She rolls over, feeling the throb throb throb of the *Haitun* going right through her. I'll just rest my eyes, she thinks, and do some of those breathing exercises that we read in the Almanac . . .

And just like Dad she's asleep in five minutes.

Bleary-eyed, she joins Charlie on the foredeck, a fitful two hours of sleep in her head. The hills have reared higher and now they climb the predawn above the river, giants holding up the sky. The stars have dimmed, the very first light bleeding over the hills behind.

Charlie gets stiffly to his feet, tiredness dragging his limbs.

'Did you sleep?'

'A bit.'

'I couldn't. I feel tired but I don't want to. Feels like I won't wake up if I do.'

He glances away upriver as the boat shudders. You can tell the current's stiffer now, the *Haitun* working harder for each chunk of water. Smoke piles from the funnel, but the bank is moving past more slowly than before.

Charlie looks back at her. 'What were you and Marlais talking about?'

'The river. He says it's different – I mean really different to normal.'

'That's what Old Lee keeps saying.' Charlie hunches his shoulders against the cold breeze. 'He wants to turn back. Heaven only knows what's coming.'

'No sign of the *Sea Witch*?'

He shakes his head, catches her glance and looks sheepishly away again. Maybe he's regretting that kiss? she wonders. Is he sorry he did it? No more shilly-shallying. We could be staved in on a rock by this time tomorrow, or God only knows what.

'Charlie?'

'What is it?'

'Are you sorry – about what happened at Full Moon Bridge?'

'Sorry?' His eyes look confused in the half-light.

'I didn't mean—'

'Why on earth would I be sorry?' he says quietly. 'It was the best thing . . .' his voice trips, '. . . it was the best thing in ages. I mean it, the *best*.'

'Can I have a hug now?'

'Yes. Please.'

They lean into each other, arms wrapping as the hills close tighter, the sky growing pale overhead. For a glorious moment she can think of nothing but the warmth of that hug, that they are together, the way everything feels right. And when he pulls his arms away she keeps hold of his hand and they stay like that, fingers gently locked, saying nothing, watching the dawn colour across the East.

'I'm glad too,' she says at last. 'Really glad.'

'I just hope we're not too late for Fei,' he mutters. 'That would be just too awful.'

It really feels like autumn now, the air coldest just as the sun finally crests the hills behind, staining the wake with rusty orange. Maybe it's just my imagination, Ruby thinks as the rays touch her face, but it seems paler than normal, not as warm.

A solitary junk passes, crew immobile, eyes looking towards the rising sun, no shouts or greeting for the *Haitun*. And the *Haitun* itself seems quieter, the crew's voices hushed in the half-light.

Another shake passes through the *Haitun*, then another – and the loudhailer crackles out Marlais' voice, his strength seemingly restored.

'All hands, all hands. Let's keep her stoked now, boys – and all eyes peeled.'

* * *

The bridge is crowded. Charlie has joined Marlais, the helmsman, McQueen, Old Lee, all their gazes focused on the water ahead. A map flaps on the chart table in the strengthening wind. Ruby looks forward into the hazy light to where huge dark walls are rearing some two or so miles ahead, the river narrowing to a gap. To the right a huge rock, painted with lines and Chinese characters, crawls past at snail speed as the *Haitun* threads her way into the first ruffle of whiter water.

Marlais tips back his cap to try to smooth the lines on his forehead. 'Don't normally get anything bad here.'

McQueen takes one more look, throws a scowl at Marlais, and then hurries down to the engine room.

'A whiff of mutiny,' Marlais winks. 'But they won't let us down. They're all feeling sorry for me—'

He pulls up sharp, eyes watering as he concentrates hard on the chart, pretending to wipe a bit of soot from the right one.

'Where are we?' Ruby says, peering over his shoulder.

The Captain's finger stabs the chart. 'Right here. First up is Horse Lung Gorge. Hardest of the three, and you get the big rapids, your Mincer, then the Grinder. Those are my names for them. And above that there's a clear passage and a little village that feeds the trackers. That's if it hasn't been washed away in that last flood.'

'Trackers?'

'Some boats need a pull. The junks can't sail up so you get hundreds of men on shore, or on tiny paths cut in the cliffs – they all hitch to a line and they haul you up, singing all the blessed way. And the drummers drumming!' His face is lighter now. 'Ah, it's a wonderful thing.'

'And what about the *Haitun*?'

'She'll do it. It's touch and go sometimes but we always get through. Maybe a little pull now and then.'

'And what if – what if we're not on the real river any more?'

Marlais winces. 'That was just my black mood, young Ruby. A bit of drink too. I was getting carried away. She's looking more normal again out there – if a bit wild.'

Ruby squints at the chart. There's a cross-hatched square on the north bank.

'Is that the tracker village then?'

'Just above the Grinder!'

'And where's the place Moonface is going?'

'Hell's Throat? Just up there.' He jags his finger across the paper. 'A thousand foot above the village. Steep path up to it, they say. You can see it from the river but I've never fancied the climb. People say that's where the demons live – the ones who throw rocks down at the boats. Particularly us foreign devils!'

The river's voice is louder now, the vibration from the battle between engine and water numbing her legs. From far ahead you can hear something churning over that, a steady pounding sound, like a distant beach on a stormy day.

In the V between the giant cliffs the sky is still dark and ominous. On the lower river, despite the Yangtze's mile-wide expanse, the *Haitun* had seemed solid, like a decent-sized boat. Now, with the rapids and their threatening names still to come, she seems smaller, much smaller. Like one of those toy boats that Tom loved to play with when he was small, mud bombing them on the pond up at the Recreation Ground until they sank.

Marlais plants a hand on her shoulder.

'She'll make it, Ruby – as long as coal holds out to the tracker village. Supplies there normally – if the bandits or Communists haven't looted the damn lot.'

Small hamlets crawl past, dwarfed by the cliffs, a few people gathering on the foreshore to watch the *Haitun* tackle the first proper white water. Marlais stands between Old Lee and the helmsman, guiding the ship full speed into the head of each snarling rapid.

'Good practice,' he grunts. 'Getting back into shape for the big ones.'

Rounding the next bend they see a heavy junk mid channel. Marlais nudges Ruby and hands the binoculars over. 'Trackers, see?'

In the shake of the lenses she sees a thin line reaching out from the prow of the junk, dipping towards the water. She follows it as it climbs again to a path beside the river. And attached to it by even finer lines, like insects caught on spider's threads, are dozens – maybe a hundred or more – men, either side of the main line, leaning forward like people do into a stiff wind. They seem hardly to be moving at all.

'Tough life,' Marlais murmurs. 'Just enough to survive on. At least as long as you survive. Hundreds of 'em drown every year.'

He frowns.

'If they're pulling this low below the gorge then the water's really bad. Might just go and have a word down below . . .'

A distant, regular drumming is coming across the water now, confused by echo and river noise. Ruby focuses again, following the line as her eyelids flutter in the lenses, and sees the steady surge and sag of each man moving in unison. For every step forward they lose three quarters of it as the rope rebounds, and the junk edges forward just a little on the river's surge.

They pass the junk twenty minutes later. The *Haitun*'s engines have taken on a heavy, serious thrum as they overhaul the junk, climbing into the mouth of the gorge. The trackers are in full view now – naked but for a loin cloth they strain on their lines, using every bit of their thin weight to gain ground. The drumming is louder, and over everything else floats a strange, ethereal whistling.

When Marlais comes back onto the bridge, he cocks his head to listen, a half smile on his face. 'It's to distract the dragons in the water. The tracker leaders got these whistling things they spin round their heads. Beautiful, isn't it?'

Old Lee turns and nods at the water ahead, and Marlais snaps back to attention.

'Mincer,' he growls. 'And it's strong today.' He grabs the loudhailer. 'Make everything fast on deck. Action stations! Piston greasers stand by!'

The cliffs squeeze the Yangtze tighter ahead, the shore closer and no more now than a tumble of enormous boulders. A path picks its way through them and thin trails of smoke ascend and swirl in the chasm from tiny shacks wedged between the rocks. Ahead the river seems to climb an abrupt step: a low wall of churning froth, sending mist up to mingle with the campfire smoke, a ramp of smooth black water lying diagonally across it like a tongue.

'FULL AHEAD!' Marlais thunders.

Their own smoke rolls over the deck mixed with the reek of hot engine oil and the ozone charge of the foaming water. Charlie's hand reaches out for hers again, his eyes full of the wild river.

'Do you think Fei got up this OK?'

'I'm sure. We haven't seen any signs of a boat in distress.'

He leans forward, craning his neck through the open front window.

'I wish we'd caught them before they got here . . .'

Marlais pulls him back. 'Hold on to something and keep away from the sides. Just in case we lose power. Can you swim?'

Ruby nods, a flash of the beach memory firing. That must be the last time, and what a mess that was!

'I not swim,' Charlie says.

'Then I'm giving you this,' the Captain growls and unfastens a lifebuoy the colour of a tangerine from the cabin wall. 'Just in case.'

They edge towards the hammering water of the rapid, the river scrolling past at speed – though when you look at the cliff wall they seem to have come almost to a halt. It's gloomy as twilight in the canyon, as if the sun's changed its mind and is setting again, and everything ahead is faded to shades of charcoal and grey. Marlais' eyes shine as he grips the bulkhead, his whole body taut, urging the *Haitun* forward. Lee's finger tips to the right and the ship swings, shooting forward diagonally, her prow cutting the black tongue of the rapid. The pounding of the water is deafening now, bouncing off the gorge walls, drowning everything else out. With a bump the *Haitun*'s prow surges upwards, shaking hard, and Ruby's eyes dart from the water to Marlais and back again, trying to judge how they are doing from his reaction.

No clue, just his hand grinding the walnuts hard. Nothing seems to happen for a long half minute, just engine noise and water flow matching each other, and then the Captain relaxes his white knuckle grip just a bit, and with relief she sees they are edging forwards, climbing the watery step.

With a jolt the ship's nose ploughs down into the foam and Marlais grabs the hailer. 'All hands to stern!'

He turns to Ruby. 'Except you two. That lot know the drill. Got to keep the props under. Shift the weight.'

Water is flooding over the foredeck, the bow under the surface and then suddenly rearing clear again as a horrific grinding from beneath sends a shadow across Marlais' face. And then it's gone, and the front of the boat is over the head of the rapid, the next stretch of river visible beyond.

Marlais slaps Old Lee hard on the back. With a final surge the rest of the *Haitun* is up and they steam into calmer water, the gorge towering above.

Marlais looks round. 'One down. But first I want to check with Mister McQueen – and make sure we didn't hole on that rock.'

Only now does Ruby feel how tightly Charlie's hand is gripping hers, his face almost white in the canyon's dusk.

'I'd rather walk from here,' he says quietly. 'Firm ground. And it might be faster.'

She squeezes his hand back, eyes scouring the cliff wall. A path leads up from where they are, clinging to the north face of the gorge, climbing a hundred or so feet above the turbulent river. Tiny tracker figures are crawling along it, some on hands and knees as they strain on their ropes pulling another junk ahead of the *Haitun*, the drop to the rocks and tumbling water dizzying.

Ruby shakes her head, glancing nervously at the cold, blue-black water.

'It'll be OK. Let's stay on the boat. If anything happens, I'll save you.'

第二十九章

SHADOWS OF MEN WHO ONCE WERE

Marlais returns a minute or so later with McQueen, the engineer wiping oil from his face with a tattered rag. The last of his words snap over the raging water ahead.

'. . . the pumps are holding up, just – JUST! – but that coal isn't good enough to get us up the Grinder. We'll need to track to be sure.'

Marlais shakes his head. 'I've promised these kids. Haven't got time to bargain and wait our turn. Could take a day. You'll stoke it as hard as you can and we'll give it a go.'

McQueen fires them a dark look, then turns and drops back into the oil and heat and smoke below.

Ruby looks at the Captain. 'I'm sorry if—'

'Don't be stupid,' Marlais grins. 'He's having a swell old time down there. We'll let the stokers get the fire really packed again and then run at the Grinder. See the whirlpools between here and there? Really big today, but I can pick my way don't you worry.'

He points dead upriver, index finger shaking just a bit.

Ahead a brown-sailed junk is hurtling down the next rapid, hazy in the murk. Seconds later it swings crazily and starts to spin, turning round and round as the sail fills and empties, seemingly out of all control. By a few feet it misses a great slab of rock and then, the sail puffs out again and takes the wind and she's coming at speed towards them, her course true and fast. It's terrifying, but exhilarating too, and for a heartbeat Ruby forgets what lies beyond, just feels the awful thrill of the rapids, the sheer rock walls, the sky slit high above.

'That's one way to do it,' Marlais smiles grimly. 'The wrong way.'

She nods, but then the full weight of what lies ahead comes surging back.

'And what about Moonface? What will we do when we're up to the next bit?'

'A few miles further and then we'll moor,' Marlais says. 'I'll pick you a decent shore party, all the decent men and all the weapons we've got, and scout out your gangster's hideout. We don't know for sure he's there yet. Or your friend.'

'And if he is there?'

'Then we'll fight. Save one poor soul at least.'

Charlie has drifted away to the rail on the starboard side, gazing up at the cliffs piled ahead. The downward-bound junk passes close as it heads for the lip of the Mincer and he cups his hands and bellows as loud as he can into the chaos.

'Have you seen a small white boat? A foreign boat?'

One of the junk crew shouts back, syllables half submerged by the river, but Charlie's back straightens.

'When? How long ago?'

Again the reply is lost to Ruby's hearing, but Charlie turns triumphantly round and beams. 'They saw her! They saw the *Sea Witch*! She's moored near the next village. Let's go! Let's go!'

But despite Charlie urging Marlais to hurry, it takes an interminable age to check the *Haitun* over.

'No point having a go until the boys have cleared and rebuilt the fire, every last bit of coal burning white,' Marlais glowers. 'And no point having a go at the Grinder if that last rapid put even a tiny hole in us. The next bump would open us like a can and we'd all be fish feed.'

Charlie casts a glance up at the cliffs, then stalks

away astern on the outer deck.

Ruby taps Marlais on the shoulder. 'Couldn't we walk on the tracker path?'

'It's a bad stretch here. Way above the river and if the trackers are working and their line breaks . . .' Marlais shakes his head. 'The whiplash can sweep all those poor souls to the rocks below. If you're not bashed in, you'd drown. Besides,' he adds darkly, 'you need my boys to go up to Hell's Throat with you.'

Ruby nods, then dogtrots down the side of the boat to find Charlie. The upriver junk they overtook is caught on the tongue of the Mincer behind, the thunder from the unseen drummers intense, the bamboo line to the trackers inching through the water and curving back up to the tiny figures on the path above.

Charlie's leaning on the rail, biting his lip as he watches the battle below them.

'It's barbaric.' He spits out the words angrily. 'Look at them. This country's got to get into the twentieth century and get dams and railways and more electricity and roads. I heard about this, but I never thought I'd see it!'

'Are you cross with *me* about it?'

Charlie shakes his head. 'No. Of course not.'

He smiles, but there's no strength in it. He still looks so tired, Ruby worries, so very pale since the fight with the *jiang shi*. Maybe there's something really wrong with him.

'How are you feeling?'

'I just want to get going.'

'They've got to get the ship ready, Charlie.'

'And what are we going to do? Against Moonface? And what if – what if he's got more of those shadow things with him? Or worse?'

'Then we'll fight them like in the tunnel,' Ruby says.

Charlie looks at her. 'I keep thinking about that man in the village.'

'What about him?'

'He just keeps popping into my head. And the courtyard where I met him looked really familiar too.'

'There are lots of places like that—'

'I felt like I'd been there before. But Mum and Dad left before we were born so it can't be right.' He shakes his head, staring at the junk behind. 'My head feels a real muddle, ever since. Ever since, you know . . .'

'Maybe you should stay on the boat,' Ruby says, half-heartedly. 'Leave the climb to the crew. To me.'

'I'm leading the way,' he says, straightening, puffing out his chest. 'Fei's my sister. I promised Dad.'

He's acting strong for her benefit, she can tell that, trying to look better than he's feeling. But no way she could face the battle to come without him.

'I'm going to get the pack and the sword. So we're ready.'

'Be quick.'

In the cabin she's surprised to find only the tiniest whisper of green glowing at the tip of Jin's sword. She had expected it to be burning full power and its pallor brings her up short. Maybe we're on the wrong track, she thinks. Maybe we are back on the normal river like Marlais said.

But just holding it feels so right. It's a link to Jin, to that moment in the tunnel when she felt the *ch'i* surging through her arms and hands, when she felt fully her old self again. Shanghai Ruby, running the backstreets from one hare-brained scheme to the next.

No fear, just the joy at each morning and what it might bring.

When Lao Jin turned up in the temple it was like they'd met sometime before, like he knew her inside out – better even than her parents. He trusted me, Ruby thinks, from the first. He believed I could do it.

She thinks of Jin summoning *ch'i*, the *ba gua* moves so fluid and light. His calm energy, his *awareness*, and she swings the blade again, trying to soften her hands, to feel the flicker of the energy reviving in her belly.

It's there, I'm sure it is, she thinks. I can feel it. I believe it.

Deep below her feet she can feel the river pulse, the engines coming back up to full power . . .

. . . her hands roll and something shifts inside her as the drums in the canyon beat louder, beating time with her heart . . .

. . . and all the thousands of pinpricks of fire go shooting across her pale, freckled skin . . .

. . . the roots of her hair tingling, goosebumps bubbling up . . .

. . . and, as if a switch has been thrown, every single inch of the spirit sword rips into dazzling green life. The stars of the Dipper and the Chinese characters shine like neon, washing the whole cabin in eerie, otherworldly light.

The door opens and Charlie stands there, his face astonished, the glasses Jin gave him reflecting the green. He swears under his breath, then takes a step in and closes the door.

'Don't let people see it.'

'Marlais already has. And Old Lee.'

313

'The rest of the crew might think we're bad luck. If it goes wrong in the rapids they might blame us. These river men are *really* superstitious . . .'

The *Haitun*'s hooter wails over everything. The bell ringing.

'Come on,' Charlie whispers. 'We're running for the Grinder. Hide it in the pack.'

Reluctant to let her grip on the sword go, she hesitates, then wraps it tight in her old cardigan and stuffs it down inside the pack. The green gleams through the opening even then. Well, doesn't matter now, she thinks, struggling into the straps and hurrying after Charlie.

On the bridge everyone is tense, bodies alert. It's as if the night has clung to the canyon and the cliffs seem higher, the river whiter, angrier. High above there are tiny dots of light jinking on the tracker path, the big black junk close behind them now.

Marlais is scratching his head, cap thrust in his pocket. 'They don't normally track this early,' he mutters. 'Must know it's going to get worse and want to beat the water. Grinder looks really strong.'

The walnuts are grating in his hand again, as he struggles with some inner turmoil. A decision to be made.

'Damn it all, we'll go!' he barks. 'Full steam ahead.

All hands ready for my orders! Let's go!'

There's a passage of smooth empty water ahead and they cut through that, smoke and sparks shooting up into the dark air. Just to their right is a great swirl of water, coiling on itself, bits of flotsam circling in its grip and then sucked out of sight to the depths below. They curve around it, lipping the edge, and then dodge a mushroom of water bubbling up from fathoms below. Marlais' eyes flick away from the river, up to the cliff path, and Ruby follows his gaze. The lights on the tracker way seem to be multiplying, glowing, casting weird shadows down into the gorge. Hundreds of them. And hundreds more when you look ahead, numberless points of light, dizzying, disorientating.

'Captain?' Old Lee says. 'Full ahead. Or turn back?'

Marlais snaps back to attention, and nods.

'We'll go.'

The wall of the Grinder is ahead of them now and the *Haitun* cuts towards the dead centre of the white water, ploughing full into the rapid's tongue. At once water floods over the bows, an awful lot more of it this time and, for a moment, it seems like they're just going to go straight under like a submarine diving. Down to the rocks, the dragons . . .

'To the stern,' Marlais barks. 'Everyone! And you two, grab on to that life ring.'

Instinctively Ruby takes a deep breath and holds it, bracing harder – but then the *Haitun*'s nose rears up, climbing the rapid, the entire boat shaking like anything, inching higher.

Come on, Ruby thinks, willing them forward. Up we go. Up, up.

She glances at Marlais and is surprised to see he's looking away to the cliff path again, not at the river. There are thousands of little points of light there as well now – like fireflies dancing. The rising sun has been obliterated by the turn of the gorge wall and in the near darkness the lights seem to be moving up and down, as well as along the track. Ruby blinks at them, sees them swim in the mist coming off the water. Must be the motion of the boat.

A terrible cough wracks the *Haitun*'s lungs, then the engine kicks hard again. For a moment, a wonderful moment, it seems they are going to do it, but then the coughing fit comes again. There's an awful hanging pause, and in that sudden silence, Ruby quite clearly hears the two walnuts in the Captain's hand crack apart. His face drains of colour.

The ship lurches backwards, sending them all sprawling to the floor.

'Brace yourselves!' Marlais bellows and then the *Haitun* is falling, turning, powerless in the river's grip as water submerges the lower decks. Side on they hurtle back towards the tracked junk behind. Charlie's arm wraps around her shoulders, gripping tight, both of them bracing for impact, but the *Haitun* shaves past it and steadies, the engines running loudly again.

McQueen is on the bridge, covered in engine oil. 'Pumps are shot,' he shouts. 'I've got to shut down . . .'

Marlais shakes his head. 'We can have one more try, Mister McQueen. We just need a better line. You do your job and I'll find the way.' His eyes dart back to the lights on the cliff. 'We're nearly there. Nearly *there*. I promised these kids. Just got to get out of the Grinder. No bloody choice.'

McQueen swears and disappears below, and once again the *Haitun* edges upriver past the tracked junk.

'Are you afraid?' Charlie whispers, leaning closer.

'Of what?'

He sweeps his hand to include everything, the darkening gorge, the snarling water.

'Yes,' she says. 'But not as afraid as I think I should be.'

He smiles in spite of everything.

'I know what you mean.'

She squeezes his hand and feels the reassuring squeeze back . . .

. . . and the horrible vibration grips the *Haitun* again as the Grinder eats into the prow.

This time the line must be better, because she sees a smile spread across Marlais' face and the *Haitun* lifts smoothly, climbing the first half of the rapid in seconds.

The river beyond is just visible through the gloom and haze.

And then the chills flood through her as she sees Marlais' eyes open very, very wide: alarm and fear – and something else beyond that. Silently he starts making the sign of the cross over and over again across his moth-eaten jersey, a string of foul language tumbling in his mouth.

His face has gone deathly white. Old Lee is shaking his head in disbelief, and Charlie's eyes are wide, wide open behind his glasses . . .

. . . and then she sees what they see.

Dozens upon dozens of shadowy boats are floating on the next reach of the river, like a weird, watery version of Nanking Road on a busy day, the Yangtze filled from rocky bank to rocky bank with dark junks flying white sails. A faint green light is coming off the water itself, the whole gorge glowing, mixed with spray and mist.

'Holy Mother of God,' Marlais chokes. 'We're there.'

And then the ship's heart misses a long beat and control is lost, the *Haitun* swinging wildly back into the rapid, water grabbing the foredeck, rolling her, the deck rearing under Ruby's feet, throwing her over, falling across nothing as a tumult of sound – coughing engine, rock roar, water, and shouts from the crew – tumbles around her. She feels Charlie's hand rip from hers, hears him scream her name and then the last thing she knows for sure is the slap and choke of ice cold water stuffing up her eyes and ears and the sounds go all weird and wobbly and her head bangs hard and—

Stars shine in her vision and there is no sound any more.

She sees, from high above just as she's always seen it, the river snaking through darkened hills. A beaten silver pathway beneath her, and then she's diving down, down and down, towards the hills, towards the water and diving silently into the turbulent blackness.

She sees the spirit sword suddenly, in front of her, right in front of her, its light gleaming, illuminating submerged rocks, weed, the broken hulls of lost ships.

It tumbles into nothing.

She sees a lifebuoy bright orange.

A body far off in the gloom.

And then that too is gone and there is nothing and no one.

No dolphins, no fish. No dragons.

Nothing but black water.

From out of the nothingness something grips her bruised shoulders. But instead of hurting, the pressure feels good, reassuring in the midst of her terror and shock. She feels herself being lifted, hurtling up from the depths, lungs straining for air – and then the skin of the water is ripping apart and river noise breaking all around her.

Through it she hears someone calling her name. No, not calling, but just repeating her name calmly, right in her ear.

Ruby. Ruby. Ruby.

She's being dragged through the water, head clear and then submerged, in and out, ears muffled then clear. She blinks the Yangtze water away, and in the half light sees a face. A familiar face, smiling, his silver eyes shining.

It's Lao Jin, swimming hard with one arm, pulling for the rocky shore.

'I've got you,' he murmurs. 'I've got you. *Mei wenti.*'

For a moment she struggles to understand.

'Where – where am I?'

Lao Jin's voice comes again – as calm and strong as it always was.

'We're there, Ruby. You did it. We're in the Otherworld.'

Ruby's adventures will conclude in . . .

THE PALE REVENANT

Coming in 2017

The river is everywhere at the same time, at the source, at the mouth, in the ocean and in the mountains [. . .] only the present exists for it, not the shadow of the past, nor the shadow of the future.

Hermann Hesse

A note about the Yangtze

How many names can a river have?

Confusions, mishearings and changing methods of putting Chinese into Roman letters have meant that the Yangtze has gone by many different names over the centuries.

Marco Polo called it the *Quiansui*, whilst on early English maps it often went as *Kian*, both of them versions of a Chinese dialect name for the mouth of the river. For a while it was called the *Blue River* (to distinguish if from the *Yellow River* further north), but that was dropped quickly as the silt laden river normally ran muddy brown.

The term *Yangtze Kiang* was adopted under foreign Postal Romanization, but was mistakenly derived from the name the Chinese gave to the lower river only. (Even spellings of that vary, from *Yangtze*, to *Yangtse* to modern *Yangzi*. Confusing, and helps to explain why I struggled with my Chinese degree . . .)

But to the Chinese themselves the main 2,500 km stretch of the river that this story explores was called the Chang Jiang or Long River. Other local names are applied to various sections – above Yibin it is known beautifully as the Gold Sands River . . .

What is not in doubt is its scale. Some 6,000 kilometres from source in the Tibetan uplands to the mouth near Shanghai, the Yangtze has shaped the destiny of China.

It is so wide that in Ruby's time no bridge crossed the river until way upriver past the three Gorges. Navigable for centuries by ocean going ships for the first 1,000 kilometres, and far further by smaller boats, it has always been a major transport artery and was connected near Nanking to the Grand Canal running north to south. The silt carried in its waters established fertile farmland to feed the country.

But the floods that often devastated the Yangtze basin caused huge loss of life. To deal with that, and to counter the dangers of navigating the whirlpools and rapids of the Gorges, the Chinese Government finally dammed the Yangtze near Ichang in 2003. The scheme has created the largest hydroelectric source in the world, but also been controversial, flooding tens of thousands of homes, dispersing millions of people and changing the ecosystems of the area. The river that Ruby experiences in the Gorges is now deep underwater . . .

And the real dolphins that once swam the Yangtze – actually called 'baiji' – are now thought to be on the brink of extinction. Or beyond.